IN TANGIER

MOHAMED CHOUKRI

IN TANGIER

JEAN GENET

Translated from Arabic by Paul Bowles
Foreword by William Burroughs

TENNESSEE WILLIAMS

Translated from Arabic by Paul Bowles
Foreword by Gavin Lambert

PAUL BOWLES

Translated from Arabic by Gretchen Head and John Garrett

TELEGRAM

First published in hardback in 2008 by Telegram
This edition published in 2010 by Telegram

ISBN: 978-1-84659-061-0

Copyright © the estate of Mohamed Choukri, 1973, 1979, 1996 and 2010

Jean Genet in Tangier
First published in 1974, by the Ecco Press in New York, USA
Translation © the estate of Paul Bowles, 1973 and 2010
Foreword © the estate of William Burroughs, 1973 and 2010
Afterword translation Charlotte Mandell, 1973 and 2010

Tennessee Williams in Tangier
First published in 1979, by the Cadmus Editions in California, USA
Translation © the estate of Paul Bowles, 1979 and 2010
Foreword © Gavin Lambert, 1979 and 2010
Note © the estate of Tennessee Williams, 1979 and 2010

Paul Bowles in Tangier
First published in 1997 by Quai Voltaire/La Table Ronde in Paris
Translation © Gretchen Head and John Garrett, 2008 and 2010

A full CIP record for this book is available from the British Library.
A full CIP record for this book is available from the Library of Congress.

Manufactured in Lebanon

TELEGRAM
26 Westbourne Grove, London W2 5RH, UK
2398 Doswell Avenue, Saint Paul, Minnesota, 55108, US
Verdun, Beirut, Lebanon
www.telegrambooks.com

Contents

Contents

Jean Genet
in Tangier

Foreword

It is my feeling that Choukri's book on Genet in Tangier needs no introduction. It is a full-length portrait of Jean Genet. Anyone who reads it will see Genet as clearly as I saw him in Chicago. To select a few quotes:

'The police have never been human, and the day they become human they'll no longer be police.' Exactly. Some police are admittedly better than others, as a cold is better to catch than rabies. But who wants either?

'There's no absolute no and no absolute yes. I'm sitting here with you now, but I might easily not be.' It was purely a matter of luck that landed Genet in Chicago in 1968 (when he covered the Democratic Convention for *Esquire*).

'I'm neither Existentialist nor Absurdist. I don't believe in such classifications. I'm only a writer, either a good one or a bad one.' I have been equally impatient of such classifications. Am I a Beat writer? a black humorist? and so on. There is good writing and bad writing. Giving names is meaningless.

'I've always been writing, even before I ever tried to write anything. The career of a writer doesn't begin at the moment he begins to write. The career and the writing may coincide earlier or later.' I did not start to write until the age of thirty-five. In an essay on Kerouac, written before I had seen Choukri's notes, I said exactly the same thing: 'I was always writing, long before I actually wrote anything.' This shared conviction made it possible for Jean Genet and me to communicate in Chicago despite my atrocious French and his non-existent English. Had he considered himself an Existentialist or an Absurdist, communication would have been impossible.

As I read Choukri's notes, I saw and heard Jean Genet as clearly as if I had been watching a film of him. To achieve such precision simply by reporting what happened and what was said, one must have a rare clarity of vision. Choukri is a writer.

William Burroughs

18.XI.68

I was sitting in the Café Central with Gerard Beatty. Suddenly he said: Look! That's Jean Genet!

He walks slowly, his hands in his pockets, unkempt. He stares fixedly at the terrace of the Café Central.

He stands still, turns completely around, and looks in the direction of the Café Fuentes. Then he chooses the Café Tanger. I said to Gerard: I've got to meet him.

No! Don't even try.

Why not?

He goes into his shell and stays there. You can't make contact with him. At least that's what I'm told.

I decided to disregard Gerard's warning. I could see Genet over at the Café Tanger, sitting down beside a young Moroccan.

We sat on for nearly an hour, listing the painters and writers who have visited Tangier over the years. One eye on the human ants milling in the square, and the other on Jean Genet's head, glistening in the sunlight. I saw him start to get up. It was about three o'clock. I said to Gerard: Watch carefully, now.

Gerard cried: You're out of your mind! I turned to him and grinned.

Behind me, I heard him objecting: What you're doing is insane!

He was walking. I went slowly towards him. He

stopped, his hands in his pockets, leaned forward slightly.

He looked searchingly at me. I said: You *are* Monsieur Genet, aren't you?

He hesitated for an instant, and without replying said: Who are you?

I waited before saying: A Moroccan writer.

He held out his hand. *Enchanté*.

I saw Gerard watching me from behind the café window, surprised and smiling.

As we walked up the Siaghines I asked Genet if he liked Tangier.

Ça va, he said noncommittally.

Don't you think it's one of the most beautiful cities in the world?

Certainly not! Whatever gave you such an idea?

I'd heard it was, I said.

It's not true. In Asia there are cities far more beautiful.

During the twenty minutes it took us to walk from the Zoco Chico to the Hotel Minzah, we talked about Moroccan writers and about some of the problems they must confront both in their writing and in publication. When we were in front of the hotel he gave me his hand, saying: I always take a nap. Tomorrow, if you like, we can meet in the Zoco Chico. Around two in the afternoon?

19.XI.68

I sat down in the Café el Menara. I was thinking: Will he come or not? For me it was still the previous day because what I was waiting for had not yet happened.

I saw him coming along, slowly, as before. I waved to him. His eyes lit up and he smiled. I rose. We shook hands warmly.

His expression is more friendly than yesterday. We sat down. He ordered a glass of mint tea, and I took a second one. Some of the passers-by go up or down the street and do not return. Others walk back and forth constantly. Most of these are youths and boys looking for tourists.

I don't understand why they haven't translated any of your books into Arabic, I said.

You mean the Arabic of the Qur'an?

I explained that Qur'anic Arabic is Classical Arabic.

I don't know. No one has asked to do it. Maybe some day they will, maybe not. It depends on whether my things interest them at that point. Personally, I think the Arabs are extremely sensitive when it comes to questions of morality.

I had with me a copy of *Le Rouge et le Noir*. He riffled the pages. Do you like this?

Yes. I read it first in Arabic. Now I'm rereading it in French. And I added: Julien's family life is like my own in some ways. One thing in particular is almost identical: Monsieur Sorel bound out his son Julien to the mayor of the town for 300 francs a year, and my father rented me for thirty pesetas a month to a hashish-smoker who ran a café in the quarter of Ain Khabbaz where we lived in Tétouan.

I see your trouble. And you're not the only one. You'll never find beauty in literature that way. You shouldn't read with that sort of thing in mind, with the idea that the life of one or another protagonist has something to do with your own life. You have to keep things separate. Your life is nobody else's life.

I thought of the personality of Basil (in *The Picture of Dorian Gray*) and his conversation with Lord Henry on the subject of art and its relation to the personal life of the artist.

What I meant was that Julien makes me see my own past in a different light, and that consoles me for the present, I told him.

Maintenant je comprends, he said. Julien's life is marvellous. He's real. Stendhal was one of the great writers of his time.

Meursault refusing to defend himself (in Camus's *L'Etranger*) reminds me of Julien in prison.

It's not the same thing, he said. And he began to speak at some length about the era in which Stendhal wrote. Then he said: But Camus was luckier. *L'Etranger* was written in an age when France was no longer run by the army and the church. The hero of today's books is more free to refuse. It's very rare that he dies for the woman he loves. She may shoot at him, but he won't feel any love for her in his cell, or repeat her name on his way to the guillotine. You could say that Kafka was the first to write about the *refus obscur*. Take K. in *The Trial,* for instance. The charges against him are grave. He must cooperate, but he has no trial. At the moment when his life is in danger, he's playing the comic lover with a woman.

After a moment I asked him about his friend Sartre. I haven't seen him in two years, he said.

I've read most of his books. I'd like to talk with him some day.

That's easy to arrange. Then he added: Postwar Sartre is not prewar Sartre. He came out of his German prison with a new skin. So did I. If we hadn't both changed our skins we wouldn't have been friends.

I walked with him to the hotel. On the way I asked him if he spoke Spanish.

No, he said. I was in Chicago in August. I learned a few words there.

And English?

Non plus.

I said goodbye to him in front of the hotel without making a new appointment.

20.XI.68

He was walking in the Medina with Brion Gysin, coming up from the Calle Bencharqi. Without greeting me, he launched into an explanation of the color red in Stendhal's novel. Listen! Red doesn't mean the army, in spite of what I told you yesterday. It stands for the judges who wore red capes. Red for the judges and black for the priests.

21.XI.68

I met him in the Zoco Chico some time after midday. We talked for an hour. He asked me questions about Morocco, from the point of view of its culture and economy. He wanted to know whether teachers and students mingled during the hours of recreation or outside school.

No. Neither the Moroccans nor the French. There's a high screen between the teacher and the pupil here.

But why?

I don't know.

He seemed disappointed. Soon we began to talk about Islam and Christianity, about what the four evangelists wrote, and the revelation of the Qur'an.

Personally, I believe the Qur'an is more trustworthy than Matthew, Mark, Luke, and John, he said.

We were silent for a moment. Then we began a new conversation. Have you read anything by any Arab writers? I asked him.

Unfortunately not. Only a few things by Katib Yacine. He's a friend of mine.

To be certain, I went on: Not even Taha Hussein? Or Tawfiq el-Hakim?

Who are they?

Two Egyptian writers. Some of their books are translated into French, and other languages. Especially Tawfiq el-Hakim.

I don't know them. Some day I hope to read them.

24.IX.69

This morning Gerard Beatty told me he had seen Jean Genet in the Zoco Chico. In the afternoon I ran into Brion Gysin at the Café Zagora. His mangled foot was still bad enough to keep him from walking. He asked me to go to the Hotel Minzah and deliver an invitation to Genet for a lunch he is giving tomorrow noon.

I spoke on a house telephone with him from the lobby. He accepted the invitation immediately, and went on to ask me if I had read *La Chartreuse de Parme*. I felt ill at ease, and laughed before I answered: Oh, no. Not yet. But I'm surely going to read it very soon.

I advised you last year to read it, he said. Forgive me if I don't come downstairs. I've taken some Nembutal pills. *A demain, chez l'Américain.*

Brion was waiting for me at the Café Zagora. I went with him to his apartment. On the way he began to complain about his foot, and about certain friends who would not let him work at the new book he was trying to write. We stopped at the Parade Bar. Brion ordered a whisky, and I had a beer. He insisted it was the evil eye of Princess Ruspoli which had caused the motorcycle accident that had ruined his foot.

I can still see that last look she gave John and me before we got onto the motorcycle. There's no doubt in my mind. She practices magic.

It seems Genet's back in town, I said to Brion.

Yes, he said. And that Nembutal's going to kill him unless he goes into a nursing home and gets treatment.

It's several years since he's written anything, I said.

I don't think he's going to write anything more, Brion said. He feels that he's done what he had to do.

He went on to say that he had been rereading some of the books. I can't believe that man didn't have a classical education, he said. There's some mystery that he's trying to hide. His life is one of the great literary mysteries of the century.

I asked him how he thought it was possible for Genet to have had such an education. He said he had spoken of it with him, but Genet would never say more than that his entire education came from the thieves and vagabonds he happened to know in his formative years. Brion told him outright that he wasn't going to accept that, and added that he suspected he'd been brought up in a Catholic institution.

You don't learn the language of Racine in the street,

Brion went on. And I wouldn't be surprised if Genet knew Greek and Latin.

I asked him how Genet had reacted to that.

No reaction, except that he got a bit pale, and looked very much astonished. Then he laughed and denied it. And he went through the same story as always. The thieves and the pimps. He claims it was a very special period that didn't last, the time when the criminals all spoke perfect French! No. You've got Genet the genius, and Genet the criminal. But there's another Genet, Genet the third, Genet the mystery man.

25.IX.69

We ate out of the pot with our hands. Genet scarcely touched the food. After lunch H. stirred things up by introducing the subject of religion. Genet seemed interested in the Qur'an. Then H. asked Genet why he stayed at the Minzah if he liked the company of the poorer Moroccans. Genet laughed.

Don't you know why?

No.

Because I'm a dirty dog. I stay at the Minzah or the Hilton because I like to see elegant people waiting on a filthy cur like me.

We all laughed. H. asked: And why should you be a filthy cur?

Because that's what they think I am.

Brion was still very much upset about his foot. I had with me *L'Etre et le Néant*, *La Chartreuse de Parme* and *Le Balcon*. Genet picked up the Stendhal: Sartre is my friend, but *La Chartreuse de Parme* is a better book than *L'Etre et le Néant*.

Sartre's book is too complicated, I said. In three years I've only been able to read a hundred and thirty pages. Sometimes one single sentence has sent me off to read a whole book.

I had trouble with it myself the first time I read it, Genet told me. One day I took the book with me to Sartre's house, and I said to him: This book of yours is difficult. He took it out of my hand and began to write notes and numbers in it, to show me the sequence in which I ought to read the various parts. And he said: I think now you'll be able to understand it without any trouble. He was right. I *could* understand it, using the method he worked out for me.

And why didn't he write it in the order he showed you, then? I asked.

He wrote it for specialists. At least, that's what he told me.

Then H. asked Genet: Do you believe God exists?

Genet laughed. I don't know. All I know is that the world exists. But only God Himself knows whether He exists.

The philosophers are right, H. said. God doesn't exist.

Genet said jokingly: So you're an atheist.

Brion's cook interrupted. H. is always like this. But he can't explain why he's an atheist. He talks like this only when he's with foreigners. When he's with Muslims he's a hypocrite and a coward. Because he knows God does exist.

And you? cried H. Can you explain your faith?

Yes. God exists. That's enough.

God doesn't exist. That too is enough.

I asked Genet to inscribe *Le Balcon* for me. He wrote the dedication in both Arabic and French.

We left the lunch table about half past five, and said goodbye to Genet in the Place de France. There we met two girls. H. knew one of them, and so we went to his apartment to drink wine and smoke *kif.* During the night a commotion woke me up. H.'s girl came into my room crying, and sat down near me half naked, to complain about how rough men are. H. followed her in, and persuaded her to go back into his room with him. Then I noticed that the girl who lay beside me was also weeping. I could not bring myself to ask her why.

From far away in the night came the music of a wedding. Distant sounds of festivity always depress me. I thought: man is very fragile.

26.IX.69

Today I met him at the Café el Menara. I had *The Idiot* and some magazines in Arabic under my arm: *al-Adab,*

Maouaqif and *al-Maarifa*. He remarked that from what he had read on the subject by non-Arab writers, Arabic literature did not concern itself with general problems, but was predicated solely upon Arab sentiment.

The humanity that lies beyond its frontiers does not interest it much.

I said: Some Arab critics consider you an Existentialist, and others say you belong to the school of the Absurd.

He looked at me, startled. Who wrote such stuff about me?

Some Arab critics.

They're wrong, whoever they are. I'm neither Existentialist nor Absurdist. I don't believe in such classifications. I'm only a writer, either a good one or a bad one.

A boy came to the table. Genet shook his hand eagerly. He turned to me: He's a friend of mine. I met him last year.

The two exchanged knowing glances, but said nothing to each other. When he did speak to the boy, Genet used a mixture of Moroccan and Tunisian Arabic. The boy laughed. Genet pointed to the worn-out shoes he was wearing, and said: How much would a new pair of shoes cost?

The boy murmured: 1,000 francs.

Is that all? said Genet. The boy nodded, and he gave him 1,500 francs with the warning: If you don't go and buy some new shoes you and I are no longer friends. I won't speak to you if I see you.

The boy smiled and ran off.

Genet turned to me. He's a bright boy. Why isn't he in school?

I explained.

I understand, he said.

After a moment I asked him if he agreed with what Sartre had written about him in his book.

Without hesitating he replied: Naturally I agree. Sartre read me the first hundred pages aloud, and then asked me if I thought it was all right as it was, and if he should go on or not.

Some people seem to think he was more interested in expounding a few of his own favorite themes there than he was in the books he was writing about. The same thing they say about his book on Baudelaire.

I disagree, he said. If Sartre hadn't been interested above all in my books he couldn't have written the book he wrote. He knows what I've written from having studied it, and he knows my personal life from the fact that we're friends. He used that knowledge to form his ideas about me.

After a moment I said: Brion tells me that Claudel, the writer's son, is planning to have an official reception for you at the French Consulate.

I shan't accept. I never go to things like that. The Cuban Consul in Paris invited me for a holiday in Cuba. Fidel Castro is a friend of mine, but I don't accept any official invitations from him. The only head of state I've sat at table with is Pompidou, and that was because he had allowed certain friends of mine who had been exiled to return to France. I hate all governments. I'm not welcome in the United States, for instance, because of my homosexuality and because of my criminal record. As if there were no ex-convicts or homosexuals in the United States! And I can't go to the Soviet Union because Zhdanov, under Stalin, forbade all my works there.

He picked up my Arabic version of *The Idiot*. Who wrote this? he asked. I told him what the book was.

I like *The Brothers Karamazov* better, he said.

Brion thinks *The Idiot* is better, I told him.

And you?

I'm just starting it. But I admire *The Brothers Karamazov*.

Later I caught sight of him in the Zoco de Fuera, with a tall, husky Moroccan whom I know slightly. I was going up from the Zoco Chico to the Boulevard, and they were walking toward Sidi Bouabid. Seeing them going alone together in the crowd made me think of *Le Journal du voleur*. He walked with his friend Stilitano like that in the barrios of Barcelona. At home I looked for the passage. *Mes vêtements étaient sales et pitoyables. J'avais faim et froid. Voici l'époque de ma vie la plus misérable.*

(Some months later I met the Moroccan and asked him if he had heard from Genet. Oh, that rich Frenchman? He told me he was going to send me a little money, but he hasn't sent anything. Those people, once they go away, they never think of you again.)

27.IX.69

We were approaching his hotel. I asked him if he had read anything by Tennessee Williams.

No, and I don't want to read anything, either.

Why not?

Everything I've read about his works leads me to think it wouldn't interest me.

Don't you know him personally? I asked him.

He telephoned me once in Paris. I wasn't very well at the time. We made an appointment for the next day, but I was too ill to keep it.

I saw Gerard Beatty coming toward us.

I introduced him to Genet, and he began to enthuse about *Le Journal du voleur*. Then they got onto Tangier and the people there. Suddenly Gerard said: Even the police are human here. Yesterday they took me to the *comisaria* because I didn't have my passport with me. But after a few minutes they let me go. They're human.

Genet, who had been visibly critical from the beginning of the anecdote, burst out: Listen to me! You're being offensive. If you've read my books, you know my low opinion of the police. In spite of that, you can stand there and tell me how human they are. The police have never been human, and the day they become human they'll no longer be police.

I'm sorry, Gerard said. I wasn't thinking in that way. I only meant –

Genet had said a quick goodbye and gone into the hotel.

28.IX.69

At the Brasserie de France. Abdeslam, a friend of Edouard Roditi, came up to our table, sat down beside me, and began to whisper in my ear. Isn't that the famous French writer? I want to talk to him. Will you interpret for me?

It looked as though he were going to ask him for money, and I was uncomfortable. I asked him what he wanted to talk to him about. About a big project, he whispered. I want him to help me finish it.

It still sounded like money to me, so I told him Genet spoke Arabic and he could talk to him himself.

Kif entaya, mossieu? he said to Genet.

Labess. Genet smiled and looked at me inquiringly.

A friend of mine, I had to say.

Abdeslam still wanted me to interpret. I'm making a book, and I want him to write a long poem for it. Very long. I'll put it in the front of the book so everyone will see it.

I translated for Genet.

What should be the subject of this long poem? he asked.

I want a poem about Tangier, Abdeslam said.

Genet smiled again. Tell him I'm here working for Gallimard, my publisher. Tell him I've signed a contract and accepted an advance to write a book, so I can't write any poems for him, either long or short.

If Genet had not continued to speak with perfect

seriousness through this nonsense, I should have burst out laughing. Abdeslam can scarcely sign his name legibly in Arabic. Probably Edouard Roditi once told him that papers in the handwriting of famous authors are worth money, and he already had a prospective customer in mind for Genet's poem. Abdeslam persisted. Tell him if he can't write it now he can write it later in Paris and send it to me.

A crippled boy came to our table, and Genet handed him a 1,000-franc note, Abdeslam watching every move. Then a dwarf named Mokhtar, who had been standing outside, burst in and rushed to the table with his hand out. Genet had nothing to give him, so he told him to share with his friend the cripple. This brought on a fight between the dwarf and the cripple, right in the middle of the café. To stop it, Genet called the waiter and asked him to lend him 500 francs. Give it to the dwarf, he told me, and he paid the bill.

When he and I were in the street, Genet said to me: Who was that character?

The one who wanted a poem? He's a parachutist, I told him. But he deserted or was discharged.

What's he doing here in Tangier? he wanted to know.

I thought of telling him the truth, which was that he earned his living by going to bed with tourists, but I remembered that Genet too had done the same thing when he was young. So I said: He doesn't do anything. There's a French writer who sends him money every month.

You mean to say that Morocco's security is in the hands of creatures like that? He wouldn't even be able to wash the dishes in the kitchen.

29.IX.69, A.M.

I saw him coming in our direction, and I said to my sister: This man coming along here is going to sit down with us.

Who is he?

Papa, I told her, laughing. Once I told him how much Papa hates me, and he offered to be my spiritual father.

She smiled. Poor man! How dirty he is!

We're the poor ones, I said. He's very rich. He's a famous writer.

It's not true! she cried.

Stand up and say hello to him, I told her. He came nearer and glanced at us. Then he smiled at her. As she got up to give him her hand, I said: My sister Malika.

Jean, he said.

How old are you? he asked her.

Fourteen.

Are you sure you're not younger than that?

As if he had offended her, she answered: No! I'm fourteen! He sat down and ordered a whisky. Looking at her glass of Coca-Cola, he said: And you? Why aren't you drinking whisky?

I don't drink alcohol. I'm a Muslim.

But some Muslims drink.

Only the disobedient ones, she said.

Mohammed Zerrad arrived. He was a friend of Genet's. We got into a long conversation about which papers were necessary in order to get a passport for the youth.

My sister stood up to go. Genet rose. *Pardon, mademoiselle.*

She's going back to Tétouan, I told him. She was smiling, and trying to withdraw her hand from his grasp.

I'll see you one of these days in Tétouan, he told her in Moghrebi.

When Malika remarked about Genet's unkempt appearance, I was reminded of a passage in *Le Journal du voleur* where he says that it never would have occurred to anyone in the Barrio Chino to wash his clothes. At most you washed your shirt, and then usually only the collar. Looking at him shuffling along today you would have said that he was still observing the same routine. He no longer lives in dirty narrow rooms, or needs a friend like Stilitano who is willing to sleep with the landlady once a week in return for the rent.

Several times he has voiced his enthusiasm for the veil and the djellaba as being the right garments for Moroccan women. *La femme a toujours été un mystère pour l'homme,* he says. It's the fact that she's hidden that makes men curious about her. Is she beautiful or not? Moroccan women look better with their faces covered.

29.IX.69, P.M.

I found him waiting for me in front of the hotel entrance. As we went in, I said: Last year they wouldn't let me in here, even though I was invited by an English friend who was staying here.

Why not? he demanded.

Perhaps I wasn't well enough dressed.

That's what I'd imagine. Would you rather go somewhere else?

No! On the contrary. I'll enjoy going with you into a place they've kept me out of.

We sat down in the garden and ordered two whiskys. There was a young man swimming in the pool in spite of the cold.

He glanced around nervously, above our heads and under the chairs, saying nothing. I had the impression that he was making certain there were no hidden microphones. Anything is possible, after all, and particularly in the case of a man like Genet.

Good. Let's talk about your writing and publishing problems, he said. I won't give you advice, because no advice that I can give will help decide your future. What I will tell you is that you must choose. Either you stay here as you are, or you go and live somewhere where you can write what you can't write here. I think the Muslims have gone beyond the ethic and traditions of the Qur'an. But in spite of that, the Qur'an is still a great book, one that's read by Muslims and non-Muslims alike. You can still read the poems of Baudelaire, Mallarmé and Rimbaud with great admiration. Why? Because their style goes right on being marvellous.

A moment later he remarked: The situation here is very unstable. Everything reeks of poverty and misery. The foreigners are the only ones here who live like human beings.

30.IX.69

We sat down on the terrace of the Café de Paris.

I had Camus's *La Peste* with me.

Do you like this novel? he asked me.

Yes. I'm reading it for the second time.

Are you very fond of Camus?

Yes. I've read a good deal of him.

There was a pause, and I asked him his opinion of Camus.

He writes like a bull.

I laughed.

Then he went on: I've never liked what he wrote. Nor did I like his personality. I was never able to get on with him.

Then you sided with Sartre in their famous controversy?

Naturally. Camus felt more than he thought.

A hippie came up to us and said to Genet in English: I'm a great admirer of your work. I'm glad to see you.

Genet looked at me. I translated what the young man had said. They shook hands, and the hippie went off waving and bowing, while Genet smiled. He turned to me and said: The American hippies are wonderful. But their fathers are insupportable.

Abdeslam the parachutist arrived. This time he made a point of sitting down next to Genet and speaking Moghrebi with him. Genet answered in monosyllables. Then Abdeslam turned to me. Tell him he has pretty fingers, he said.

Pretty fingers! I repeated, startled.

Yes, fingers! Tell him his hands are beautiful.

Tell him yourself, if you want to say it. Speak slowly, and he'll understand.

What's he trying to say? Genet asked me a moment later.

He says your fingers are pretty.

Genet stared at his hands with surprise. Then he looked at Abdeslam and burst into laughter. Abdeslam reached out and touched Genet's hand with his fingertips. Then he told him it was a beautiful hand.

Genet turned to me. Ask him what he thinks of my bald head. What does it look like?

Tell him his head is beautiful, too, said Abdeslam.

I translated.

Tell him he's crazy, said Genet. It looks like a baboon's ass.

1.X.69

We were sitting on the terrace of the Café de Paris.

You seem sad today, I said to him.

I'm always sad, and I always know why, he replied.

I accepted his sadness and did not press him further. I have my own sadnesses.

3.X.69

At the Café Zagora.

Did you have a hard time writing your first novel? I asked him.

No, not very. I wrote the first fifty pages of *Notre Dame des Fleurs* in prison. And when I was transferred to another jail they somehow got left behind. I did everything I could to get them back, but it was hopeless. And so I wrapped myself in my blanket and rewrote the fifty pages straight off.

I know you didn't start to write until after you were thirty, I said. Thirty-two or thirty-three.

That's right.

You'd never thought of writing before that?

I've always been writing, even before I ever tried to write anything. The career of a writer doesn't begin at the moment he begins to write. The career and the writing may coincide earlier or later.

You haven't written anything for several years, have you?

Do you consider your literary silence and your assumption of a political position another kind of creation, part of your writing?

Literally, I've said what I had to say. Even if there were anything more to add, I'd keep it to myself. When I was a convict, the judges had good reason to keep me in jail. In spite of that, they let me out. Whether they were afraid to keep me there any longer, or whether they let me go of their own free will, I don't know. In any case, the time had come for me to get out. But I might just as easily still be in jail.

You mean that sometimes luck wins out over the law?

Yes, it's possible for it to. There's no absolute no and no absolute yes. I'm sitting here with you now, but I might easily not be.

Later he recounted the story of a French painter who was eating in a restaurant and was asked by the proprietor to make a drawing of a flower so he could hang it on the wall of the restaurant. The painter drew the flower and then told the restaurateur how much it was going to cost him. What! the man cried. You dare ask such a price for something that took you five minutes to do?

Not five minutes, forty years, said the painter. Do you want the drawing or don't you?

The restaurateur said: Not at that price. The painter tore up the drawing and continued to eat.

10.X.69

At five o'clock we met at the Café Zagora. He asked me what my hunch was: would they give a passport to his friend Mohammed Zerrad, so he could accompany Genet to Paris?

I tried to convince him that bribery was the most practical way to go about trying to get a passport for a young Moroccan who was not in the government and had no contract to work abroad.

That sort of situation doesn't exist in any other country, unless the man is a criminal or a deserter or a spy, he said. They renewed my passport in London in three hours, without making any reference to my career.

That couldn't happen here, I told him. Not yet.

At quarter past five we took a taxi together to the Amalat. There was a long line of people inside, poorly dressed and with anxious faces. A thin man burst out of the office in a state of great excitement. His voice was nervous and hard. Genet turned to me. That's the man who told me to come back at five.

They shut at six, I said.

This official in charge of passports would come out now and then and push those who were waiting. Then he would mouth a few curses and go back inside. Genet was upset. He took a few steps along the corridor, stopped, and muttered: He's an animal, that one. What does he mean, shoving and insulting the people that way? He's a brute!

We waited until all the functionaries had left. All, that is, except those in the passport office. The thin man kept up a steady stream of vituperation against the people waiting. Genet asked me to explain some of the words he was shouting as he went up and down the line. Sometimes he spoke to them in the tone of one who held their very lives in his hands. He pushed one man with particular fury, and literally screamed at him. Again Genet asked for a translation.

He's telling him that as long as he's working in this office he'll never get a passport.

Why not?

Perhaps the bribe wasn't big enough. Sometimes, if a man argues with him, he locks him up. By the time he gets to court his fingernails are like claws and he has a beard down to here.

I told Genet I thought he should try to see the Governor himself, but he would not even discuss it. I hate those bureaucratic chiefs, he said.

At the last moment before the building closed, the thin man spoke to Genet, telling him he could expedite the passport if all the Moroccan's papers were in order.

On the way back in the fine rain that blew against us, he asked: What that man wants is a fistful of banknotes. Isn't that it?

Exactly, I said. You've got it right.

We sat down at the Café de Paris and ordered two

whiskys. He puffed on a Pantera cigarillo. I accepted his invitation to dinner at the Minzah.

The dining room was full of American tourists. The Moroccan waiters served Genet with great gusto, treating him as a friend rather than as a man staying at the hotel, and he never ceased to joke with them in his halting Arabic. The American tourists ate, and talked without respite.

Un moment ... écoutez, said Genet. Can you hear them? They're chewing on the motors of the planes they wish they were in. In Vietnam, or in the Middle East.

The pianist finished one piece and went into another. I've never heard a pianist quite that bad, Genet said. He plays the way they chew their food and their words.

Genet was happy, but he ate scantily. His only appetites are for alcohol and Nembutal, as he says.

I asked him: What are you reading these days?

If you mean books, I'm not reading anything. All I take with me when I travel is a few clothes and my papers.

You seem to like this hotel.

I know the manager, he said. He's read my books. Sometimes we talk about them, about the ideas behind them. At least in this place I feel at home, and not like just another client.

A Moroccan friend who works at the Minzah has told me a bit about Genet's behavior there. Sometimes he wanders down into the dining room barefoot and in his pyjamas, to ask a waiter for a match. He will go back upstairs, and soon reappear to ask for something else. It does not seem to occur to him to use the telephone beside his bed.

After dinner we walked for a half hour on the boulevard. He bought a few newspapers and some magazines, and went back to the hotel.

12.X.69

I met him about half past eleven in the morning at the Café de Paris. Mohammed Zerrad was with him. Genet asked us both to have lunch at El Mirador. He is suffering with a kidney ailment, he told me, and called in three different doctors to see him this morning. Each one gave him an injection and then left.

We said goodbye at four o'clock. He had been delightful the entire time. Then he went to take his siesta.

13.X.69

I picked him up at the hotel at six this evening, and we went to the Brasserie de France. He was still in pain, and walked very slowly.

14.X.69

I met him at the hotel. His health seemed to have improved. He gave me a copy of the Qur'an in French, saying that he did not fully understand it.

In order to know what most of the commentaries mean, he said, one would have to have studied the history of the Arabs. You've read the book in Arabic, of course? It must be marvellous.

It's the only great work in Arabic, I said.

He began to discuss Mallarmé, for whom I know he has boundless admiration. Among the lines he quoted there was one I particularly liked, and I asked him to write it out for me. Having no paper at hand, he sought out a blank page in the Qur'an, and wrote: *Et le vide papier que sa blancheur defend ...* He was not absolutely certain of his quotation, and he put a question mark after it. (Later when I checked, I discovered that he had written *et* where he should have written *sur,* and *sa* instead of *la.*)

I asked him what, if anything, the name Mallarmé meant in French. He grinned. His name indicates impotence: *mal armé, n'est-ce pas?* Poorly equipped sexually, but with a brain that made up for it.

Then I asked him if *Esquire* had published the complete text of his report on the 1968 Democratic Convention in Chicago. He said they had published only half of it. But I sold the other half to a different magazine, he went on. I know they only buy what I write because it has my signature on it, and not because they want to hear what I have to say about democracy in the United States.

15.X.69

Mohammed Zerrad has gone to the country town where he was born, somewhere near Tétouan, to fetch the papers he needs in order to get his passport.

Genet was troubled. Do you think they'll really give him those papers up there in the mountains? Or will it be the same story as it is here when you try to get something from the officials?

But I told you, I said. Everything depends on his personal relationships with the officials themselves or with whoever has contact with them. And if he doesn't know anybody, it can only be solved with money.

Hassan Ouakrim came into the café and sat down with us. It occurred to me that he might be able to help. He knows several functionaries at the Amalat, and never seems to have difficulties getting official papers when he needs them. (Ouakrim runs the Troupe Inoziss, a local dance group.) I introduced him as a friend who might possibly be of use to us. Genet's face showed interest when Ouakrim assured him that he would do everything he could for us, and it showed more interest when he told him he headed a group of dancers. Then he spoke at length of the difficulties of running a project that combined music, dance, and theatre. Genet warned him that the artist must be on guard against whatever has influence on his work from the outside. Otherwise, he said, he will constantly be wanting to make it more up to date, which, here in Morocco, means more European. You must keep your music and dance intact, he told Ouakrim.

16.X.69

At the Brasserie de France. Mohammed Zerrad has come back from his trip, bringing the necessary papers with him. He says he got them quickly only by paying a good deal of extra money. We congratulated him on his success. We were waiting for Ouakrim to arrive and go with us to the Amalat.

Do you think he can be of any help? Genet asked me.

I think he may. He knows a few people who work there, perhaps because of his dance group.

I see. But is he trustworthy? I mean, can one talk about Moroccan politics in front of him?

I don't think he could do us any harm, I said. All I know about him is that he's always busy with his group. What he wants is to go abroad and study.

When Ouakrim arrived, he took only Zerrad with him to the Amalat. The black waiter came and stood by me. I hear he's a famous writer, he murmured to me.

That's what they say, I told him.

He's a real gentleman, he said.

Genet gave him a friendly smile. The waiter stepped forward and offered him his hand. Speaking in *darija* he said: You are a fine man.

You're a good man too, answered Genet, also in *darija*. Someone called to the waiter, and he left the table.

Aren't you going to ask the French Consul to help you at all? I asked. In case you can't get the passport in the ordinary way?

Never, said Genet. That's the one thing I won't do. I'd rather pay any amount of money than have to ask at the French Consulate for anything.

17.X.69

I was carrying a copy of *La Peste* with me, having almost finished reading it. We sat down on the terrace of the Café de Paris.

You're still reading that *Peste?* he asked me.

I'm almost at the end.

And my *Balcon?* Have you read that?

Not yet, I said.

Why not?

I'm waiting for the end of the month, so I can buy another copy, I told him.

But what for?

Because my copy's inscribed. You signed it for me.

What's that got to do with it?

I told him I did my reading in cafés, and I was afraid something might happen to the book if I took it out with me. I said I was keeping it as a souvenir.

He reached out and seized my copy of *La Peste*. Then he ripped out the first page.

Do that with my book, he said. Tear out the page that has the inscription on it. Read the play. Then paste the page back in. It's certainly better to read the book than leave it on the shelf for fear of losing the signature.

This made me smile. We talked about the price of books, and I complained that all of his were too expensive.

I make more money that way, he said.

But why don't they bring out your works in a cheap edition like *Le Livre de Poche*, for instance?

I don't know.

But you know that most students can't afford to buy your books.

It's not my fault, said Genet.

I decided not to say any more.

You told me the last time you were in Tangier that you hadn't seen Sartre in two years, I said.

That's true. And I still haven't seen him. One day last year when he was giving a lecture at the Sorbonne I tried to get in and hear him, but a girl at the door told me there was no room inside the hall. A lot of other people were trying to get in, but it was impossible.

The girl must have recognized you, I said.

She was a student. I didn't want to insist.

Later, as we were walking along the Boulevard Pasteur, Genet asked if we could go to the bookshop that was the local agency for Gallimard. He had spent the money he had brought with him. I was not certain whether the Librairie des Colonnes was the right one or not, but since we were very near it, I pointed to it and said it might be the one he wanted. We went into the Librairie des Colonnes.

The two ladies who run the bookshop, Madame and Mademoiselle Gérofi, overwhelmed us with courtesy. Genet asked Madame Gérofi if he might speak with her alone for a moment, and she led him up to her office on the balcony. I could see them sitting up there talking. Then Madame Gérofi began to use the typewriter. Brion Gysin says that Genet never uses banks. Gallimard acts as his bank, with the main office in Paris and branches in any bookshop that acts as a Gallimard agency. When he needs money in Paris, he goes to Gallimard to get it, and carries it out with him in a little bag which he hides under his overcoat, at the same time looking around him furtively just as if he had stolen it.

When we were outside in the street again he said: The lady's husband may be able to help with the passport. I've got to meet him in a little while. Let's sit down here and wait. She called him on the phone and he's coming right over.

We went into the Claridge. Once again we began to talk about poetry, from Baudelaire to Verlaine and Rimbaud. Finally we reached the shrine of Mallarmé, where he had been leading the conversation.

I wish I had *Brise marine* here, he said. I'd like to read it to you.

I said I would run and ask Madame Gérofi for it, and he thought that a good idea.

At the bookshop I found Madame Gérofi very busy with her accounts. I told her Monsieur Genet wanted to see the book. She handed me the poems of Mallarmé. Tell Monsieur Genet that my husband will arrive immediately, she said.

As I was running back to the Claridge I caught sight of Ouakrim, who said he had been looking for us. At the table he told Genet that he thought there was at least some hope of getting the passport. Genet asked him if he believed Monsieur Gérofi might be of help. It was possible, Ouakrim said, since, being an architect, he had many friends in the government offices.

He can help you if he wants to take the trouble, he told Genet.

Monsieur Gérofi arrived at five o'clock. He is seeing a certain official tomorrow morning and will speak to him.

Ouakrim said that he too had an appointment with someone who might be useful. We got into Monsieur Gérofi's car. Genet still had the borrowed copy of Mallarmé in his hand. He was astonished at the number of difficulties involved in trying to get a simple passport in Morocco. Monsieur Gérofi merely nodded, and said from time to time: That's the way it is here.

We arrived at the Amalat. Ouakrim went in alone

while we waited in the car. Genet began to leaf through the Mallarmé volume. If you'll excuse me, I'm going to read this poem to my friend here, he told Monsieur Gérofi.

Mais je vous en prie, said Monsieur Gérofi.

Genet began to read *Brise marine* in his high, thin voice. When he had finished, he said: Isn't it a miracle, that poem?

We agreed that it was extraordinary. Then he singled out a line that particularly pleased him: *Et la jeune femme allaitant son enfant.*

Ouakrim came back saying that the man he had had the appointment with could not be found. I had noticed that Genet was growing increasingly concerned about getting the passport, and seemed more determined than ever to see it through.

19.X.69

I met him around eleven in the morning. We walked down to the Avenida de España and sat at the Puerta del Sol. Genet's friend Georges Lapassade happened to pass by. He seemed perturbed and spoke with great nervousness. I did not particularly like his personality.

In the afternoon I met them both again at the Brasserie de France. We're invited to tea at Madame Gérofi's, Genet told me. You're invited too.

I was tempted to refuse, in order not to have to be

near Lapassade, whom I found truly disagreeable. But Monsieur Gérofi arrived then, and we all got into his car. At his apartment we found Emilio Sanz. I had met him at Edouard Rotiti's. He was another whom I found insupportable – the sort of man who waves a flower in the air as he talks, and sniffs it before answering your question or giving what he considers a shattering opinion.

The room encouraged relaxation, and I was tired. I asked Madame Gérofi if I might have a glass of whisky instead of tea. The conversation came around to the illustrious persons in the arts and letters who have lived in Tangier. Madame Gérofi spoke of Tennessee Williams, saying that he used to come often, but now had not been here since 1964. The whisky helped me to relax. I drank it slowly. I was practically asleep when I heard Genet exclaim: I've gone into the literary graveyard!

They were talking about the theatre. Genet said that it was no longer a viable art form. I asked him what form he thought more valid today.

Something that doesn't yet exist. All the forms used so far have worn out.

Yes. He can say that now that his complete works have been published, I thought. But if he had thought that back in the forties, he wouldn't have written his books, and there would have been only Genet the beggar and thief, Genet condemned to life imprisonment.

As we got up to go, I saw Emilio Sanz take a book from a bookshelf. He handed it to Genet for him to autograph. Genet glanced towards me, asking a question with his eyes. I shrugged slightly, as if I were saying: It's your responsibility. You know how you feel about that sort of man.

I'm sorry, Genet told him. I don't feel well. I can't sign any books today.

Bravo, I thought. What an intuition!

Going down in the elevator Genet asked me: Who is he, the Spaniard with the moustache?

I said he was the son of a banker.

I didn't like him at all, he said.

I don't like him either.

20.X.69

I was with Brion at the Brasserie de France. Genet came at about half past six with Mohammed Zerrad. Brion left immediately. We talked for two hours. Mohammed Zerrad also left, and I went with Genet to look for Georges Lapassade in the Zoco Chico. We found him with some Moroccan youths in the Café Central. We went to Maria's restaurant and ordered a bottle of wine. Genet took only one glass. He did not want to eat dinner. Georges and I accompanied him to the hotel, and then I took Lapassade to meet Brion. I talked with them for a half hour or so. While they discussed the old days in Tangier, I fell asleep. When I awoke at two in the morning, they were still talking. I left Lapassade there listening to Brion's discourse on Morocco.

21.X.69

Genet, Lapassade, Brion Gysin and I took a walk through the alleys behind the Zoco Chico. We went into the Bencharqi quarter. There we found Manolo's house. Inside the door old Alberto the Italian was sitting, watching to see who came in. He brought us some ancient chairs that creaked when we sat in them. The *sala* was like an icebox. Mildew on the walls. Everything damp and dirty and old. Brion began to talk about the place as it had been in the days of the International Zone.

This city is completely dead, said Lapassade. What's left of it?

I was reminded for some reason of what Genet had written in *Le Journal du voleur*, when he falls asleep leaning against a wall, seeing Tangier in his mind's eye as a *repaire de traîtres*.

The old Italian offered us what remained of a bottle of wine. We thanked him and got up to go. You can see for yourselves, he said. There's nothing left here. Was it dead like this twenty years ago? In those days there were always five or six clients waiting to get in. Nowadays if we get three during the whole day we're lucky. Sometimes nobody comes in for twenty-four hours straight.

We agreed that the past had been better than the

present, and that nothing resembling the past would ever be seen again.

About half past five we went to the Amalat, Genet, Ouakrim and I. Ouakrim had arranged an appointment with the Governor's private secretary, who gave us a cordial reception. It was the first time during any visit to the Amalat that I had seen a happy expression on Genet's face. The man asked him what sort of work Zerrad would be doing in Paris, and Genet said he would be using him as gardener. I laughed to myself, since he has no garden and no house.

So he will come under the category of servant, the secretary said.

Genet reflected for a moment. *Je vous demande pardon,* he said. I should never think of considering anyone a servant. He would only be working in the garden. In any case I intend to try to find someone who can give him instruction in French.

The man smiled. Apparently he understood Genet's attitude in not wanting to label anyone *servant*. He said he would need a letter from Genet declaring himself financially responsible for Zerrad during his absence from Morocco. The letter would be kept at the Amalat as a guarantee. Genet agreed to take him the letter tomorrow, and the man promised to do everything in his power to see that the document was ready in a day or two. We felt better when we went out into the street. Genet was reflective. He seems to be a civilized man, he said, as if to himself.

22.X.69

I met Lapassade, Genet having gone off to take his siesta. We went to Maria's restaurant. As we were eating Lapassade said: It looks to me as if Genet were finished. Where's Genet the adventurer, the Genet of Barcelona, Tunis, Greece?

Lapassade was right, I thought. He was only telling the beads of the past. Whenever I asked him about one of his books, he answered: Oh! I wrote that years ago. One afternoon I said to him: You don't look too well today. He gazed at me with lifeless eyes and said: You're right. I'm very low.

Later at the Brasserie de France, Genet whispered to me, indicating Ouakrim, who sat at the table with us. Does he expect me to pay him for his help?

I put the question to Ouakrim.

Non, monsieur Genet, he said. Then he went into Arabic. We're friends. But you might be able to help me. There's something I'm very much interested in.

Genet said he was ready to help him in whatever way he could.

What he wanted, said Ouakrim, was a letter of introduction to someone in the United States who might be able to get him into a dance school there.

Genet said he would write a letter. We walked to the Minzah and sat in the salon while Genet went up to his room to look for his address book. A letter of introduction from Genet is worth more than a million francs, said Ouakrim.

I agreed that accepting money would have destroyed the friendship. When Genet came back he sat down and wrote two letters, one to Barney Rossett and the other to Richard Seaver, both of Grove Press in New York. I could not help noticing that he ended one of them with the phrase: *et puis, j'aime tellement les dollars américains!*

23.X.69

Mohammed Zerrad got his passport today. Larbi Yacoubi decided to celebrate the occasion by arranging a Gnawa party for us. It started about eight o'clock. There were Moroccans, both Muslim and Jewish, French, English, and Americans present. The chief of the Gnawa, black as charcoal, got on friendly terms with Genet during the first rest period between numbers. The music was Sudanese, of course, and the dances expressed basic emotions.

The boy sitting beside me occasionally jumped up and took part in the frantic dancing. From time to time he translated a fragment of the text of a song from the Bambara into Moghrebi, and I retranslated for Genet.

Genet asked the chief how old he was. The old man said: I don't know exactly, but when Kaiser Wilhelm the Second came to Tangier in 1905 I was just beginning to walk.

Genet turned to me: He's handsome, very handsome, that man. Look! He's smoking *kif* as if he were a young man of twenty!

A photographer among the guests got up and began to take one picture after another. I noticed that Genet seemed delighted to be snapped with the Gnawa musicians, and annoyed whenever he was caught while talking with a European. For the first time his behavior rather put me off. It seemed to me pretentious, but I accepted it as a part of his personality.

Lapassade smoked *kif* constantly, moving his head in time with the Sudanese rhythms. The party went on until half past two in the morning. I saw that Genet resented the presence of the Europeans. He kept moving around, changing his seat continually.

When we left, he pulled out a handful of bank-notes and put them into the chief's hand. (The musicians already had been paid.) As the money passed between them they exchanged glances. Peace be with you, he said to the black man, who echoed the phrase smiling.

In the street he turned to me, saying: They were wonderful, those Gnawa, weren't they?

Yes. Personally I don't like Gnawa parties.

But why not?

They're primitives. I hate everything primitive.

So, what kind of music do you like? he asked me.

Oh, Mozart, Beethoven, Tchaikovsky, Berlioz, people like that.

It seems to me you've been westernized.

Maybe.

Well, I far prefer those Gnawa we just heard. I used to be like them myself. They're fantastic!

Lapassade turned to me. You simply don't realize their value.

Their value is of no interest to me, I replied. I just don't like them.

Genet told Lapassade: Let him alone. He's free to like what he wants to like.

When we were almost at the Hotel Minzah, Lapassade said to me: I'm going down to the Zoco Chico. Do you want to come along and have some tea?

No, I said curtly. No thanks. I think I'll go to bed.

I said goodnight to Genet and went on my way.

25.X.69

Genet and I said our farewells down on the Avenida de España. He was accompanied by Lapassade and a group of French teachers who were up from Rabat on holiday. He and his friend Mohammed Zerrad are setting out today for France via Spain.

I told him that I had left some of the photos taken at

the Gnawa party for him at the hotel. They had not given them to him, but he thanked me, and I walked away.

2.II.70

I ran into Mohammed Zerrad in the Zoco de Fuera. We both laughed when we saw each other, even before we spoke. He seemed to be in a good mood. I asked him where Genet was. He did not know, he said. He had been working in Gibraltar for the past month.

I asked him about the trip through Spain. A group of newspaper men came to greet them at the airport, including photographers. He said Genet seemed to know some of them personally, and joked with them as if they were old friends. Then they asked him questions and took down his answers. I asked him if they put any questions to him, too. He said they did, but since he speaks practically no Spanish, he merely said he was a friend. They were taken to someone's house, where they lived a luxurious life during their stay in Madrid. But when they got to Paris, he said, nobody paid any attention to Genet, and this surprised him. He said they went to a big building full of books, and that Genet told him: This is where I live.

Genet introduced Zerrad to some of the people who were sitting at desks there. Then he asked a girl if she would take his Moroccan friend out in her car, to show him the city. Paris was a fine city, he said, but it was too easy to get lost in. They spent an hour driving around in a beautiful car. It went like a dove, he said. And she was a dove too. A dove driving a dove.

I asked him how they communicated with each other.

Just with smiles, he said. And sometimes we made signs. She was very well educated. You don't have to talk to a girl like that. Afterwards we went back to the book house, and Genet took me to a little hotel and rented a room for me.

It seems that later Genet introduced Zerrad to a French student he was paying for, and the two got into the habit of going out together when Genet was too busy to see either of them. The student lived in the same hotel where Zerrad was staying.

One day Genet came to see Zerrad and handed him some money, saying he was going to a country that was 'very far away' to see a production of one of his plays. But as soon as Genet left, the student moved into Zerrad's room. And there was only one bed, he added. But the boy kept saying it would be cheaper.

The student took Zerrad all over Paris with him. Zerrad said he was always afraid they would get separated. The size of the city terrified him. He said the young Frenchman was all right for the first three days, and then he suddenly changed. He began to go into shops and buy things, and Zerrad had to pay for them.

The money was flying out of my pockets! he said. And I'm not Genet. I can't go and get money wherever

I happen to be, like him. All I could think of was getting out of there fast while I still had enough to get out with. I kept seeing myself lost in the streets, with my hand out asking for money. So I came back to Tangier and gave my wife the money I had left. Then I went to Gibraltar and got a job the first week.

I said it was strange. Then I asked him what he thought of Genet.

He's a good man, but I don't understand him, he said. Anyway, he did a lot for me, and I won't forget it. If it hadn't been for him I'd still be here earning five or six dirhams a day. That is, if I had work at all. You can't tell.

Afterword

After 1969, Jean Genet returned to Tangier many times, alone or with El Katrani. Brief visits, since he was now living in Larache in the house he had bought for El Katrani, whom he had encouraged to get married so that, as he told me, he would finally get rid of the whores.

On February 13, 1980, I was in Paris to talk about *For Bread Alone* on the television show *Apostrophe*. Genet, who usually lived in hotels, big or small, was living then in a modest studio apartment in Pigalle.

He was barefoot when he welcomed us, Tahar Ben Jelloun and me. After a warm embrace, he said to me, 'You have written a very good book!'

There was just a single bed there, and books were stacked up on the floor; in one corner, a telephone on a little table, an ashtray next to the bed and a little rug for visitors. No chairs. A smell of urine emanated from the bathroom and the window was closed, since he had a cold.

Genet stretched out on the bed and Tahar and I shared the little rug.

El Katrani had one son, Azzedine. Genet adopted this boy. He enrolled him as a boarder in a school in Rabat and, until his death on April 15, 1986, paid attention to the boy's education. It is said that, afterwards, Aniss Balafrej, faithful to the promise made to Genet, has looked after Azzedine, who is continuing his studies in the same school.

In Rabat, Genet had come to know Mohammed Barrada and his wife Layla Chahid.

They invited him over to their place, but only for lunch, because Genet went to bed very early, especially in the last years of his life.

And he who didn't like staying with other people sometimes stayed with them for ten days or more.

Cancer was eating into his throat and suffocating him, but he never stopped smoking Gitanes. When I met him at the Hotel Royal in Rabat, with El Katrani and his son Azzedine, his voice was weak and rasping.

I didn't see El Katrani again until my last visit to Larache. He told me that he had entrusted some letters of Genet's to a professor in the Literature Department at Marrakech who was writing an essay on him.

'Did he give them back to you?' I asked.

'Not yet.'

He very much regretted having lent these documents. I added that he would do better to sell Genet's letters to a French university to keep them from getting lost, since he didn't know how to preserve them.

'I won't make a mistake like that again. I hope poor Jean will forgive me.'

Several times I almost told El Katrani how bothered I was by this word 'poor' to describe Genet, who was all dignity and who confronted death alone, without asking for anyone's help. But for El Katrani, 'poor' meant 'good'.

The last time I saw El Katrani he told me with great bitterness, 'He came to Larache and we went to see my son Azzedine in Rabat. After that, he went back to Paris to die there, suffocating in a little hotel ... The poor man, he died all alone, over there.'

Everyone who knew El Katrani and his relationship with Genet knows that he adored him.

After Genet's death, the press revealed that he had expressly asked to be buried in Larache. El Katrani told me that was wrong.

Genet had told him, in the presence of Jacky (another friend he'd adopted): 'I can be buried anywhere but Larache.'

Fate willed it that he rest in an old cemetery where most of the dead are Spanish soldiers.

It is in fact quite close to an old Spanish army barracks. I asked El Katrani why they had buried Genet in Larache.

'It was Jacky who decided at the last moment,' he replied. 'Probably so that his grave would be closer to us – to my son and me. And also, Jacky often comes here to see us.'

When I visited Genet's grave in the company of El Katrani, he said to me, 'I come to this grave three or four times a week. I sit down here, alone or sometimes with Azzedine, when he's on vacation, and I contemplate the sea, reliving my memories of Jean, in Morocco or abroad.'

Georges Bousquet, the director of the French Cultural Centre in Tangiers, thinks Genet's death devastated El Katrani's spirit for ever, and that it will be very difficult for him to begin a new life. What's more, El Katrani seems like the living dead. It's a tragedy, but who could free him from his hallucinations?

El Katrani died a few months later, in a car accident. He was on his way to see his son in Rabat.

1993

Translated from the French by Charlotte Mandell

Tennessee Williams
in Tangier

Foreword

Choukri's book describes a close encounter of the third kind. Hearing that Tennessee Williams had been sighted in Tangier in the summer of 1973, he immediately decided to investigate this famous visitor from the large and remote planet America. (A few years previously, when Jean Genet landed in Tangier, Choukri spotted and interviewed him, but the spatial distance between them was far less, for the Moroccans and the French have not been strangers since the turn of the century.) Choukri was a young-old Moroccan of thirty-eight that year, and had recently written the extraordinary story of his life. *For Bread Alone,* translated by Paul Bowles, recounts the most desperate, squalid, poverty-stricken childhood and adolescence imaginable; and then how Choukri at the age of twenty-one created a future for himself as writer and teacher by learning to read and write. But imagine, in spite of his resolutely acquired sophistication, the distance between Choukri and Tennessee. Choukri had travelled very little and America remained to him, as to most Moroccans, a kind of legendary terra incognita, just as it appeared to the early European immigrants. There was a language problem – Choukri speaks good Spanish and adequate French as well as Arabic, but his English (like Tennessee's Spanish and French) is minimal to fragmentary. And their temperaments are opposite in two important ways. Tennessee's humor is immediate and explosive, Choukri's concealed and reluctant; Choukri likes searching literary discussions ('I was about to say that Alma Winemiller seemed to me like a granddaughter of Hester Prynne'), Tennessee does not care for them. Add to this some more obvious polarities – of lower-class Moslem and middle-class Southern upbringing, of sexual preferences, of relative obscurity and extreme celebrity – and the odds against successful contact seem almost impossibly high.

When we say that opposites attract, perhaps what we really mean is that similarities emerge in spite of the opposites. Both Choukri and Tennessee are fugitives from their backgrounds, outsiders and loners. (Driving down the Boulevard Pasteur, the tacky main street of Tangier's European section, I have often glimpsed Choukri alone, thin and sharp-featured, walking or sitting at a café, always with a stack of books.) I don't know whether there was anything special about Choukri's mood that summer, but certainly Tennessee was not at his most buoyant. He had arrived in Tangier with the Wrong Companion, whose wrongness Choukri amusingly records. ('One would have said that he felt nothing, like the statue of the angel in *Summer and Smoke*.') He was pre-occupied with trying to finish a play, *The Red Devil Battery Sign*. He was exceptionally restless, having cut short a stay in Italy, as he would cut short the stay in Tangier. At first it threatened to become one of those impromptu visits in which nothing turned out right; perhaps not a great deal did; but the encounters with Choukri were an unexpected success. Obviously Choukri's admiration touched Tennessee, and he sparked a personal curiosity. He took Tennessee's mind off the Wrong Companion (from time to time, at least), and showed himself a fine example of the kindness of strangers.

At any rate they clicked – and the result is this series of bright verbal snapshots, unposed and relaxed yet sharp. At first Choukri is puzzled by Tennessee's wonderful capacity for laughter, no matter what the circumstances. 'Your works, especially your plays, are depressing,' he tells him, 'but you always seem to be happy.' Tennessee (rightly) denies that his work is depressing, and adds: 'Sadness can be funny, and sometimes joy can be depressing. Not all sadness is depressing, or all happiness pleasant.' So Choukri realizes that 'he can forget his fatigue and discomfort by laughing', and after first finding Tennessee 'not at all like your writing', changes his mind.

The loner also senses that 'Tennessee likes solitude, but he's afraid of being alone', and elicits a memorable response when they talk about critics: 'They flay us,' Tennesse remarks with the wisdom of the true survivor, 'but we know how to grow new skin.'

By the end a genuine affection has grown up between them, and it touches because it's so clearly transitory. 'Perhaps we'll meet again one day,' Tennessee says with a goodbye hug, before his spaceship takes off. (Perhaps they never will.) Most of their meetings have been haphazard and unplanned – in the street, at a café, at Paul Bowles's apartment – but Choukri's impressions have a remarkable coherence. Like so many Moroccans, he is a natural storyteller; incidental characters and local atmosphere (Tangier café life, a dreadful apartment that Tennessee is offered, a bureaucratic trauma at the post office) are described with a seemingly casual precision; and Choukri's account of Tennessee's touchdown during two weeks of a Tangier summer achieves its effect by the collecting of moments, the compiling of fragments, by sympathy growing out of curiosity. 'Tennessee's way of expressing himself makes me feel good,' he says at one point. How right he is, and how well he conveys it.

Gavin Lambert

16.VII.73

I went to see my friend Paul Bowles at his apartment. Tennessee will be here on Sunday, he told me.

Aha! I said. So he's coming back at last.

He has not been to Tangier since 1964. I was drinking black tea with lemon. It's a long time since I've drunk anything alcoholic at Paul's. The last time he offered me anything, it was vodka. An old friend of his from America brought it to him from a Soviet ship on which he was a passenger. I went each day and got drunk on it. Bottle after bottle, until we finished the translation we were doing. It's almost twenty years since Paul has taken any alcohol, which is why he very seldom offers drinks to the people who visit him. Tennessee likes to drink, so Paul will have to buy a few bottles of something while he is here.

I did not stay long at Paul's because I had an appointment with Mohammed Zefzaf at the Café Manila. I found him running his fingers over his beard between swallows of beer. He tried to smooth his uncombed hair.

Tennessee Williams will be here Sunday, I said. I just got the news from Paul Bowles.

He smiled. But I saw him a few minutes ago at Yacoubi's studio, he told me. He was with a young American or Englishman. I don't know which, because he didn't open his mouth.

Ha, that's strange. He's already here! And what was your impression?

I think he's afraid of strangers. But I think he's attracted to them once he knows them. He had a nice suit on, and it was clean. Not one of your careless dishevelled writers. His friend had a fine camera with him. Tennessee seemed happy enough. Whatever Yacoubi said or did made him laugh.

And Yacoubi himself? What did you make of him? I asked him.

I don't think he wanted us there, my friend and me, once Tennessee arrived, he said. But he'd invited us when we were at the Café de Paris. It was his idea.

Zefzaf looked like a ghost with his dark skin and his bushy hair and his black clothing. You probably scared him, I said, with that pointed beard and that eagle's nest on top of your head.

Oh, he stared at me, all right, Zefzaf said. But I could see that he approved of me. If Yacoubi hadn't hurried us out I could have come to be friendly with him. We said goodbye and I came here to have some beer. I think Yacoubi wanted to have Tennessee to himself. You'll meet him at your friend's house.

You still look like a dangerous criminal to me, I told him. (This is our regular routine, to keep sadness at arm's length and make life seem worth living.)

You should try to get to know Tennessee, he told me. Then you can write about him the way you did with Genet.

We sat drinking beer and talking until around three in the morning.

17.VII.73

A very hot day, even at half past ten in the morning. I went to the Café de Paris and sat down on the terrace. He was at another table, reading an English-language newspaper. At his right sat a young man. I looked at the photograph on the jacket of *Cat on a Hot Tin Roof.* I had a copy of it in Arabic translation with me. Then I stared at him for a long time. From what I could see, his eyes still held the same dreamy expression I had noted in the photographs, taken many years earlier. The pictures show him in his forties; now he is in his sixties. I am almost as old as he was when the photograph on this book was taken. He was born on March 26th, and I on March 25th. One day of difference in temperament between us? It can be wonderful to know someone without that person being aware you know him. Shall I surprise him as I did Jean Genet in the Zoco Chico? He's a writer and I'm a writer. He's famous and I'm not famous. That's the difference. The apprentice thief usually learns from a master thief. I've worked at some of the same jobs that he has, back in his early days.

The waiter came with the drinks for their table. He set down two bottles of Coca-Cola. Then he poured Fernet-Branca into Tennessee's glass. (I tried that bitter stuff once, but never since.) Tennessee wore thick glasses to read his paper, hurrying from one page to another, as if he were merely glancing at the headlines. After about half an hour the two got up and walked in front of me. Both of them wore light blue suits and espadrilles. Tennessee walks jauntily, his newspaper under his arm. The young man, a leather envelope in his hand, tries to keep up with him. I sat thinking that soon the game of human contact would begin. It might turn out to be a friendship or otherwise. Then I saw Yacoubi about to greet them. That should make the game of human contact easier to play. Yacoubi is not a friend of mine, but I know him, and have given him my opinion of his paintings.

I walked along behind them. By the time they came to the Café Manila I was almost abreast of them. Yacoubi turned and saw me. He stopped and said: Ah, Choukri! How are you? This is lucky.

He introduced me to Tennessee and his friend Baxter, explaining that I was a Moroccan writer.

We're looking for a house for Tennessee, Yacoubi said. Can you help?

I said I would be pleased to do what I could.

You know more about the town than I do, he said. You live here all the year round.

We walked here and there, looking for estate agencies. I thought of a nearby one, and we set out to find it. As we walked, I showed Tennessee the Arabic translation of his play, and explained that the title in Arabic meant 'A Cat on the Fire'. I added that several of his plays, both full-length and one-acts, had been published in Arabic, as well as some of his short stories.

I heard his noisy laugh for the first time. Many books, many boys!

As we passed Madame Porte's tearoom, he asked Yacoubi: is that agency very far?

I assured him that we were nearly there, that it was in the Calle Moussa ben Nusair.

Why don't we take a cab? he asked.

I told him it was not worthwhile. He laughed again. I was not sure why he laughed. Either he was tired, I thought, or he hated walking in the heat. The sun made the air heavy and immobile.

At the agency I explained to the blonde Moroccan girl what we were trying to find. She told us she had several flats. Then she telephoned another agency. I was standing by the door. Tennessee and his friend had stretched out in two chairs. Yacoubi excused himself and went back out into the street. I told Tennessee that Paul Bowles was a friend of mine, and that he had translated various of my works into English: my autobiography, my book on Jean Genet, and several stories. He said he would like to see the book on Genet, and I promised to lend him the part of it that had been printed in the magazine *Antaeus*. He looked me up and down, and said: Where *is* Genet?

I have no idea, I said. His friends don't seem to know, either. I've asked several, but none of them could tell me. He may be with some political group like the Black Panthers, helping them in one way or another.

He laughed, and said: I like what he writes, even though

I don't understand him. He has a fantastic imagination. But I don't even know whether he still writes these days.

I don't think he does, I said. He hasn't written anything in several years. Only a few magazine articles and interviews.

I know about them, he said. But I'm talking about books.

When he was here he told me his place was in the literary cemetery.

Tennessee laughed. His friend Baxter had not budged. He seemed to be congealed.

He considers that he has nothing more to write, I went on. That's what he gave me to understand. He's disillusioned about literature, and even more about the theatre, from what I heard him telling Madame Gérofi one day at her house.

He stared at me for a long time, looking straight into my eyes. I remembered then that Zefzaf had mentioned his strange way of looking at one, and I said to myself: He's surely forming an opinion of me right now.

He may be ill, said Tennessee. I too stared down at him, trying to see his eyes over the rims of his sunglasses.

He suffers from chronic insomnia, I said. And he takes Nembutal.

The girl finished her telephoning. She turned and told us in French: You'll have to go to the other office in the rue des Vignes. Then she explained to me which building the agency was in, and we went out into the street. Yacoubi was talking with another Muslim in front of a restaurant on the opposite side. When he saw us, he ran over to join us, and we started to walk.

Is this other agency far? Tennessee wanted to know.

No. It's just behind that hotel there. I pointed to the Hotel Chellah.

Once again we went along under the broiling sun. I could see that he had a real dislike of walking.

Yacoubi remarked to me in Arabic that he thought it was going to be difficult to find a furnished apartment in summer.

You can get anything here, I told him. It's a question of paying for it.

Yacoubi smiled. Our companion is very rich and very generous, he said. He's a good man. He's willing to pay any price if he finds what he's looking for.

I know that, I said. He glanced at me as if it surprised him that I should say I knew anything at all about Tennessee.

I've read a lot about him, I explained.

Good, he said, still smiling.

We walked in the sun and in the shade. From the shade into the sun and from the sun into the shade, and the air was perfectly still. The Spaniard in charge of the other agency was standing outside the door at the top of the steps. He said he had just sent his assistant to the first office with the keys to three apartments so that we could inspect them. They were all in the Calle Quevedo.

Annoyance was clearly visible on Tennessee's face. The Spaniard asked us to step inside the office, which Tennessee and I did, leaving Yacoubi and Baxter outside in the street. The office was filthy and everything was covered with dust. Tennessee sat down in a chair facing two poorly dressed Moroccan women who apparently were also hunting for apartments. A child with them stared at us with wide-open eyes. There was nowhere for me to sit. We waited, saying nothing. From time to time the Spaniard went outside to see if the man with the keys was in sight. I amused myself studying an old map of Tangier showing sections of the city scheduled for urbanization.

The Spaniard began to call out: Come on, Antonio! A turtle can get around faster than you can. Turning to us, he indicated the old man who was coming in. He'll take you to see whatever you want.

Tennessee awoke from his reverie.

About how much do these apartments cost? I asked the Spaniard. He looked first at Tennessee and then at me. There are three apartments, and they're all the same price, he said. Two hundred dollars a month.

I translated this for Tennessee. He nodded and said: We'll see. The important thing is that it should be comfortable.

Once again we began to walk in the heat. This time there was no shade. The shady places always seemed to be far away. It was not a great distance to the apartment house, but having to walk without the solace of an occasional bit of shade bothered Tennessee. Moreover, there was no hope of catching a taxi, as the way went exclusively along back streets, where it would have taken us a half hour or more to find one.

The apartment building was divided into two sections, each with its own entrance. We went in, and were faced by a Moroccan concierge. The elevator's not working today, he told us.

When I explained to Tennessee, he exclaimed: Oh, no! Let's go.

I looked at the elevator. It was ancient. Once Tennessee had been an elevator operator, but now he was over sixty and did not relish having to climb a hundred steps or more in order to get home.

Let's look at the other part of the building, said the old Spaniard.

Now we left one place of shade and went into another. This section of the house had no elevator at all. The old man said he thought we would like the flat on the second floor. Yacoubi and I climbed up with him, while Tennessee and his friend waited below. I could hear him laughing down in the lobby. I leaned over the balustrade and called to him: Mister Tennessee, come up!

But where *is* the apartment, for God's sake? he cried.

On the second floor! It was like shouting down into a well.

Then I saw him looking up at me, laughing. Mister Tennessee, come on! We may find a good apartment here.

He began to climb, still laughing. Baxter, behind him, neither smiled nor frowned. One would have said that he felt nothing, like the statue of the angel in *Summer and Smoke*. I said to myself that his thermometer was out of order, like the elevator. Tennessee can forget his fatigue and discomfort by laughing.

The apartment consisted of one room. There were two alcoves facing one another, each containing a bed. The old Spaniard went to one alcove and pulled back a sliding door to disclose the bed. This is one bedroom, he said. The other one is over there.

The room's three windows looked onto the Calle Quevedo. There was also a small balcony with washtubs on it, giving onto a vacant piece of land. Tennessee leaned out over the landscape of refuse and garbage, and exclaimed: Oh, no! This is not a place where I could live and work.

We went out into the street. The old Spaniard was following us, saying: Don't you want it? Don't you like the apartment? There's another one. His voice held a note of entreaty.

We're sorry to have bothered you, I told him. This gentleman wants a really good apartment, a place with luxury. He'll pay for it if he finds it.

We haven't got anything more luxurious than that one, he said dejectedly.

Once again we walked, stopping in a patch of bare sun to hail a taxi that would take Tennessee and his friend to the Hotel Minzah. Three or four drove past, all occupied.

Each time Tennessee saw one coming, he would signal to it, crying: Here comes one! And each time I would say: Yes, but it's full.

The best place to get one is on the corner in front of the main post office, I told him.

These little annoyances are part of life. We started to walk through sunlight and shade, and finally stood on the corner opposite the post office. There we stopped a cab, and Tennessee and Baxter jumped into it. The taxi started up. We saw Tennessee waving to us, a blissful smile on his face. At his side Baxter sat like the statue in *Summer and Smoke*, whose invisible inscription could be deciphered only by running the fingertips over the letters.

What are you doing now? Yacoubi asked me.

I looked at the waves of heat dancing above the tarred street. I'm thirsty, and I'm hungry, I told him.

He smiled and said: I'll invite you to a bowl of *baisar*.

In the market of the Fondaq ech Chijra we found a restaurant that specialized in *baisar*. It was full of ill-dressed, famished Moroccans. We ordered two bowls of *baisar* and a loaf of wholewheat bread. The serving-boy, who apparently was a friend of Yacoubi's, said they had no real wholewheat bread, and Yacoubi asked me to go out and buy a loaf. The bread-sellers were just outside the restaurant in the courtyard. I bought the bread at the nearest booth and came back in looking at it. I saw Yacoubi staring at it, too.

The man said it was pure wholewheat, I told him. He

broke the bread in half and sniffed of it. No, he said. It's not pure wholewheat. He robbed you. It's a fake. I know bread that's made with wheat. It's a sin the way the bakers adulterate their bread here. The man who cheats on bread goes straight to hell.

I grinned and agreed with him. I was interested in eating, not in discussing real bread and false bread. Real bread, false bread, an annoyance like looking for a taxi.

He handed me half the loaf and we began to eat. I shook a little red pepper over the hot soup. There was fire in my mouth, and my throat became a hot stove. I began to cough. There was a tin oil-can full of water on the table which served as a mug. The other three men at the table were drinking out of it. I got up and asked the boy for two empty bowls, and filled them up at the water tap, while I went on coughing.

You shouldn't drink water with *baisar*, Yacoubi told me. It's better for you without.

I had to have water at that moment, and I did not want to discuss the advisability of drinking it or not drinking it. All I wanted was to stop coughing.

He began to tell me how beneficial *baisar* was for the entire body, particularly the stomach, intestines, and nerves. In order to have something to say, I asked him what the two drops of blood meant in one of the recipes for chicken in his cookbook. He smiled and said: Ah! That's a secret. A lot of people have asked me about that in America, but I didn't answer them. Everybody can imagine what he wants. If I tell the secret, the recipe loses all its meaning.

I thought to myself how pleasant it would be if human beings had no intestines and no glands. We set out for Yacoubi's studio.

There was an unfinished painting on an easel. I stood in front of it, looking at it. Yacoubi hurried over. No, he said courteously. Please don't look at it. I don't like anyone to see a painting that isn't finished. Look at the other ones.

I excused myself for having seen the painting, and ran my eyes over the ones that were hung on the wall, half expecting him to tell me not to look too long, or to wait until he put them on exhibit. He ran downstairs and came up immediately with two shirts. Here's a gift for you, he said. They're for summer.

I wondered if he was giving me the shirts because he had decided that the one I was wearing was not suitable for summer wear. He put on a record by Ali Akbar Khan. Then from the cupboard he brought out a pile of letters that Tennessee had written him from Rome years before. Some were typed and others handwritten. He extracted one and held it out to me, asking me to read it aloud. He said that he and Tennessee had been close friends for many years, in spite of the fact that many people found it impossible to get along with Tennessee.

And now, I asked him. Are you still close friends?

Of course. And now he's not so difficult, even with

people he doesn't know very well. Everything's different today. It's hard to explain. We're still friends, but not the way we were. Perhaps because now we meet only by chance, either here or in the United States.

He showed me an old letter from Timothy Leary, and a new one written from jail, sent through his female lawyer. I read them both.

The second one was very touching in its description of his life in prison, and with the hopes it expressed of his being granted his freedom.

Then he showed me a recent photograph of his daughter. She's grown up, I said.

That's right, he agreed. Girls grow up faster than boys.

18.VII.73

Yacoubi and I were sitting on the terrace of the Café de Paris. The sun was making me feel sick. We were on the side opposite the French Consulate, and it was afternoon. I turned to him and asked if we ought not to be leaving in order to go and pick up Tennessee.

He smiled. No, I'm waiting for the sun to go down. I always sit in this spot and watch it set over the Consulate.

But why in this spot precisely?

That's a secret only Allah knows.

And you? I said. Don't you know it?

Now he laughed. Let's go and get Tennessee Williams.

We met Tennessee coming out of a shop near the Minzah. He greeted us warmly, with great bursts of laughter, and we started to walk back up the street. When we got to the Café de Paris, Yacoubi pointed to a Moroccan sitting inside and said: There he is. Then he told Tennessee that the man, a friend of his, could show us a villa on the mountain with garden and swimming pool. Tennessee let us hear his marvelous laugh, and cried: Right! A villa with a pool in the garden! That's what I want!

We went into the café, and Yacoubi introduced us to a very elegant Moroccan, whom I have known by sight for years. He did not have much difficulty expressing himself in English and French to Tennessee. It was arranged that Tennessee would visit the villa. Having nothing more to say to each other, they smiled back and forth two or three times. Yacoubi took out a letter he was going to send to Ellen Stewart (La Mama) and asked Tennessee to write a greeting to her at the bottom of the page. I looked out the window at the tourists, of whom there are more than usual this year.

Tennessee was reading over in a low voice what he had written to La Mama. Then he burst into his usual loud laugh. I asked Yacoubi what he had said.

Smiling, he said: Does it interest you?

Tennessee's way of expressing himself makes me feel good, I told him.

He smiled again. Well, he wrote: I'm a dirty old man

who hopes you will present one of his plays in your theatre.

We took leave of Yacoubi's friend and went out of the café. Tennessee wanted to buy a rubber bathing-cap, and we went from one shop to another along the boulevard, looking for it. All the caps they had were for women. Each time they brought out one of those he burst into laughter. Finally in one place the proprietor showed him several kinds. One had a wig attached. The hair looked like the fur of a baby donkey. He held onto it, laughing. When he caught his breath, he exclaimed: The place to wear this is the Café de Paris!

Yacoubi and I laughed. The proprietor stared at us with surprise, and then decided to laugh along with us.

I was thinking that I had never seen a writer who was as amusing as Tennessee, and that nonetheless he was the man who had written *Summer and Smoke* and *Cat on a Hot Tin Roof*.

Eventually he bought a blue cap which could be worn by either sex, although he had hoped to get a white one. But the only white one was covered with what looked like fish scales, whereas he wanted it to be smooth. He handed fifteen dirhams to the proprietor, saying: Your bathing-caps are very expensive. This wouldn't cost four dollars in the United States.

Back in the street, he wanted to know how to get to Porte's. I knew that he used to frequent the place on his earlier visits. It was where he always went with Jane

Bowles. But now he gave me the impression of never having been in Tangier before. As we walked along, I showed him my Arabic copy of *Cat on a Hot Tin Roof. A Cat on the Fire,* I said. That's the simplified title they gave your play. Do you like it?

What matters is that the character should *feel* like a cat on a hot tin roof, he said.

He must like hot things and sweet things, I thought. I felt like asking him if that was why he likes to give his works titles using words suggesting heat and sweet things, such as *Summer and Smoke, Sweet Bird of Youth, Suddenly Last Summer, Hard Candy, I Rise in Flames, Cried the Phoenix.*

Have you ever wanted to see one of your plays done in Arabic? I asked.

I don't know whether I'd enjoy it or not. I never thought of it. I don't know what they're like in other languages. Probably in Arabic they'd give them the kind of production they like, and not the kind *I* like. So it doesn't really matter whether I see them or not.

We arrived at Madame Porte's and went in. I've been missing this place, he told me. We took a table by the open window, from which we could see both the Calle Goya and the Calle Moussa ben Nusair. Tennessee sniffed the afternoon air, and remarked: It's nice to be here.

It's a comfortable place, I said. The best tearoom in Tangier.

I've always liked it very much, said Tennessee sadly. Jane liked it too.

There was a moment of silence at our table. I saw his half-shut eyes behind his sunglasses. He's either planning something new, or remembering things that happened here, I thought. But he's enjoying his reverie. Perhaps he's thinking of Jane Bowles. She had a happy disposition. I was surprised when I read the French translation of her novel *Two Serious Ladies*. Only a genius could have written such dialogue at the age of twenty-one. As Christina is about to dance, she says to her friend Mary: 'Now, don't take your eyes off me. I'm going to do a dance of worship to the sun. Then I'm going to show that I'd rather have God and no sun than sun and no God. Do you understand?'

'Yes,' said Mary. 'Are you going to do it now?'

'Yes. I'm going to do it right here.'

The young waitress arrived, bringing a flurry of movement to our silent table. Yacoubi ordered black tea, I coffee, and Tennessee a pot of tea and a glass of white rum.

I said to myself: He still likes to visit and drink from the spring of memory. But I don't know whether he still gets drunk. There was an evening here at Madame Porte's with Tennessee and other friends, back in 1961. Tennessee was drunk, and fell backwards in his chair onto the floor, making a great racket that attracted the attention of everyone in the establishment. Madame Porte was among those who hurried over to his prostrate form, only to ask:

Qui est-ce personnage? I know I've seen his picture again and again in magazines, but I can't recall his name.

She was told the name of the man spread out on the floor in front of them. Ah, so that's who he is, she murmured. They left him lying there on his back, until he got up by himself, laughing uproariously.

The waitress brought the drinks. Tennessee tasted the rum first, then poured himself a cup of tea. I decided he liked rum better than tea.

He began to talk to Yacoubi. Have you met any nice girls since you got back from America?

Only one. Just one. She's a Moroccan who's studying in the States.

Isn't one enough? said Tennessee.

No. Or yes, but only if I've chosen her among dozens of girls.

What Yacoubi'd really like is a complete harem, I said. We laughed.

One handsome boy is enough for me, said Tennessee. A boy who just happens by.

So you don't want a harem, I said.

No. Harems are always very tiring. They're no fun. He turned to Yacoubi. Listen, Ahmed. You've got to find that handsome boy for me. One boy for me, and a whole harem of beautiful girls for you. Years ago at the Hotel de Verdun there were some marvellous boys. He laughed. There must be others now who've taken their place. The ones who were there wouldn't be boys any more.

And prostitution here still starts at the age of four, as Brick's father tells him in *Cat on a Hot Tin Roof*, I said.

Where is this hotel? Yacoubi asked me.

I don't know. I don't think it exists any more. The man who owned it is very rich now. He's in jail for having committed some crimes. I laughed. I'm more interested in hotels where there are girls.

Tennessee patted Yacoubi's shoulder. You've got to find me a boy, remember. Only one. And you'll have a harem full of wonderful girls.

Yacoubi laughed abruptly and said nothing. I passed Tennessee Colin Wilson's *The Outsider* in Arabic translation, and asked him if he had read Wilson.

Ah! Yes, he said. I've read *The Outsider*.

He's a good writer. Have they translated much of him into Arabic?

Almost everything, I told him. He's greatly admired in the Arab world.

Fine!

Yacoubi took the book in his hand. Does he know his books have been published in Arabic? he asked me, speaking in English.

Of course he knows it. I believe the two translators were even in touch with him while they were working. And in an introduction to one of the books one of them remarks that Wilson was delighted to have his works appear in Arabic translation.

TENNESSEE WILLIAMS IN TANGIER

And he must collect royalties on them, said Yacoubi. Tennessee was following our conversation.

Maybe, I said. I don't know how it works.

He must get royalties, Yacoubi exclaimed. Since he knows the books are being published. He turned to Tennessee. Why don't you write to the people who published your plays in Arabic and ask them for your royalties?

Who, me? It's too much trouble. I only want them to give me a camel to ride, and a boy. I've got unpaid royalties in the Soviet Union, too, and some of the other socialist countries.

When he was here, Genet told me the same thing about his royalties in those countries, I said.

I wonder where he is now. When was the last time he was here?

At the end of October 1969.

How was he then?

Tired and sad. Sometimes he felt well enough to forget his sadness. But nothing like the way he used to be, of course. Nembutal had clipped his wings. He may have been having nice dreams with it, but he never spoke of them.

I take Nembutal myself, said Tennessee. But only one, to fall asleep.

You got very sick once from taking sleeping pills and drinking at the same time, didn't you?

He opened his eyes as wide as they could go, for an instant, but did not reply. I waited for him to laugh, or at least smile. Then I decided that the very memory of those days terrified him.

Yacoubi asked me about Paul Bowles and his friend Mrabet. He and Paul have known each other for more than a quarter of a century, but since Yacoubi moved to America they see each other much less frequently. Furthermore, said Yacoubi, Mrabet seems always to be at Paul's apartment. Tennessee began to speak of his own long friendship with Paul. He spoke warmly of Mrabet, whom he had known in California.

I told Tennessee: Tomorrow I'll give you the issue of *Antaeus* that has the first chapter of my autobiography in it.

Does Dan Halpern pay for the contributions you send him? he asked me.

No. He's never paid for anything of mine he's put into his magazine. He did give me an advance on my book about Genet in Tangier.

He didn't pay me, either, said Tennessee. After he'd published one of my stories without paying, I sent it to another magazine that paid very well.

He let out a huge laugh. I reflected that he looked healthiest at the moment of laughing, and thought: He knows how to make himself happy. He doesn't expect anyone else to do it for him. He's over sixty, but he looks under fifty.

Yacoubi turned to Tennessee and said: Mrabet's someone to be careful of, don't you agree?

Who, Mrabet? Oh, no! He's very *simpático*. He's good-hearted. I'm very fond of him.

Are you a student? Tennessee asked me suddenly.

How would you expect me to be a student, when I'm thirty-eight years old? I work for the Department of Education.

He studied me for a moment and said: You don't look thirty-eight.

Perhaps that's because I've known how to live.

He went on looking, and said nothing. Then he glanced at his watch. It was quarter to eight. I think I'm going to be on my way, he said, and he called the waitress. Pulling dirhams from his pocket, he laid fifty on the table.

Yacoubi immediately said: That banknote's worth about twelve dollars, you know.

Tennessee laughed. And will it buy a *chico guapo*?

On the way back to the Minzah with us, he stopped to get a *Herald Tribune*. He glanced at it and said: It's impossible to find a recent newspaper here. This issue is days old. He turned to Yacoubi. And the Zoco Chico? How is it these days? The same as before?

It's more dangerous than it was. It's full of bums and *maricones* and thieves.

My God! The world gets worse all the time!

I'll take you down for some mint tea whenever you like, Yacoubi told him.

Yacoubi's exaggerating, I thought. He's lived so long

MOHAMED CHOUKRI

in America that he's begun to have the same sort of fear that keeps foreigners from coming here.

I don't think the Zoco Chico is quite as bad as you paint it, I told him.

He glared at me. Are you crazy? he cried. Tennessee can't go down there alone! He'll have trouble. We've got to go with him, or at least one of us, to keep the hoodlums away.

Ah, I said. You're right. Of course. But even if he did go alone, nobody'd bother him. The ones who were here twenty years ago are all gone. They're in Europe working. Or they're given up hustling. They're grown up now!

That doesn't matter. The Zoco Chico is dangerous for Tennessee, Yacoubi insisted.

You're right. And I know Tennessee doesn't like dangerous hoodlums. I've heard about how he hates to be accosted in the street. I think he got a bad impression of Tangier years ago. Paul told me how he used to say: Look! There he is again, that one! It's sinister!

I did not want to seem to be contradicting Yacoubi. I know he has a tendency to exaggerate. And it may be that his long residence in other countries has made it difficult for him to accept life in Morocco. He smokes hash, and most *hashishin* suffer from fear and a sense of being persecuted.

Yacoubi and I said goodbye to Tennessee near the Minzah, and went on our way. He's a very good man, and a serious one, said Yacoubi. He hates lies and flattery. He always remembers his old friends, and if they need help, he helps them. But he breaks off very fast if anyone tries to trick him. I've known him for twenty-five years.

Yes, I've heard all that about him, I said.

You mean you've read it?

I've read a lot about him.

19.VII.73

I saw him sitting with his friend Baxter on the terrace of the Café de Paris. It was about half past eleven in the morning. I shook hands with them, and stood by their table. Tennessee asked me to sit down and order something.

I asked for coffee. I didn't have a centime on me to buy breakfast with. At least, I thought, I won't have to smoke on an empty stomach.

He had been reading the *Herald Tribune*. Now he passed it to Baxter and said: How are you, Choukri? What's new?

I smiled. I had *Orpheus Descending* with me, as well as *After the Fall*, both in Arabic editions. I held out the former book to him, saying: This is *Orpheus Descending*. I admire it very much.

He took the book and laughed. Oh! he cried, pretending to be disappointed. They haven't put a beautiful picture of me on the cover the way they did for *Cat*! Is it the same translator for this one?

Yes. His name is Mohammed Samir Abdelhamid.

He laid the book on the table. Baxter picked it up and asked me how many of Tennessee's plays had been published in Arabic.

I know of four or five, but there may be others. Then I showed him the front of the book, where there was a list of all of Tennessee's writings that were in translation.

Have you read any Arab writers in English translation? I asked Tennessee.

No, he said. And then suddenly: I've read Mohammed Mrabet's short stories, translated by Paul.

I showed him the Arthur Miller play. He read the title and pushed the book away. He's a bad writer! he said, making a grimace.

I wondered if he disliked everything by Miller, or only this sadistic play about his wife. Perhaps Marilyn Monroe was a friend of his.

Tennessee recovered his calm expression. Was he serious, I wondered, or only joking? I was astonished, and looked at him in perplexity, waiting for him to add something to what he had said about Miller. Then slowly, as if he were choosing one of those warm titles for a play of his, or selecting the final perfect line of dialogue for it, he said: No. It's not true what I said about Miller. I was only joking.

He was smiling and speaking very slowly. I decided that he and Miller must have had a falling-out. By now I had got over the shock I had felt at his words.

Arthur Miller is a good writer, he went on.

Where his shirt opened at the neck I could see that he was wearing a gold cross set with black stones.

It might be that he doesn't like what I write. He laughed. At least, that's what I think. But it doesn't mean anything, whether he likes it or not, any more than all the stupid things the critics write about both of us. They flay us, but we know how to grow new skin.

I hoped he would continue in this vein. He seemed at ease, and I believed in his indifference to what might be written about him.

Yacoubi arrived and sat down with us. I let them talk together, and heard Yacoubi suggesting that they visit Madame de Meuron. He added that her garden was one of the most beautiful in Tangier. Then he asked me to go to the telephone book and get her number so he could call her and tell her we were arriving.

When I got back to the table, I found that Tennessee had left with Baxter. I gave Yacoubi the number. He said that Tennessee had agreed to go to Madame de Meuron's later in the afternoon.

In the afternoon I found Yacoubi again on the terrace of the Café de Paris. He was with his Moroccan girlfriend. She explained that she was studying in the United States and thus had forgotten how to speak Moghrebi. Yacoubi had already asked me for my opinion of her, and I had told him I thought she was pretentious, and did not want to see Moroccans. I also said I thought it strange that four or five years of study in America should make her forget her own language. Then I asked him what he thought of her himself. His reply: I swear I don't know! She always insists on speaking English with me, too. Sometimes I say something to her in Arabic, and she answers me in English. She's a woman. They're always impossible. They have devils in their heads instead of ideas. She knows more about me than I know about her. They take their time studying us. I always have to ask her to say everything over again more clearly. But she never asks me to explain what I say.

Then either she understands you very well, or not at all.

I don't know. I don't trust women, he said.

I had a copy of *Summer and Smoke* with me, and *Antaeus 7*, with the first chapter of my autobiography in it. Baxter arrived at about a quarter to six. His clothing was simple, immaculate. He sat down, saying that Tennessee would be right along.

After a moment Tennessee appeared, wearing a dark brown suit whose shiny texture varied with the light. He was in a jaunty mood, which contrasted with the dark suit. He ordered a bottle of Oulmès. Baxter seemed abstracted, as always. The sun was almost ready to set. I wondered if Yacoubi were waiting to perform his ritual of watching it go behind the French Consulate.

I brought out the magazine and inscribed it for Tennessee. He read the first few lines of the work and burst out laughing. These had to do with my uncle's death and my tears on account of it. You begin your life story by crying, he said. He laughed some more. I must read this chapter.

What about this woman we're going to see? he said to Yacoubi.

She's a nice widow who's lived here for many years.

And has she got a lot of money? Tennessee went on.

I don't know. But she's certainly not poor.

Well, I am, said Tennessee.

If she's not rich, at least she has a title, I told him. She's a countess.

A title's not enough nowadays, he said. You have to have money as well.

We all laughed, except Baxter and Yacoubi's girlfriend. They're of the same clay, I thought. She makes you want to rape her, and he needs a man like the cannibal in *Desire and the Black Masseur*.

The sun had already gone behind the gables of the French Consulate when Yacoubi stood up and announced that we should be leaving if we wanted to get to Madame de Meuron's. He handed me a ten-dirham note to pay for what we had drunk.

We got into two small cabs, Yacoubi and his girlfriend in one, and Tennessee, Baxter and I in the other. As we drove along, Tennessee hummed. I had never imagined that any writer could be so consistently light-hearted.

Paul Bowles was living in Acapulco in 1940 when Tennessee first called on him. At that time Tennessee was not known. This was in the month of August. He arrived at Paul's door late in the morning. Paul and his wife had been invited by friends to have lunch on the beach, and she was nervous about getting to the appointment on time. It was a very hot day. Paul and Jane spoke with their servants, telling them that the *señor* would be staying until they came back, and to give him drinks and feed him if he wanted to eat. In the afternoon when they returned from the beach he was stretched out in a hammock looking very happy, with a bottle of rum beside him and several parrots squawking in the trees above, squawks to which he was responding in kind.

I had already met Louise de Meuron at Paul's apartment, and had liked her friendly way of speaking. Following Yacoubi's cab, we drove through narrow curving streets. The children of the quarter greeted us with delighted cries, and waved at us.

My God, there are a lot of children around here, said Tennessee.

It's the summer holidays, I told him.

He was gratified to see that we were getting a friendly reception from the urchins. Baxter continued to be the statue of eternity, and Tennessee went on humming.

Did the original Miss Winemiller sing 'La Golondrina' well? I asked him.

Oh, yes. Very well.

I laughed. And Val? Was he a good guitarist? Did he sing 'Heavenly Grass' well?

Ah, Val.

What I had meant to ask was whether Alma Winemiller and Val were actual people he had known. But it seemed unimportant. Good writers usually improve upon places and characters, making them larger and more important than they are in reality.

I have *Summer and Smoke* with me, I told him. He turned and smiled. At the very end of the play there is a short dialogue in Spanish between Alma and the young travelling salesman. Do you speak Spanish?

They're just words. I don't know Spanish well.

I was about to say that Alma Winemiller seemed to me like a granddaughter of Hester Prynne. On the tail of Yacoubi's taxi, we began to go down an extremely steep incline. The house was beautifully situated, facing the old mountain, and above Merkala Beach.

I think I've been here before, Tennessee said. Many years ago.

This place is right out of paradise, I murmured.

We got out of the taxi. Yacoubi and his friend walked ahead, down towards the house. Tennessee and Baxter followed, leaving me with the taxi-driver. I had four dirhams left over having paid for our drinks. Tennessee turned, saw me about to pay the driver, and came back, calling out: No! No! How much should I give him?

Whatever you like, I said.

He produced a ten-dirham note, and the man began to dig for change. Keep it, Tennessee told him. The Spaniard beamed and thanked him. I know how taxi-drivers hate it when a resident interferes and tries to arrange the same price for a foreigner as he would pay himself, particularly if the foreigner looks well-to-do. Tennessee stood still at the top of the steps leading down to the house, and stared across at the mountain. It is a fine landscape. At that moment of twilight the mountain was very green, and above it there were clouds varying from pink to the color of almond-flowers. Tennessee stopped on each step and looked across at the mountain or out towards the sea. Finally he said: This woman has some sort of sweet-smelling flower in her garden. What a view!

He's seen the world, I thought. He must have seen thousands of better views than this. But some day I want to visit Bali or Java.

Madame de Meuron and her daughter greeted us cordially. Yacoubi and his friend were already standing there with them, talking.

Where would you rather sit, in the garden or in the pavilion? she asked Tennessee.

I think the pavilion.

Before we went in, Madame de Meuron asked us to order our drinks, giving a list of what she had in the house. Tennessee asked for vodka. So did I. Baxter wanted a Martini. Yacoubi and his friend wanted only tea.

We reclined on comfortable low divans. I think I've been here before, years ago, Tennessee told Madame de Meuron.

Of course you have, she said. I remember very well. But it's true that it was a long time ago.

He asked her about a Russian woman who had once lived on the property.

Ah, Sonia Kamalakar! That mad woman! She's in heaven now. She died years ago.

Tennessee grimaced. Mmmm, he said.

Madame de Meuron launched into a story illustrating Sonia's craziness, and Tennessee laughed from time to time, putting his hand over his mouth, or rolling his eyes.

She ruined my best flowers, she was saying.

I had heard from a Moroccan friend who knew both women that Sonia used to walk naked around the estate, singing very loudly, and sometimes dancing, with no heed to whether anyone was watching or not.

They began then to talk about Barbara Hutton and her illnesses and her husbands. I heard Tennessee say: Her health has always been poor.

As Madame de Meuron talked on, she pronounced the word 'Nembutal' several times. Finally she said: And yet I've used it for years, and it hasn't hurt me in any way. But I take it only as a sedative, and not for the sensation it gives.

Madame de Meuron's daughter and two Moroccan maids brought our drinks. The girls were beautifully dressed and well trained in their work. The daughter called down to her children, who were playing near the tennis-court. They arrived and were introduced to us. Their perfect behavior made one think of the children of centuries ago.

Suddenly Madame de Meuron began to cry out: Amadou! Amadou! *Viens ici!* Two impeccably dressed black youths came into the pavilion. They kissed Madame de Meuron's hand and that of her daughter. Then they greeted us and went out again.

Are you French? Tennessee asked Madame de Meuron.

No, I'm Swiss. German-Swiss.

Then I heard them speaking sadly of the death of Jane Bowles. She was a fine writer, said Tennessee at one point. I picked up the notebook in which all this is being written, and he saw that I was about to speak.

I like this that you wrote about her. Then I read it aloud in English: 'I am not alone in my belief that Jane Bowles is the greatest prose writer of the century.'

That's right. I did say that. But where did you get it from?

It's in your *New York Times* piece about the death of William Inge.

Ah, yes. Inge was a good writer too.

I asked our hostess's daughter for more vodka and tonic. I felt totally relaxed. Yacoubi was telling a tale about a young Moroccan who had gone to the house of a European homosexual. The young man refused to go to bed with the man. Since the man kept insisting, the Moroccan took out his knife and went after the man's sex. Tennessee made a face. You mean he cut it completely off?

Yacoubi laughed. No. He only wounded him.

Tennessee looked relieved. My God!

Madame de Meuron began to discuss the residents of Tangier. Once again I heard her mention the strange behavior of Sonia Kamalakar. Tennessee listened to her as if he were astonished, rolling his eyes now and then. Finally he glanced at his watch.

I'm afraid we've got to be going. We're invited to Paul Bowles's.

Madame de Meuron's daughter offered to drive us all back to town in her big car. On the way she began to tell more stories about her mother's friends. Tennessee laughed. I was drunk.

The car stopped in front of the apartment house. Tennessee, Baxter and I got out. I had not been invited to Paul's. I was thinking: The fun is going to continue, and I want more to drink. Paul must have bought some wine for Tennessee this evening.

He opened the door for us and we went into the *sala*. Tennessee immediately asked: Where's Mrabet?

In the kitchen getting dinner.

Tennessee took off his jacket and Paul laid it on an old Moroccan chest. Mrabet came in. Tennessee cried: Hello, Mrabet! They embraced warmly. Then Tennessee held him at arm's length and said: You seem to be well.

Mrabet smiled and said: Thanks. And you look much stronger than before.

Oh, not all that strong, Tennessee said, sitting down on the couch. Mrabet excused himself and went back to the kitchen. I sat on the rug, facing Tennessee. Baxter sat beside Paul, who began to fill a cigarette with green tobacco. Tennessee was speaking of the difficulties of finding a place to live. I heard him asking about the Baron de Favier's house where he had lived in 1962.

The doorbell rang. I think it's Carol, said Paul. Mrabet opened the door. She came in, accompanied by Gavin Lambert. They were loaded down with bottles of wine and mineral water.

Gavin sat down beside Tennessee, and Carol set some bottles on the *taifor* in front of them.

I haven't turned into a frog yet, to drink mineral water, I said to myself.

Gavin crossed his legs, placed his elbow on his knee, and rested his chin on his hand. His way of sitting made me think of a bird in its nest. Even his hair looked like the crest of a bird.

Mrabet and Carol were setting the table. Carol's face was flushed, and Mrabet's eyes were almost shut as usual. I noticed that Tennessee looked at Mrabet delightedly.

Carol poured the wine for us. Paul was drinking his tea with lemon. Omar Khayyam once wrote: If I die, wash me with wine, and make my litter of grape branches.

Tennessee and Gavin were talking together. From time

to time Paul put in a remark. Mrabet came in, carrying a chicken tajine. Tennessee sniffed the air. I love Moroccan cooking! he exclaimed.

Paul had once told me that Larbi Layachi, the author of *A Life Full of Holes* (which he signed with the pen-name of Driss ben Hamed Charhadi), had served as cook for Tennessee when he was in Tangier in 1962. As Mrabet filled the plates, he told me: You were right to come. I'm always glad to be with a Moroccan at a party where everybody else is a foreigner.

The tajine was delicious. I know that Mrabet is proud of everything he does. It is not an exaggeration to say that it is all the same to him whether he has prepared a meal, published a story in *Rolling Stone,* caught a big fish at the Caves of Hercules, cut a batch of *kif,* bought a canary, passed all other cars on the highway, or won a bloody fight. He thinks more highly of what he is able to do with his hands than he does of the imaginative powers he uses when he invents a story.

Mrabet tried to heap more food onto Paul's plate. *No, grácias,* said Paul. I have enough. Mrabet laughed, saying: Eat, so you can put on a little flesh.

But I can't eat, Paul complained. You know that.

I know. You don't eat as much as one of my canaries. Mrabet has great respect for anyone with a big appetite. The size and amount of everything has to be exaggerated. He is not logical. He functions only in terms of emotion and naive imagination.

Carol kept pouring wine for us. Each time I emptied my glass I would say to her: You forgot to give me any.

You mean you've drunk it all, she would say.

No lucidity either tonight or tomorrow, I muttered in Arabic.

What'd you say?

Nothing.

Once she made a mistake and poured mineral water into my glass. I did not notice until after I had drunk it. Then she filled the glass with wine.

When he had finished eating, Tennessee went into the bathroom. He came out. Raising his hands over his head, he struck the pose of a flamenco dancer and sang a few words in Spanish. (I thought of John Buchanan and Rosa Gonzalez in *Summer and Smoke*.) Then he spun quickly around, undid his collar, and sat down.

You're nothing like your writing, I said.

How do you know that?

Your works, especially your plays, are depressing, but you seem always to be happy. How do you account for that?

It's not true. My works aren't depressing. The troubles my characters have are part of their lives. Sadness can be funny, and sometimes joy can be depressing. Not all sadness is depressing, or all happiness pleasant.

Mmmhmm, I see. (Then what do Alma Winemiller's sufferings mean? I thought.) I don't understand your conversion to the Catholic Church when you were released from the hospital, I told him.

I believe in God. That's all.

It wouldn't be that you believe in order to please your public? I suggested.

He burst out laughing. But there's no connection between my religious beliefs and what I write, he objected.

I looked at the cross he wore on his chest. I was surprised when I first noticed you wearing that cross, I told him.

He touched it. My mother's ill, he said sadly. I'm hoping God will make her better. He leaned back. I'll bet you're a poet. Don't you write poems?

I used to scribble them a long time ago, yes. But only a few of them have been published.

But you have the imagination of a poet.

Maybe, I said.

You have a good face. The face of a poet. Or a Spaniard.

I laughed. And you have the face of a German, I told him.

It could be, he said. One of my grandparents was German.

He looked over at Mrabet. Hello, Mrabet! Are you still strong?

Mrabet's black shirt was open at the neck. He jumped up, pulled off the shirt, and struck some athletic poses to show off his muscles. Tennessee applauded, crying: Bravo! You're still as strong as ever.

Mrabet put his shirt back on and sat down. Then I stood up and took off both my shirt and my undershirt. I pounded my chest and said: I'm strong, too. Everyone laughed and applauded.

He's a good sport, said Tennessee. I like a man who undresses easily.

Carol got up to fetch something from the kitchen. I blocked her passage, seized her by the waist, and lifted her into the air.

Yes! cried Tennessee. You're strong, too.

When I had sat down again, Tennessee looked at me for a moment, and said: You must come to Florida. I have a house at Key West. Come and stay a while. You could work. It's not for sex! I know you only like women.

Thank you, I said. I'll think about it.

(Later Gavin told me that Tennessee had turned to him at that point and said: If he does come, do you think he'll destroy me? And Gavin had replied: I doubt it.)

Tennessee drained his glass and announced: I think I'll go home to bed.

Baxter was curled up on the floor like a Persian cat.

I'll drive you home, Mrabet told Tennessee.

We got up to leave, Carol, Gavin and Paul remaining behind. At the door Tennessee mentioned to Paul how good the dinner had been.

Tell Mrabet, Paul said. He cooked it.

A good boy, said Tennessee.

On the ride into town he talked with Mrabet in English. Are you always busy working on a book? he asked him.

Mrabet answered in French. Yes, but I'm still poor. My books don't make enough money for me to live.

But you have your own car!

It's not mine. It's lent to me by Paul.

Tennessee laughed. Paul has two cars! A Mustang and a Karmann-Ghia. And I have no car at all! I'm poor, like you.

I remembered how Paul had told me that Tennessee always complained of having no money. He would assure his friends that all he possessed was thirty or forty thousand dollars.

We drew up outside the Hotel Minzah. Tennessee looked happily drunk. He hugged Mrabet and me. Baxter bade us a chilly goodnight. I got back into the car.

Where do you want to go? Mrabet asked me.

To the Mirador.

I got out near the cabaret.

Choukri, you kill yourself every night, said Mrabet. You should stop drinking so much.

Some day I'll try to stop, I told him. But in the meantime you should try not to smoke so much *kif.*

He looked at me through his nearly shut eyes, and said: Alcohol does more harm than *kif* or *majoun.*

I was not in a mood to enter into a discussion with him as to the relative dangers of alcohol and *kif.* I said goodnight, and decided to go up to a little bar called the Hole in the Wall.

20. VII. 73

I met him with his friend Baxter on the boulevard. He seemed perturbed, and his smile expressed weariness.

21. VII. 73

He was better today. He has an appointment with a Moroccan doctor. He wanted to buy some vitamins. He said he had enjoyed the first three chapters of my autobiography.

In the afternoon I met Edouard Roditi at the Café de Paris. I was sitting there, making an entry in this journal. I told him I was going to make a book out of it. At the same time I asked Edouard if he knew Tennessee personally.

I met him when he was an unknown poet, he said. We both published our poems at New Directions. But we've never been friends.

23. VII. 73

Sitting at the Café de Paris this morning making notes in my journal, I looked up and saw him standing on the sidewalk, looking around for a chair to sit in. I got up and went out to him, and we set out in search of newspapers. They had not yet arrived. He complained volubly about

Baxter. He's an idiot! he cried. He thinks only of himself. A narcissist. All that interests him is buying expensive suits and kaftans, like some stupid girl who gets excited by any pretty material.

He's probably very unhappy, I said. He practically never smiles.

I know. That's why I'm thinking of shipping him back to his mother. He's a mother's boy. I ought to look for another friend.

We went into the Librairie des Colonnes. Mademoiselle Gérofi was working at her desk. Tennessee took down a copy of *Le Monde* from the newspaper rack.

Look! There are other French papers, I told him.

There's as much in *Le Monde* as there is in all the other French papers combined, he said.

He paid the Spanish salesgirl, went over to one of the shelves containing French books. Seeing a volume of Rimbaud's poems, with a picture of him on the cover, he put his finger on the spine of the book. A great poet, he said. I'm very fond of him.

When we were out in the street, I said: I like Rimbaud too. Of all the poets who insisted that poetry comes out of man and not from the gods on Parnassus, he was the best.

I agree, he said. I read an excellent book about him by an English woman.

He tried to recall the name of the author. Ah! he said. Enid Starkie.

Does Baxter help you with your typing? I asked him.

Sometimes he does. But he'd rather lie back and dream. I've got to look for another companion to go through Europe with me. I'd rather be alone, though, than stuck with another one like him. I'm perfectly capable of living alone. He must be miserable here in Tangier. I'll send him back to his mother. She can take care of him better than I can.

We arrived back at the Café de Paris and sat down inside, since it was hot out on the terrace.

He's still young, I said. And besides, he hasn't had much time to get to know you.

I know. He's only twenty-five.

Tennessee ordered a Fernet-Branca and ice, and I asked for a glass of milk.

Still, some people are mature by the time they're twenty-five, I said.

Of course. But he's not.

I was thinking that Tennessee was going to find it difficult to find another friend like Frank Merlo, who helped to keep him organized, and that it could have been his death that impelled him to drink to such excess that he was finally hospitalized. He considered Frank Merlo his brother. At first it seemed inconceivable that Frank should have lung cancer. He suspected Merlo of having invented the illness, and subsequently felt guilty for having had such a doubt at such a time.

It seems to me your friend Baxter has no interest at all in literature or art, I told Tennessee.

He doesn't read at all. He likes music. It helps him to daydream about himself.

He glanced at my notebooks, and at the copy of Henry Miller's *Le Colosse de Maroussi* that I had with me. What's new? he said.

I'm working on the second volume of my autobiography, I said. And I'm reading this book.

He picked it up. I haven't read this one yet, he said.

Paul thinks it's his best book. Do you like Miller?

Oh, yes. He's a good writer. He had a very hard life before becoming one. He suffered a lot.

I thought of saying: So did you. But I said: Do you know him personally?

I met him years ago.

The waiter brought our drinks. I finished my milk at one gulp.

Do you like milk? Tennessee asked me.

Not much. I woke up at five o'clock this morning, and I'm trying to replenish all the energy I used up working.

I did not add that usually I consider milk something only for children and invalids, and that to drink it makes me feel either like a child or an invalid.

Haven't you found a house yet? I asked him.

Yes! An agent has found me one. The owner is going to spend the summer in Hong Kong.

Is it Sanche de Gramont's house?

No, it's not his. Another man. The house is a long way from the beach. But there's a phone and I can call a taxi for that. I like to swim every day.

Paul says you swim all year around.

That's true. Swimming keeps me well. I work every day, too. It's a habit. I get sick if I don't work each day.

Like Hemingway, I thought to myself. He liked to swim, and worked every day, too. A moment later, I asked him: Have you read any more chapters of my book? I'm eager to know what you think.

Oh, yes. I'm enjoying it.

It's the first book of mine to be published.

Do you write only in Arabic?

That's right. I can't write in any other language. I'd have no style. It took me years to be able to write in Arabic.

I understand. He looked at his watch. Can I get lunch here? he said.

You can, but it would be better to go to the Zagora or the Claridge.

I think I'll swim for a while in the hotel pool before I eat.

About half past five I was writing at the Café de Paris. I looked out and saw Tennessee sitting on the terrace. I picked up my coffee and books and went out to sit with him.

He saw *Le Colosse de Maroussi*. Ah, it's the same book you were carrying this morning! he exclaimed.

I'm reading it slowly, I said. Then I handed him the issue of *Antaeus* that had my piece on Jean Genet in it.

I'll read it, he said.

At one point I asked him to write his address on one of the pages of the Miller book, so that I could send him copies of my books when they came out. He ordered a Campari and some ice. I asked him if he had seen any of Genet's plays produced in the United States.

Only *The Balcony*. It was a very obscure play. About prostitution. I didn't understand it entirely, but the writing is poetic.

He inscribed a copy of that for me, I said.

Does Genet know Arabic?

He knows *darija*, and he can write a few sentences correctly.

Marvellous! Tell me, what happened here between Genet and the blacks? Did they let them into the hotel with him?

I laughed. How do you know he likes blacks?

I know he does. He likes them to look like Idi Amin.

I saw him here once walking with a black boy. And another time with a fairly dark one, I said. I don't think he has much of a sexual life now. He liked to joke with the children in the street and give them money. He's generous. He always handed something to beggars.

Does he go on stealing the way he used to, simply to amuse himself? asked Tennessee.

I never heard anyone mention such a thing. But people

still refer to him as a likeable scoundrel. I think his hosts enjoyed seeing him slip a silver spoon into his pocket and afterward pretending they'd seen nothing.

He laughed. When I was in Bangkok I was invited by a very fancy prince to have dinner at his palace. In the dining-room there were paintings of naked men showing off their buttocks. I was already drunk before we sat down to eat. He brought out a lot of rare jewels to show me. Then he left them on a table. When I thought he wasn't looking, I grabbed a few of them and dropped them into my pocket. The other guests burst out laughing, so that the prince realized what I had done. He waited for me to put the jewels back. When I didn't, he decided I really meant to steal them, and he began to ask the others to try and persuade me not to. I put my hand into my pocket and rattled them around. The prince was so worried that he changed the seating at table later, and sat himself down beside me.

And did you give them back?

Of course! I was just having a little fun. I'm not sure that at first I didn't mean to steal them, though.

The trouble was, you didn't know how, I told him.

After a moment he said: I'm invited to York Castle tonight. Do you know the owner of the house?

No.

25. VII. 73

In the morning at the Café de Paris with Yacoubi and a
television announcer who wanted to tape an interview
with Tennessee. He had already taped one with Yacoubi
in his studio. We caught sight of Tennessee going past,
alone. Yacoubi jumped up and brought him to the table.
The three of them began to discuss the project. Tennessee
did not appear eager to give the interview. His face
showed annoyance. Turning to Yacoubi, he explained that
he wanted no more journalistic experiences. He gave the
impression of being in a hurry, and he spoke abruptly.

Tell your announcer friend that I'm still busy moving
into a villa on the mountain, he said. When I'm all settled, we'll see about doing it.

30. VII. 73

I sat with Yacoubi in the café. He seemed to be in a bad
mood. It could be because his girlfriend has left for Tunis.

I won't speak to her if she comes back, he told me.
From now on no one's going to get into my studio.

I knew he was not serious, and that he was referring
only to a few individuals who bothered him.

Tennessee arrived and asked Yacoubi to go to the post
office with him, to help him get a parcel that had arrived
from America. Yacoubi said he was only waiting for the

waiter to bring him his change. It was five minutes to twelve.

Then Yacoubi asked me if I would go in his place. I agreed, and we found a cab. On the way Tennessee commented on Yacoubi's ill-humor.

I think he gets glum when he has no girl living with him, I said.

Why doesn't he look for a boy, then? said Tennessee.

He uses the girls as secretaries, I explained. He always needs someone to read his mail to him, and to write his answers for him.

Baxter has been suffering from an upset stomach. I asked Tennessee if he was better, and it seems he is.

He's a great dreamer, he added. And a narcissist. And narcissists are always feeling sick somewhere.

We got out of the taxi at the post office and went in. It looks as if they were already shut, I said.

An employee told us to come back at four o'clock.

As we stood waiting for a taxi to take Tennessee to his hotel, I said to him: Haven't you found that good-looking boy yet?

No, not yet, he said, laughing. One afternoon on my way to Paul's house, I passed a café near the Iberia Airlines office. There were a lot in there.

I know the café.

I'm afraid of the ones who sit at the Café de Paris, he went on. They look dangerous.

We got into a taxi. At the Place de France I said

goodbye and got out. Yacoubi was still sitting on the terrace of the Café de Paris, but now he was with an American girl I know. I waved to him and went inside. I know it annoys him if he is with a girl and someone speaks to him. It's true, he can't live without a woman.

About four o'clock I ran into Tennessee on the Avenue Mohammed V. He was on his way to the post office to get his package. I offered to go along with him, and he was pleased. Immediately he hailed a taxi. Even though the place he is going is next door, he will still take a taxi.

He presented the form at the desk. The girl looked at his passport, and said: Your passport gives Thomas as your first name. The package is addressed to Tennessee.

He explained that he was a writer and used a *nom de plume*. Then he pointed out the place lower on the page where the pseudonym was written.

The box was full of letters, magazines and clippings. The customs officer pulled out a copy of *Playboy* and cried: Ah, no! This is forbidden in Morocco.

Then he began to leaf through it, and to exclaim with disgust at the photographs of naked men and women. Two other officers came up, accompanied by a nervous-looking girl.

Look! cried the first. Can this be possible? These are filthy pictures! No! No! No! This pornographic magazine can't come into the country.

But they sell it here in Tangier! Tennessee protested.

No! No! *C'est défendu!* Look! Look! There are photos

here of nude men! Even the men in this magazine have begun to show themselves!

He began to examine the clippings, trying to read the English titles of the articles. Then he opened all the letters, and set to work studying the contents, page by page.

Tennessee clapped his hands together. Oh, no! he cried. This is impossible! I'm going to get out of this country as fast as I can.

He turned to the girl, who was staring at him worriedly, and said to her in French: This sort of thing doesn't happen anywhere else in the world.

That's what you think, she said. Go to Paris and you'll see what they do to your mail.

He looked back at the man who was reading the letters. But those are only personal letters! he said. There's nothing dangerous to you in any of them. I don't think my friends have sent any letter-bombs.

The inspector said to me in Arabic: The new law insists that all letters be opened and read.

I explained this in English to Tennessee.

Why not call the police? he shouted at the man. What are you waiting for? Call the police!

Part of this was in French and part in English. I saw a check protruding from one of the envelopes which had been torn open but not yet emptied of its contents. As he often seems to do when a situation becomes difficult, Tennessee suddenly relaxed, and seemed to take an amused view of the proceedings. Each time the inspector or one of his assistants said anything at all, he would burst into laughter.

The inspector was growing impatient with having to go through such a large quantity of mail. Take the letters and put them back into the box, he told me. I'm going to do him a favor. I'm going to allow the rest of the letters to enter the country without being read. It's strictly against the rules.

I had a copy of the page-proofs of *For Bread Alone* with me, and I was worried that they might take it away from me and want to examine it.

All right, Tennessee was saying to the inspector. Keep the magazine. Just let me tear out the pages that have my story. I don't want the naked photographs.

No, that's impossible, the man said. Then he turned to me and said in Arabic: Wait a minute. I'll see if the chief has come in yet.

I translated for Tennessee. This whole thing is impossible, he said. They're insupportable!

The inspector came back immediately. No. He's not here yet. He ought to be coming in any minute.

Tennessee went on trying to convince the man that he had a right to tear his own story out of *Playboy*. My story has nothing to do with nudity, he kept assuring him. Then he took up the magazine and showed him the pages he wanted to tear out. The inspector carried it over to the chief's deputy. He returned and said impatiently: All right. Cut out the pages with your story.

While Tennessee was busy doing this, the inspector asked me in Arabic: Has he got the disease?

What disease? I said innocently.

He looked at the careless way I was dressed, in an old pair of trousers and a shirt. I mean, is he one of them?

I was annoyed. I don't know. That's his business, not mine. I'm a teacher and he's a friend of mine. I've got nothing to do with other men's sex lives.

I'm glad to meet you, he said. I was just wondering.

I was still annoyed. If you're interested, I'll ask him for you, I said.

No! No! I was just asking you. I don't want to ask him.

Tennessee had his story, and I began to tie up the box. Then a second inspector with more epaulettes than the other came up to me saying: Untie that. Let me look at what's inside.

I'm tying it up, not untying it, I told him, pointing at the other inspector. He's already looked at the letters.

That's right, said the other. I've examined them all.

Where's my passport? said Tennessee. The inspector handed it to him, and he slipped it quickly into his hip pocket. He was not wearing a jacket.

I picked up the box and said to the inspector: Thank you for the favor.

They were all watching us as we went out. Once we were in the street, Tennessee began to laugh. That was a strange experience. I'll never forget it. I think they wanted those photos in *Playboy* for themselves.

It's an expensive magazine here, I said.

How hot it is! Let's go and have something cold at Madame Porte's. Where can we get a taxi?

Porte's is very near.

Really? Let's go, then.

He remarked again: What a ridiculous story!

Madame Porte, who sat facing the entrance, greeted us as we went in. She seems to know you, I said.

Oh, yes. I've been coming here for years.

There were only seven or eight people in the place. We went to the middle of the big room, sat down, and ordered two chilled white vermouths. Have some pastries, Tennessee said.

Thanks. I will.

I was hungry, and I had no money on me. I had taken nothing all day but a glass of milk and a cup of coffee. This is what happens when one drinks all night every night, and sleeps between the legs of whores afterwards.

Tennessee called the Spanish girl. This gentleman would like some pastries.

She came with a tray laden with many varieties. I chose a sort I had never tried before.

He pulled out the pages containing his story and laid them on the table. Then the girl brought the vermouth in very tall glasses. In each glass the convoluted length of lemon peel ended in a shape that resembled a serpent's head. Tennessee sipped from his glass with relish.

This is a good drink, he said.

I tried mine. It is, I agreed. It's cold and the flavor is delicious. I looked at the shape of the lemon peel and then at the book I was carrying with me: Lawrence's *The Plumed Serpent*. Then I showed him the book.

Yes, I've read it, he said. It's a good book about Mexico. Will you excuse me? I'm going to read my story. When a thing has been published and I read it, it's as though I were reading it for the first time.

I see. You read it as a reader rather than as an author.

More or less. He began to read. I divided my time between looking around the tearoom and daydreaming. As he finished reading each page he passed it to me. Sometimes I read an entire line, and sometimes only a word here and there. The story took place in Italy. I read and took sips of my drink, smoked and nibbled on the pastry like a child. The flavors of the vermouth and the pastry blended beautifully. The people at the other tables spoke in very low voices, and the soft music that came out of the walls was calming. Now and then a car or a motorcycle went past. The rest of the time it was quiet. Every page took Tennessee several minutes to read. Each sip of my drink or puff on my cigarette or taste of my pastry killed a moment of time. Now and then Tennessee chuckled to himself.

When he had finished reading, he stuffed the sheets of

paper into his pocket. Then he glanced at the Lawrence book and said: How do you like it?

I like all his books, I told him. I know you do, too. You adapted one of his short stories and made a play of it.

You Touched Me, he said. Lawrence was a great writer.

I asked him if he still liked the ambience of Tangier.

Oh, no! Tangier has changed terribly. I used to have friends here. Now there's only Paul Bowles.

Do you know Brion Gysin? I asked him.

Ah, yes. That American? Where is he now?

I've heard he was living in London. He was collaborating on a film script with Burroughs.

He's a strange man, he said, getting to his feet. I'm going to the hotel and lie down for a while. I'm invited to the mountain with Paul and Carol tonight, and I'm tired. I had a lot to drink last night at the Rembrandt.

31.VII.73

Late in the afternoon I met him not far from the Café de Paris. He looked a bit wan. I've got to go and see a doctor, he said. I haven't slept well for two nights.

The same way Genet felt when he was here, I thought. I handed him *Antaeus 10*, which contained my piece on Jean Genet.

I. VIII. 73

I met him walking with Baxter on the Boulevard Mohammed V. He handed me a sheet of paper on which he had typed his opinion of *For Bread Alone*, to be used in connection with the book's publicity.

I read it and said laughing: I think this blurb is going to help the book sell. I'll make hundreds of dollars with it!

You will? he said.

I think so.

Will you share it with me if you make more than you expected?

If you like. Why not?

I'm not serious. Your book is good. I think there'll be an American edition of it.

He was annoyed by what Genet said about him in my *Antaeus* article. We were standing opposite the belvedere that overlooks the harbor.

Genet's a liar, said Tennessee. I never called him on the telephone as he says I did. Françoise Sagan was the one who was trying to arrange a meeting between us.

I'm writing a diary about my meetings with you, I said suddenly. Is it all right for me to put in what you just said?

Oh, it doesn't matter. He was probably ill that day. He's a very sick man. Perhaps he takes so much Nembutal that by now he can't remember what really happened.

I thanked him for his blurb and said goodbye.

Gavin Lambert was sitting in the sun on the terrace of

the Café de Paris. I stopped to talk with him, and mentioned Tennessee's annoyance over what Genet had said about him.

We all know Genet lies, said Gavin. I know Tennessee very well. He doesn't lie. And he's not arrogant like Genet. You should make that clear in the diary you're keeping.

Later I went to Paul's and showed him the blurb. He told me Tennessee had found a pleasant villa.

4. VIII. 73

I was with Edouard Roditi, looking for a good table on the terrace of the Café de Paris.

There's Tennessee with his English friend, I said.

They were coming from the boulevard. When they saw us, they walked over to where we were standing. Tennessee and Edouard talked for a moment about Tangier. Then Edouard turned towards me and said to Tennessee: It was I who suggested that Paul translate something of Choukri's.

A good job, said Tennessee. I've read his book *For Bread Alone*. It's excellent.

He and Baxter shook hands with us once more, and continued toward the Hotel Minzah.

We don't get on together, Edouard told me in French. But among writers it's necessary to be conciliatory. I knew him when he was a completely undiscovered poet.

9.VIII.73

This morning I was at the café. Tennessee came along with Baxter. They sat down, and Tennessee told me: I'm leaving tomorrow.

So soon? I said.

He seemed in a rather bad humor, perhaps because of Baxter, who was still a fine statue, but for whom he did not feel like playing Pygmalion. It was stiflingly hot. He ordered a Coca-Cola and a glass of Fernet-Branca. I went on sipping my very bad coffee. I had with me only the amount of money the coffee was going to cost. I longed for a glass of cold beer. To calm my frustration I smoked furiously. My mouth tasted like earth.

I'm going to do the same thing with your visit to Tangier that I did with Genet's, I told him.

On me? What is there to write?

A diary. I told you about it the other day.

He laughed.

A woman from the Djebel walked past. Baxter snapped two pictures of her back. Then I asked him to take one of Tennessee and me, so I could append it to the text I was writing.

I'm sorry, he said blandly. I've only got three or four pictures left on the film, and I want to take more snaps of country people.

A young Moroccan Jew, accompanied by a short Frenchwoman, stopped in front of our table. The man greeted us, and began to talk with Tennessee about music. He spoke in English very rapidly, only stopping to draw breath. Tennessee listened, looking astonished. Now and then he moved his head a little and murmured: Ah, I see. I see.

I puffed on my cigarette and looked at the young man through the cloud of smoke. He stood there beside the woman, and his lips were the only part of him that moved. The woman seemed to be agreeing with everything he was saying, but without ever uttering a word. They were like creatures from another world. A man and a woman who have dropped onto the earth, I thought. Two robots. I could not seize anything of what he was saying. I got only an isolated word now and then: *jazz, blues, young, movement, new experiences, future of music,* and *help.*

I don't know anything about music, Tennessee said. I think Paul Bowles might be useful to you.

I've known Paul Bowles for years.

Thank you. And he and his friend went on.

Tennessee turned to me. Do you know him?

I've heard that he is a musician. And his friend tries to paint.

I didn't understand anything he said. Did you?

I said: No, I didn't.

A man sitting to Baxter's right suddenly called out: Hello, Mister Tennessee! I knew you more than twenty-five years ago. You used to come to the Zoco Chico. You remember me?

I'm sorry, I don't remember you. That was long ago, said Tennessee.

That's right. More than twenty-five years ago. Life was wonderful then, especially in the Zoco Chico.

Tennessee whispered to me: Do you know him?

Yes. He sits here all day. At night he goes from one bar to another.

What does he do? What's his work?

I don't know exactly, I said. I've heard that he likes to make love to women with his tongue.

We laughed, and he said: He's an idiot.

We were quiet for a moment. Then Tennessee said: The world is full of stupidity.

You can look for a good friend but you won't find one. It would be better to be dead than to have to live surrounded only by stupid people.

Tennessee likes solitude, I thought. But he's afraid of being alone.

Once more he wrote out his address for me, this time in the volume of Rimbaud I was carrying, and rose to go back to the hotel. He hugged me, saying: Perhaps we'll meet again some day. Keep on writing.

Baxter held out his hand and said a cold goodbye. Tennessee walked down the street with his usual springy step, while Baxter advanced beside him like a robot.

It is an adventure full of surprises to find yourself observed in print by another writer, especially one of such an alien culture as the Moroccan Mohamed Choukri's. There have been past instances when the surprises were brutal. I am grateful to both Mohamed and his translator-editor Paul Bowles that in this instance the tone is gently humorous and discreet with a reticent sympathy implicit.

Tennessee Williams

Paul Bowles
in Tangier

If you are my enemy, I'll kill you for money,
but if you are my friend, I'll kill you for free.

A proverb from the Petit Socco (Little Market) of
Tangier, quoted by Ira Cohen in an article on Paul
Bowles titled 'Mimbad Sinbad'.

The Myth of Tangier –
Where Does It Come From?

The intense nostalgia for the Tangier of yesteryear, the Tangier of the International Zone, seems utterly absurd to me. Within the history of each city or country, every epoch has its own significance and beauty, just as every stage in the life of a human being has its own kind of magic. But the lamentation over the mythical Tangier, the yearning for a Tangier that no longer exists, and by those who never even lived there, is the peak of absurdity. According to the most pessimistic and lachrymose of these whiners, 'Everything marvelous about Tangier has vanished!'

Does Tangier have the aura of a myth? Yes, undeniably; but in whose eyes? Is Tangier a lost paradise? Certainly, since those who once witnessed its opulence are still here to speak of it, but who are they who mourn a world that is no more? Can one speak of the irresistible magic of Tangier? Yes again, but also, once again, magical for whom?

Among all of those who have spoken or written about Tangier, most only did so from the viewpoint of the frivolous pleasures they sought and found there. It was an optimal backdrop for their petty amusements, their whims and self-indulgences; or simply a place in which they could try to forget their own misery. Consequently, to them Tangier was little more than a bordello, an endless beach or a huge sanatorium.

But when we consider the Tangier described to us by Paul Bowles and his wife Jane Auer, we feel their nostalgia for the city's lost innocence was justified. Their ruefulness was authentically rooted in Tangier's past, a past they themselves had experienced. Nevertheless, the general run of such jeremiads and wistful reminiscences – of both recent and ancient origin – can be found at their most ludicrous in the numerous articles and second-rate studies written about the city's past.

Most of the texts written about Tangier today are more like postcards than books. A writer will spend a few weeks in Tangier, and then produce what is, in fact, a pamphlet about it, simply to flaunt his deep knowledge of the city's secrets, clandestine geography, glorious past, and the celebrities who lived there, or passed briefly through. Not to mention those writers who, in search of an instant and meretricious fame, produce the sort of 'postcard' on Morocco that is muddled and inept, aimed at readers easily enthralled by all that is exotic and far-fetched, or those besotted with *The Thousand and One Nights*: 'Because in the Tangier of the twentieth century, the magic of *The Thousand and One Nights* is always ready to re-erupt.'[1] Such people are to be pitied. They are as risible as the tourist who has himself photographed on a camel that has been plucked from the desert and deposited on a Tangier beach (unless it was actually born there!), so that he can mail the picture to his nearest and dearest with some asinine effusions about 'the beauty of the Moroccan desert', and so forth. These are essentially rest-stop writers. They exchange a room in their own home for a room in a Moroccan hotel, and then claim to have visited our country! While here they continue to eat the same food they do at home. Only the most intrepid of them will venture on a couscous or a kebab. But far more appalling than this superficiality is their writing about Tangier – writing imbued with hatred, racism, and a contempt for the perceived simplicity of the city's native inhabitants. The best example of this is the book *La Pequeña Historia de Tánger* by Alberto España,[2] the Spanish fascist. Despite the inclusion of a few noteworthy historical points, this writer was interested exclusively

---

1 Hélie Lassaigne, 'Zestes de Tanger', *Libération*, December 28, 1989.
2 Alberto España, *La Pequeña Historia de Tánger* (Distribuciones Ibéricas, 1954).

in the indigenous and foreign ruling authorities and the segment of Tangier's native elite that was utterly subservient to colonial domination and hegemony. The most important unbiased historical and sociological document about Tangier remains *Memorias de un Viejo Tangerino*, by Isaac Laredo,[1] the outstanding journalist of his time.

Paul Bowles has said: 'As far as tourism is concerned, I think it's participating in the destruction of the world. Tourists leave nothing behind them; they destroy all the countries through which they pass. We know that very well. Tourists nowadays can go wherever they want, due to that invention called the airplane. It's a horrible thing.'[2] In my opinion this kind of transport is only appropriate for livestock, to speed cattle and sheep on their way to the slaughterhouse. Maybe the airplane is useful for rapid movement, but it's hardly suitable for traveling. Traveling requires that one be prepared for a journey that may last months, not hours. Tourists find this idea ridiculous. Wherever they're going, they want to get there as quickly as possible and settle in a hotel. That's it. They're

---

1 Isaac Laredo, *Memorias de un Viejo Tangerino* (Madrid: C. Bernejo Impresor, 1935).

2 It's known that Bowles had a crippling fear of air travel and renounced it a long time ago. Today, however, he's no longer afraid, since he's been forced to travel repeatedly by air as a result of illness and his acceptance of a number of invitations from different television stations. He's now flown to France, the United States, and Spain.

not interested in discovering a new country. In the age
we live in, people are only concerned about time. They
take a vacation that will last six weeks, or even only three.
What's the good of that? Wouldn't they have been better
off staying at home?'

Bowles developed this idea more fully in *The
Sheltering Sky*, a novel set in the latter part of the forties.
The protagonist, Port, declares: 'Another important
difference between tourist and traveler is that the former
accepts his own civilization without question; not so the
traveler, who compares it with the others, and rejects
those elements he finds not to his liking.'[1] Here Bowles
pities the man constricted by his epoch, allowing it to
shape his life without offering any resistance. In the same
vein he says: 'Whereas the tourist generally hurries back
home at the end of a few weeks or months, the traveler,
belonging no more to one place than the next, moves
slowly over periods of years, from one part of the earth to
another.'[2] But Bowles knows perfectly well that the true
traveler, with his journeys grounded in the exploration
of other cultures and civilizations, disappeared in the
twenties and thirties, to give way to recreational tourism.
People who leave their country to seek adventure in
another land no longer exist, except for those with specific

1 Paul Bowles, *The Sheltering Sky* (New Jersey: Ecco Press, 1977),
   p. 14.
2 Ibid.

occupational reasons for doing so, be they scientific, literary, journalistic, or artistic.

This 'Tangier', for whose foundational origins historians and researchers scrabble in vain, sprang from the Flood, according to a *Tanjawi* legend. The dove returned, Noah cried out 'Tīn Jā' (land is here), and shortly thereafter his ark docked near the plateau of Charf. Myth and history merge in Tangier. Yet it never divulges its eternal secret, enfolded in the enduring silence of its memory – a blend of enigma, magic, and wisdom. Milan Kundera accounts thus for this retreat into mystery: 'Man's struggle in life is the struggle of memory against forgetting.'

Those who come to Tangier today, hoping to recover the experiences of those who preceded them, or who simply sojourned here a while, are unlikely to be disappointed. They will be happy to find echoes of those tales from the city's past which have so captivated them. The important thing, for them, is to tune in to the reverberations left humming by those who went before.

Paul Bowles's Arrival in Tangier

Tennessee Williams has said: 'Paul Bowles is far more important than the places he inhabits.' And, in a letter to Alec France, Bowles wrote: 'I never felt I knew the place well enough to write about it.'[1]

From the beginning of the fifties onwards, the founders of the Beat Generation began to invade Tangier: William Burroughs, Allen Ginsberg (he visited Bowles here for the last time in December 1993), and Jack Kerouac (he came in 1957) among them. Their writing expressed the rebellion of a new generation of Americans who felt lost and disillusioned after the Second World War. This was not the case with Paul Bowles, however, leaving aside his impulsive decision to join the Communist Party. This he later regretted, and was ultimately expelled in

1 Paul Bowles, *In Touch: The Letters of Paul Bowles* (London: Flamingo, 1995), p. 463.

1940 after a lengthy dispute. He was, though, infatuated by traveling from the early days of his youth, and was further propelled in that direction by his parents' severity. Regarding Bowles, Virgil Thomson observed: 'But it seems that in 1939, if you wanted to work in the theater, which Paul did, you had to be smart and opportunistic. It was preferable to be a member of the Communist Party that controlled the union. You would be expelled if you didn't join the party. And not just that, you had to be Stalinist as well, because the New York party branch was Stalinist and sympathized with the left.'

Bowles derived most of his books concerned with exoticism from his various travels: his stories and novels are hardly ever devoid of some kind of journey, long or short. As Daniel Rondeau has said: 'He is a peripatetic writer.'

Paul Bowles first came to Tangier with Aaron Copland (a student of Nadia Boulanger), a pupil accompanying his teacher in a relation of apprenticeship. They arrived via Ceuta and Tétouan on August 8, 1931, after a two-day sojourn in Oran. It had been Alice Toklas, supported by the domineering Gertrude Stein, who had advised Bowles to make the trip.[1] Stein had made it a habit to invite her

---

1 Hemingway mentions that she was overpowering, and dicta-
torial in her opinions, but occasionally her advice was sound.
Bowles once told me that she didn't want Ezra Pound to visit
her, because whenever he went to her house he broke whatever
was there that could possibly be broken just by touching it. As a
result of her volatile nature, she lost all her friends one after the
other, as Hemingway confirms.

close American friends to Paris, particularly the artists among them, often encouraging them to undertake various adventures and travels to far-off places. Bowles would behave in a similar fashion towards his own friends once he had finally settled down in Tangier with his wife Jane Auer in 1947. The impetus, however, behind Bowles's constant traveling was the desire to discover new ideas, not the wish to participate in a revolution, like Byron in Greece, or Malraux and Orwell in Spain.

Bowles had merely come to spend a summer in Tangier, like many of those before him, yet in the end he stayed. It is worth noting that most of the foreign artists who visit Tangier come in the summer, and then leave after a sojourn of shorter or longer duration: a brief encounter, an infatuation, or even a temporary marriage – without witnesses. But Paul Bowles, how can his decision to remain here for so many years be explained? The climate? The simplicity of life? The hot *majoun* served with glasses of mint tea? The availability of *kif,* sold at that time even in the tobacconists' shops? Or was it the city's lingering cosmopolitanism, the freedom of life in the International Zone, and the charm of its myth and exoticism? In any case, his decision to pass the rest of his days here is never explained, or made precisely clear. He only answers evasively and with ambiguity, as if he wanted his secret to be as elusive as his shadow. He would often say, with his well-known sense of irony: 'I came and I stayed.'

'And why did you stay for your entire life?'

'Oh! That's how it is. You're not the first to ask me this question, and I've nothing to lose by answering you now. Life was very good at that time [from the thirties until independence in 1956]. You could listen to the sounds of the cicadas in the eucalyptus trees while sitting on the terrace of the Café de Paris. Today, though, you won't hear anything but the deafening noise of traffic.'

With variations in phrasing, this is how he answers everyone who asks him about his decision to remain in Tangier, something which he has never regretted. But, if Bowles would have preferred that Morocco stay as he knew it in the thirties and forties, that's because there is something in him that is purely colonialist. In a letter to his friend Alec Franc (March 2, 1975), he says: 'One of the reasons I'm here is surely that on arriving I found a people admirably attuned to my own fantasies.'[1] And, from his novel *Let It Come Down*: 'It was one of the charms of the International Zone [Tangier] that you could get anything you wanted if you paid for it. Do anything, too, for that matter – there were no incorruptibles. It was only a question of price.'[2] And towards the end, when he thinks everything is over, he writes to Regina Weinreich (August 2, 1989): 'It's difficult to live as a non-Moslem in a Moslem land.'[3] At one point in *Let It Come Down*,

1 Bowles, *In Touch*, p. 465.
2 Paul Bowles, *Let It Come Down* (Santa Rosa: Black Sparrow Press, 1994), p. 26.
3 Bowles, *In Touch*, p. 537.

Thami's father-in-law comments: 'Only bad things can happen when Nazarenes and Moslems come together.'[1] Bowles finds it hard to believe that 'everything that comes to pass is merely a symbol', as Goethe said. He tries to transcend the dying of the light, the inexorable decline into darkness, by constantly invoking the past, in the interviews he has given since he became too ill to write.

Paul Bowles loves Morocco, but does not really like Moroccans. About this, there can be no doubt. Even in his attempt to defend them, in his novel *The Spider's House,* his disappointment in them is clear. He assumed that, after independence, they would return to their traditional way of life. But he was taken aback by their rejection of it in their attempt to become more and more Europeanized. The Morocco that Bowles loved will never return; with the establishment of independence, it was over. The image that continues to be deeply rooted in his mind is not just of *Tanjawis* (natives of Tangier, or 'Tangerines') but of all Moroccans. In Sebastian Hirt's documentary on him, he reads this paragraph from his book *Points in Time*:

> An English privateer sailed into the bay at day-break. We dispatched four men to bring the ship into harbor. Then we all went quickly to the shore at the foot of the cliffs and waited. When the prow hit the reef we swam out and climbed aboard. Some of the passengers dived into the

1 Bowles, *Let It Come Down*, p. 261.

water. The captain and crew were on deck. This
time we had orders to kill as few as possible. We
took them all alive save one English woman who
drowned when she jumped overboard. We had
the chains ready, and we drove them ahead of us
through Tangier.[1]

Then, he adds:

They had had orders to seize all European ships
crossing the open shores of Morocco in order to
capture their crews and enslave them. This story
was told from the viewpoint of simple citizens
who had been able to capture the crew of a small
ship. I don't know to exactly which period it goes
back, I think to the sixteenth century. They cap-
tured thousands of men and transported them
to Meknès to work underground, in the depths
of the earth, digging narrow dungeons and
caves for the palace. They were brave and reck-
less in that period too. They would be ready to
do it again if it were possible. But these days it's
become impossible. They talk seriously about re-
claiming Andalusia from Spain. Perhaps they'll
do it; they hate Spain, and all foreign countries
for that matter. They're very xenophobic. I do
believe it's possible that they'll try unsuccess-
fully to invade the South of Spain. They did
that while Franco was in power and he took ap-
proximately 55,000 Moroccans captive whom
he later used as the spearhead of his army. They

---

1 Paul Bowles, *Points in Time* (New York: Harper Perennial), p.
32.

won a lot of victories, but what fatalities! They began to attack peasants in small villages. They were confident of success; Franco encouraged them by giving them permission to do whatever they wanted: they began to burn the villages, to loot, and to rape the women. They had unlimited freedom to do whatever they pleased. They took full advantage of that, and with the greatest pleasure; they killed religious men, nuns, and burned churches and villages. They destroyed everything that was in their way, because they loved that kind of thing.

In the story 'The Hours after Noon', Mrs Callender, in reference to her daughter, says to Mr Van Siclen in a weary voice: 'You wouldn't talk that way, so playfully, if you knew the hazards of bringing up a girl in this place ... With these Moors all about, and strange new people coming to the pension every day. Of course, we try to get good Moors, but you know how they are – utterly undependable and mad as hatters, every one of them. One never knows what any of them will take it into his head to do next. Thank God we can afford to send Charlotte to school in England.'[1]

So Moroccans, in Mrs Callender's opinion, are savages, though she adores the Moroccan sun and the country's splendid natural scenery. Mrs Lyle in *The Sheltering Sky* is even more reprehensible and ridiculous

1 Paul Bowles, 'The Hours after Noon', in *The Stories of Paul Bowles* (New York: Harper Perennial, 2006), p. 236.

than Mrs Callender when she addresses Port: 'They say in the mountains here it's better to carry a gun. Although I must say I've never seen an Arab I couldn't handle. It's the beastly French one really needs protection from.'[1] Later, while the porters of the hotel are bidding Port, Mrs Lyle, and her son Eric farewell as their car pulls away, Mrs Lyle says, settling into her seat: 'I noticed several people staring at me when I left.' She follows this with: 'They're a stinking, low race of people with nothing to do in life but spy on others. How else do you think they live?'[2] When Tunner wants to change rooms with Kit so that she can be across from Port, he is hardly less malicious, as he says, in reference to the hotel's employees: 'Righto. We'll get one of these monkeys to make the shift for us.'[3] Mrs Lyle insults everyone, first and foremost her idiot of a son, Eric, who at one point while talking to Port comments: 'She wouldn't know what to do if you put her down in a civilized country.'[4] Later, she says to the buffoon: 'I've discovered the sweetest mosque, but it's covered with brats all shrieking like demons. Filthy little beasts, they are!'[5] Bowles is outstanding at describing the material and spiritual dregs of humanity while leaving his own feelings and judgments out of the picture.

1 Bowles, *The Sheltering Sky*, p. 70.
2 Ibid, p. 71.
3 Ibid, p. 94.
4 Ibid, p. 60.
5 Ibid, p. 54.

He loves places rather than people, and he is only happy with himself when he is in a specific location. From Tangier he wrote to William Targ: 'Places have always been more important to me than people. That is to say, people give landscape scale; the landscape is not a backdrop for them. My dreams are seldom of people; they are almost always of places, directions, relative positions of objects around me. The human beings in them are faceless, anonymous. I accept this as a basic condition of existence.'[1] Bowles always considers himself an exile, regardless of where he is living, even in New York, his birthplace. He is at home everywhere and nowhere. Jane, though, was the opposite; she wanted to engage in conversation wherever she was. As she frequently admits in her letters, she was only marginally interested in location, quoting Antonin Artaud: 'Life consists of burning up questions.'

'Pack of lazy buggers, lolling about, smoking their pipes and cadging food. Useless sods.'[2] These are the words Sir Nigel uses to describe Moroccans. Small-framed, base, and utterly repulsive, he is an Englishman with eyes set too close together, like those of a chimpanzee, and a face embedded with wrinkles. He engages in a kind of sadism with five adolescent Moroccan girls who come to him from Tangier's surrounding villages. They

---

1 Bowles, *In Touch*, p. 440.
2 Paul Bowles, 'Dinner at Sir Nigel's', in *The Stories of Paul Bowles*, p. 620.

are supervised and prepared for action by a sixth, who is black, and older than the rest. Sir Nigel lashes them with his whip while they scratch each other, tearing one another's hair and clothing until they can take no more. When the scene reaches a pitch of hysteria they are given a signal to stop, a wave of the sixth girl's hand. She then drags each of them to their respective rooms. The scene, observed by a group of English and Canadian journalists, is described by Bowles, with his usual skill, in the story 'Dinner at Sir Nigel's'. One of the journalists who knows Sir Nigel confirms that the girls come to him of their own free will. They are sequestered for a month and perform the spectacle for the sake of good food and the expensive kaftan with which he compensates each of them. Another of Sir Nigel's opinions is that his cook – who is also his butler and gardener, and whom he brought with him from Zanzibar – accomplishes on his own the work for which he would need 'half a dozen Moors'. It's clear that the story has been engendered by the kind of imaginative scenes found in *The Thousand and One Nights,* but in the style of Sade, even though Bowles claims he has never read Sade. In 1950, he tried to read the latter's *One Hundred and Twenty Days of Sodom,* but found the book not worth the effort, as he wrote to John Martin at Black Sparrow Press (January 12, 1978), in reference to an introduction by Gore Vidal to a collection of Bowles's stories in which Vidal alludes to Sade's influence.

Bowles says about storytellers: 'The people who have

told me their stories have done so for the pleasure of it, not for any other reason. It was a normal thing to do. People used to love to tell stories and to listen to them, and that wasn't so long ago, perhaps fifty years or less. With the introduction of television, no one thinks about it anymore. The television has nearly killed everything. It's practically done away with music, oral literature ... and what else? Of course, there are other things. It's the pattern of life that rises from commercial television that kills culture, nothing more.'[1]

Had things remained the same as they were during one of the happy periods of his life, Bowles would have rested content. Geographical and historical changes and the rise of new cultures ruined the pleasure of life for him, and would have done so no matter where he was living. Maybe he chose to stay in Tangier because, when he arrived the first time, it was a place almost wholly devoid of the concept of time (the axiom, 'Time is money', never having penetrated there), and of the West's compulsion to be constantly on the go. 'What's a week to them? Time doesn't exist for them,'[2] as Port says to Kit in *The Sheltering Sky*. One could think of his stay in Tangier as a kind of search for a cure for pollution, an attempt to escape from the pressure of time that makes people become obsessed with speed. Bowles wants to recover the

1 From Sebastian Hirt's film *Le Titan de Tanger: Paul Bowles, une légende* ("The Giant of Tangier: Paul Bowles, a Legend"), 1993.
2 Bowles, *The Sheltering Sky*, p. 177.

past to which he clings so desperately; but it has already slipped away from him, for ever. All he can do is pine for it, which he does in a sour and maudlin manner.

In a letter to Charles Henri Ford (November 2, 1947), Bowles clarifies his concept of place: 'As you know perfectly well, I've never yet felt a part of any place I've been and I never expect to. But naturally, the fewer people there are in a place, and the less there is happening, the less conscious I am of missing what is going on under my nose. Which is why I like the most difficult places ... in fact, if there is no one at all, I can say that the reason I am ill at ease is that the place is such that no one could live in it, therefore it can't be surprising that I too should be unable to stay there. In other words, it's a question of finding uncomfortable situations and putting up with them for as long as possible before escaping; the desire for escape then can be called perfectly natural.'[1]

Through his writing, travels, and unconventional lifestyle, Bowles played a significant role in hippie culture, although he strenuously denies having any connection with the Beat Generation. All the same, he welcomed many beatniks into his home, where he would converse with them at length, despite the large amounts of his time they took up. He was like a spiritual father; he understood their rebellion against their families and societies (he had behaved similarly toward his own

---

1 Bowles, *In Touch*, p. 179.

family and country). He was tolerant of them, even with all their inanities. It reached the point where they would leave their bags at the entrance of his small apartment, languidly saying: 'Hey man, we've come to see you.' Eventually he grew tired of them and had to turn them away. He charged the ever capable Mohammed Mrabet with the execution of this task.

Every summer, a group of students aspiring to be writers came to the American School in Tangier, and Bowles would help them with their texts. Not a single one of them had talent, however, and they ended by disappointing him – with one exception, and who that was we do not know. They came thinking they would enrich themselves through writing, without even having mastered the basic grammar. Bowles continued to work with them for years, until he was incapacitated by illness (so far he has had two operations for sciatica), and worn down by the decrepitude of age.

In his work, Bowles remains both less mystical and less profound than Hermann Hesse, a writer who, because of the light in which he presents the exotic and the numinous, also had a significant influence on the hippie generation (particularly his two novels *Steppenwolf* and *Siddhartha,* the former for its remarkable pessimism and the latter, conversely, for its optimism). Unlike Paul Bowles, Hesse had no need to resort to *majoun* to stimulate his imagination. In *The Sheltering Sky*, Bowles relied on the drug to depict his protagonist Port's death scene; likewise, in *Let It Come Down*, *majoun* helped him create the scene in which Dyar Nelson, anxious to be rid of his friend Thami out of an irrational fear that he is planning to seize all his money, hammers a nail into the latter's ear.

Norman Mailer would later write: 'Paul Bowles opened the world of Hip. He let in the murder, the drugs, the incest, the death of the Square ... the call of the orgy, the end of civilization.'[1] The question I would therefore pose is: Was Bowles, in fact, triumphant in fulfilling the dream harbored by so many of the American artists and pilgrims who came to the world's cultural capitals – Paris, Berlin, Rome, and Tangier – once he, himself, arrived? Further, did he succeed in realizing his own personal dream, distinct from those of the other adventurers who came before him, as seen in his statement: 'like any Romantic, I had always been vaguely certain that sometime during my life I should come into a magic place which in disclosing its secrets would give me wisdom and ecstasy – perhaps even death'?[2]

Here I remember Malika, the heroine of Bowles's story 'Here to Learn', a girl out of whom Tim (Pygmalion) would like to shape his own Galatea. After the death of her husband, an inheritance frees Malika from her

1 Paul Bowles, *Conversations with Paul Bowles* (Jackson: University Press of Mississippi, 1993), p. 180.

2 Paul Bowles, *Without Stopping: An Autobiography* (New York: Ecco Press, 1985), p. 125.

material destitution, yet her biggest challenge still remains. Having inherited nothing from her family but metaphysical darkness, how is she to overcome her spiritual misery?

Shakir Nuri asks Paul Bowles: 'Are you afraid of death?'

'No, I'm not afraid of death. Of course, I don't want to die, but at the same time I'm not afraid of that fatal moment. All of us are going to die. This is a human reality that we have to accept just as we accept life: death is part of life. Nothing else would be realistic.'

Bowles was born with a compulsive longing to escape. We also know that there were those in his family who wished he did not exist. When he was just six weeks old, his father, wanting to be rid of him, left him on the edge of a windowsill one cold, snowy November evening. Another account says that his maternal grandmother, Winewisser, wished him dead, because she was jealous and wanted to monopolize her daughter's affections, not wanting her daughter to have children at all. But his greatest enemy was his father, a man who, unrelentingly hostile, rejected all the indications of his son's early intelligence. 'Jealous of my immense talent he ordered my piano removed from the house,'[1] as Bowles writes in reference to his father in a letter to his friend Bruce Morrissette from Italy in 1932.

---

1 Bowles, *In Touch*, p. 95.

Paul Bowles's childhood was spent in the world of adults, though with a family so devoid of warmth he was hardly ever embraced by them. His life was strictly governed, regulated, and repressed in ways that were often maddening and terrifying. Only on rare occasions did his father show him any kindness. One of the torments to which his father would subject him, with compulsive scrupulousness, was the injunction that every mouthful of food be chewed forty times before swallowing, for the good of his health. It seems obvious that Bowles derived his story 'Ice Fields' from his familial environment, for there is a clear resemblance between himself and the story's protagonist, Donald.

Until he was seven, Bowles was not allowed to play with children of his age. Once he began school, he continued to be friendless, isolated from the other infants. This apartness would be the reason why he had no trouble surpassing his classmates in his studies. In these circumstances, it is hardly surprising that all the characters in the first story he wrote were animals. After putting him to bed, his mother would sing to him, as lullabies, songs that were far above his mental age. She liked to read him the horror stories of Edgar Allan Poe, an author who continues to be his favorite to this day. On his own initiative, he early came across Lautréamont – a writer whose work is no bloodier than Bowles's own writing – and he was duly impressed. Faulkner, however, he did not like. 'I read the books, but didn't believe them,'[1] as he wrote to Allen Hibbard from Tangier (January 1983). He never finished *Guignol's Band* by Céline, and, as for Joyce, he admitted to Millicent Dillon that: 'I envy you if you're able to sustain a uniform degree of interest throughout *Ulysses*. People are always saying they do. People also claim to be clairvoyant and to levitate.'[2] He continued to be an avid admirer of Rimbaud until he was fifteen years old, at which point he began to prefer the latter's adventures to his poetry. He found Francis Bacon's style of painting disturbing, and William Burroughs's *Naked Lunch* bewildered him.

His mother's health was frail, and as a result his father would repeat to him: 'You're the reason for your mother's constant illness. Never forget it!' In one of his interviews, Paul Bowles speaks of his desire to be a child once again, but not the child he was, to be sure: 'I would like to be a child again, because the air smells better. Now that I'm eighty-one [at the time of this conversation], there are fewer possibilities to enjoy life. The child is free; he goes out, he sees the sun and the flowers, and he is able to really breathe. At my age, a person goes out and he feels any number of little aches and pains. This isn't important. The child has the feeling that the world is a wonderful place; he's not afraid because he's innocent, maybe I'm longing for that innocence. This doesn't mean

1 Bowles, *In Touch*, p. 510.
2 Ibid., p. 506.

that the life of children is paradise; children suffer more than adults. Children suffer, and they feel and experience pleasure more acutely.'

Bowles loves to experience fear, but he doesn't know why. It is his belief that: 'Fear is what runs the world. It's the most powerful stimulus, more powerful than love, because love doesn't drive the world; it propagates the species. It's not important like fear, which occupies the preeminent position. Fear is what characterizes life, because obviously all of us want to continue living. Everything that is outside threatens you; if you weren't afraid you wouldn't breathe.' Of course, this idea is influenced by Oswald Spengler's *Decline of Western Civilization*, a text Bowles is very fond of.

In his novel *In the Spider's House* he does not raise the question 'Why live?', but rather, how is living possible, since the worm is in the fruit? It is clearly a fatalistic novel.

Paul Bowles does not see a solution to the fear of death, unlike Epicurus, who said: 'As long as I am living I have no fear of death, and when I come to die I will not feel anything.' But in Bowles's understanding of fear, an emotion he considers more important than love, isn't there a refusal to stand up to the challenge of life? Apparently, there is another way to get rid of fear: suicide.

In the same vein, Bowles uses the bourgeoisie as an example: 'They have money, every material comfort, yet they have the same fear of death. Nothing can protect a person from death. Nothing. There are people who believe in immortality. It seems that these people are less afraid, but why? They should have the same fear, because no one has proved, nor will anyone ever prove, that immortality exists.'[1] Bowles neglects to mention that fear is an emotion that has no prescribed boundaries.

In Sebastian Hirt's documentary, Bowles says about death: 'I think that one should die as one lived. If one lived in a catastrophe, then he should die in a catastrophe. This is preferable. As long as we're going to die one day, it doesn't matter in what way this occurs. I believe that those who are afraid of death are those who believe that there is an afterlife. They don't know what will become of them after their physical deaths. If you believe in God, how will He measure what you did in your life? How can you be certain that you'll obtain His approval? So you're worried, you're afraid of death. But there's no need for this.' I wonder to what degree does Bowles accept the idea of Emile Cioran: 'When a human being dies, he becomes master of the world'?

---

1 From an interview held in Tangier with *El País*, March 29, 1992.

Tangier: Various Opinions

When Mark Twain visited Tangier, coming directly from Spain in 1876, he only stayed for thirty-six hours. In his book *The Innocents Abroad* he remarks: 'Tangier is the spot we have been longing for all the time ... We wanted something thoroughly and uncompromisingly foreign.'[1] He believed it to be the second oldest city in the world. The day he arrived, it seemed like paradise to him, as he wrote to his friends; the suddenness of his departure remains a mystery to this very day. None the less, Tangier did not disappoint him. And Paul Bowles chose to remain here, whatever irritations he might have encountered.

Aaron Copland declared, after he and Bowles had been in Tangier for a few days: 'It's a madhouse, a madhouse'. He was disturbed by the loud, tense way

---

1 Mark Twain, *The Innocents Abroad* (New York: Harper & Brothers Publishers, 1906), p. 113.

Tanjawis spoke, and by the sounds of the drums and the *ghayta* that continued day and night. When he and Bowles visited Fez, he found it even more disconcerting than Tangier, thus confirming his aversion for Morocco in its entirety. Bowles was less sensitive than Copland and, after being befriended by some of Fez's bourgeois families, he preferred Fez to Tangier, and began to enjoy his expatriation. In 1949, Truman Capote came with Jane Bowles, behaving like a frightened child dragged along by his older sister. He was twenty-five years old and had simply come to spend the summer in Tangier, not to begin work on a book, or finish or revise one, like most of the other young writers who were there. After returning to New York, he wrote, warning those leaving for Tangier, of three essential things: 'Be inoculated for typhoid [Bowles had contracted it], withdraw your savings from the bank, say goodbye to your friends – heaven knows you may never see them again. This is serious advice ...'[1] He fled the city, afraid that he too would fall under the spell that kept others from ever leaving: 'I feel that time, if it isn't completely static there, moves extremely slowly and doesn't leave one [like Bowles] the ability to choose his own destiny.'

Bowles describes Capote thus: 'He was quite plump. He had a strange voice (like a goat), and an odd way

---

1 Michelle Green, *The Dream at the End of the World: Paul Bowles and the Literary Renegades in Tangier* (New York: Harper Perennial, 1992), p. 70.

of speaking. He joked around a lot and would make us laugh. The only problem was that no one here knew who he was. He was waiting for everyone to say, "Look! It's Truman Capote." But no one did. Finally ... he refused to go to the old city or the Kasbah ... he was afraid. "No, I won't go there" [Bowles likes to imitate his voice very much]. That's how he would speak. His voice was like a goat. I asked him, why don't you want to go? He said, "Who knows what will happen to me!" Nothing would have happened, but he refused to go.

'Truman Capote went to a soirée. It was a masquerade party. Everyone was wearing a costume. I don't know what he was disguised as. He was carrying garlands of flowers, and wearing some kind of dancer's outfit. Ada Green was there; as soon as she saw him she inquired: "And what are you supposed to represent?" "The spirit of spring!" she was told. "Well, you don't look it!" she snapped. And here they stopped speaking to each other.'

In 1950, Brion Gysin arrived,[1] and was fascinated by the *cha'bi* music performances to which Bowles introduced him. By this time, Bowles had become the cicerone to

1 Brion Gysin (1916–86). A painter, inventor and writer, he initially came to Morocco on a grant from the Fulbright Foundation in July 1950. Planning to stay for the summer, he ended up in Morocco for twenty-five years. A former student of the Sorbonne, he wrote *The Exterminator* in collaboration with William Burroughs in 1960. Bowles had invited him to Morocco and they travelled together for several months before Gysin finally settled in Tangier.

all the Americans who came to Tangier (the 'Dream City'), and even to those who were not American. He had entrenched himself there like the Sphinx, and acted as their accredited sponsor, their authoritative source on all Morocco. Brion Gysin, like Mark Twain, compared Tangier to paradise, as he said to Bowles, and hoped to remain in the city for the rest of his life. To bind himself to the place, he opened up the restaurant '1001 Nights' in a wing of the Menebhi Palace in the Marshan (the most beautiful of the old quarters outside the city's walls). He set the *Jahjouka* musicians up in Tangier and disseminated their music throughout Europe and the United States, eventually bringing the Rolling Stones to Tangier to hear them. In comparison with Bowles, he was on more intimate terms with Moroccans, whom he genuinely liked and treated as friends. He learned Moroccan Arabic and spoke it better than Bowles.[1] 'If I become Muslim one day,' he confided to Bowles, 'it will be because of this *cha'bi* Moroccan music.'

Brion Gysin wrote just one novel, *The Process*, but it lacked marketability. For twenty-five years he stayed in Tangier, until the daily medical care required by his cancer forced him to move to Paris, where he died in 1986. He never abandoned the idea of returning to visit his

---

1 Bowles mispronounces even the easiest of words: *hammaam* he pronounces *hamaan*, *mijmar* becomes *mijmah*, *ghaitah* is *raitah*, and *muqaddam* is *muqaddan*; there are many others, as is clear in his autobiography and other books.

friends and acquaintances, and his last will and testament contained clear proof of his love for both Tangier and Marrakesh. Anne Cumming Felicity, whom he considered a kindred spirit, carried his ashes from Paris in small vials and scattered them amongst the rocks of Hercules' cave and in the Jamaa El-Fna market square in Marrakesh, a place he greatly loved. Ashes here, ashes there, ashes all over!

Brion Gysin may have been the only well-known foreigner whom I have never heard complain about Moroccans. Once he had left Tangier for good, he told Daniel Rondeau in Paris: 'The Tangier of those years was paradise. We'll never see its like on earth again.'

Bowles recorded a number of different kinds of *cha'bi* and Andalusian music in Morocco. Regarding some of the difficulties that impeded him in this, he says: 'I needed help from the Moroccan government; whenever I settled down in a different city, I called whoever was in charge. I let him know my identity and I asked him to gather the musicians for me. Sometimes they refused, saying, "No, by no means, we don't want Moroccan music to be exported. We don't want foreigners listening to what we do." Some of them were really badly mannered, but most were nice and ready to help me. The support of the government had to be obtained in order to bring the musicians, because sometimes a truck had to be sent to search for them a hundred kilometers away up in the mountains. They had to be brought to a place where

I could do the recordings with them. Occasionally it happened that they were on hand in the village, but more often than not you had to go search for them wherever they were.'

It was in the early sixties that I first began to hear and read about the names of all the foreign writers and artists who had visited Tangier: those who came fleetingly, those who came from time to time, and those who left without ever coming back, like Truman Capote, Jack Kerouac, and Alfred Chester. The latter chose to commit suicide in Israel, after being expelled from Tangier and Asilah as a result of all the trouble in which he enmeshed himself with the local authorities. He behaved like a madman, no matter where he was. Among his many stunts, he tried to convert the roof of an old house that he had rented in Asilah into a swimming pool. He enlisted children from the quarter to help him implement this project, and had them carrying water up to the roof in buckets. Bowles would recall the insanity of it and laugh.

From a distance I used to see Bowles, the founder, and his clique, but I didn't know any of them personally yet, and I hadn't read any of their works. They were writers and I still hadn't published my first story. I was immersed in reading the classics and Romantics, both Arabic and foreign. In the field of literature, I still had to sow my first seed, and I didn't share their tendency toward homosexuality. Later, I would realize that, in regard to his sexual orientation, Paul Bowles, like Jack Kerouac, is more discreet than the rest of them. But with Kerouac there was always the possibility that he would expose himself when drunk. Once, he stood up in a bar shouting, 'I fucked Gore Vidal.' In the forties and fifties, amongst writers and artists homosexuality was considered a kind of national sport, especially in the New York scene. It was something intimate that could strengthen a friendship. Allen Ginsberg and Peter Orlovsky visited Kerouac one time when he was sick. As a show of friendship, they had sex with him. When Kerouac protested that he wasn't gay and they shouldn't have done it, they answered him in an exaggeratedly sweet tone: 'We only wanted to make you happy, dear Jack!' In recounting the incident, Orlovsky remarked dolefully that Kerouac had been too drunk to have an erection.

After his novel *On the Road* was published, Kerouac became the Marlon Brando of literature. Suddenly 'the men wanted to get to know him personally and the women desperately wanted to sleep with him'. Anything that he wrote was published and would sell extremely well, but he paid a high price for this sudden fame and lionization. Kerouac would boast of his celebrity to all and sundry, egged on by the young guys who frequented the bars to drink to the health of their adored idol. He would stop at nothing to promote his literary career. William Burroughs once said: 'Jack Kerouac was gregarious, social. He loved to go out, drink and talk, always wanting to be surrounded by people. He was ready to bray about being a famous writer to anyone who would listen to him, and would shout out: "I'm Jack Kerouac!'"

William Burroughs has admitted that the reason he first came to Tangier from San Francisco in 1952 was to visit Bowles,[1] the writer of *Let It Come Down*[2] – something that Bowles denied in an interview. On another occasion, he claimed that he came for the young boys, the Spanish ones in particular, and the hashish and *majoun*. In *Naked Lunch* he says: 'The Spanish boys call me El Hombre Invisible – the Invisible Man.'[3]

He could be seen in the Petit Socco, sitting in a café, leaning against a wall, or walking around. A little later he might be spotted wandering around the streets of the new city. There was always something severe about his bearing. Anyone who saw him then would get the impression that he was a spy surreptitiously gathering information, the collar of his overcoat perpetually raised, his fedora tilted slightly downwards on his forehead, his gaze steady, one hand clutching the front of his coat, the other in his pocket, or both hands plunged deep in the pockets of his

---

1 In the spring of that year Burroughs had killed his wife Joan during a party. He put a glass of champagne on her head, fired his gun and missed, smashing her skull. This was a game he had played with her before.

2 The title of the novel is taken from *Macbeth*, Act III, Scene 3: Banquo: 'It will be Rayne to Night'. 1st Murderer: 'Let it come downe' (They set upon Banquo).

3 William Burroughs, *Naked Lunch* (New York: Grove Weidenfeld, 1990), p. 61.

coat. This was when he was daily ingesting any number of different drugs, whether by injection, swallowing, or smoking. Bowles and Brion Gysin would often visit him in the Munirya Hotel where he was writing *Naked Lunch*. They would gather up the papers strewn all over the floor and organize them. When Allen Ginsberg and Jack Kerouac visited Tangier, they helped Burroughs put what he had written of *Naked Lunch* together. It is said that Kerouac[1] would type the drafts on the typewriter, while Peter Orlovsky got high smoking *kif* and prepared the food with Burroughs.

---

[1] It should be mentioned here that the legitimate curator of the true drafts of *Naked Lunch* was Allen Ginsberg. Burroughs would send him everything he wrote, and Ginsberg arranged the papers into what would become the manuscript.

William Burroughs in Tangier

When William Burroughs arrived in Tangier he greeted *Tanjawi* society, both the Moroccans and the expatriates, with hostility. The former he saw as intellectual inferiors and swindlers, while the latter were ostentatious, boastful of their comfortable financial situations that allowed them to frequent all the best restaurants and bars. Everyone – those who were permanent residents like Paul Bowles, and those who visited frequently like Tennessee Williams – avoided him. Burroughs lived in isolation. He trusted no one, to the degree that whenever he went out in the street he carried a knife or a gun – which he liked to polish in full public view. Behind his self-protective barrier, he consoled himself in his loneliness by indulging his paranoia to the utmost. At Dean's Bar, the owner Dean considered Burroughs's arrival in Tangier to be an evil omen. He thought Burroughs looked like a troublemaker with the mark of Cain on him, and would grudgingly serve him a drink only if he was with a good customer like Kells Elvis, one of Burroughs's old school friends, who had encouraged him to write at the beginning of the thirties.

The mistake Burroughs made, which prevented him from getting on with Moroccans and living among them, was that he trampled on their traditions and customs without the slightest concession to civility or courtesy, in contrast to Bowles, who was astute enough to adapt to the local culture. Burroughs, however, considered himself above this kind of humility, as he wrote to Brion Gysin in Paris: 'I have to leave before I open fire on Tangier's ridiculous people with my laser gun.' He lived like a cowboy in a Western who steps off the stagecoach in a town where no one knows him. But once he discovered some of the secrets of life in Tangier, he changed his mind and grew to be happy there. He wrote, 'I don't see how anyone could be happier than I am right now ... I hope to God I don't have to leave Tangier ... Tangier is my dream town. I did have a dream ten years ago of coming into a harbor and knowing that this was the place where I desired to be ... Just the other day, rowing around in the harbor, I recognized it as my dream bay.'[1]

Burroughs's dream here is analogous to the dream Bowles had while in New York, in which he imagined a

---

1 *The Letters of William S. Burroughs* (New York: Penguin Books, 1994), p. 330.

place (Tangier) that would give him wisdom, and maybe even death. Yet Burroughs did not stay in Tangier for reasons of anthropology, as Bowles did; rather, he had found a safe haven where he could indulge his chronic drug use free from interference. In a letter to Allen Ginsberg he explains (August 18, 1954): 'Come to think of it the Tangier police are a model for just what the police should be and do. They don't care at all about your sex life or whether you take junk (of course everybody smokes tea [*kif*] in the street like tobacco). All they do is maintain order (and do a pretty thorough job too). I haven't seen many fights and when a fight occurs the police are there in a matter of seconds. They were however not able to prevent a murder that occurred recently in the main drag, but there was no warning. One Arab walked up to another and stuck a knife in his stomach. And prevent theft (there is not much of that either).

'In an altercation an American is automatically right against an Arab. I like that, and I don't abuse it. If I hit someone you can be sure he deserves to be hit, because I am naturally good-natured and easy-going to a fault. It is nice to know the cops will take your side if you do have trouble. I haven't had any to speak of here. One Arab tried to rob me, but a good hard shove ended the attempt. The tribunals don't even make a pretense of not discriminating. An Arab always draws more time than a European for the same offence. All sentences here are relatively light, however – 5 years about maximum.'[1]

This is the Morocco that Burroughs, Bowles, and those from their generation who lived in Tangier miss today. When Burroughs first came to Tangier, he was only comfortable in the company of those Moroccans who worked as shoe-shines. Understanding nothing of their chatter, he would smoke *kif* and drink mint tea with them in the *cha'bi* coffeehouses. He had no curiosity about their culture, nor any desire to understand their traditions, and so he wrote to Allen Ginsberg: 'What's all this old Moslem culture shit?'[2] Only when he was clinging to his lover Kiki's body was he truly euphoric. They would smoke *kif* and have sex. One of their erotic embraces, he claimed, lasted for sixteen hours. Burroughs was aware that *Tanjawi* society was going through a period of starvation, so he wasn't stingy with Kiki. In exchange for his body, he gave him almost two dollars a day: half was for him and half for his sick mother, who knew about their intimate relationship. In his blissful paradise Burroughs had little cause for worry, apart from the paucity of the financial resources he received from his parents, most of which he spent on drugs. He was most seriously disturbed by the symptoms of addiction that afflicted him from time to time. 'Last night', he wrote, 'I

---

1 William Burroughs, *Letters to Allen Ginsberg* (New York: Full Court Press, 1982), p. 55.

2 Burroughs, *The Letters of William S. Burroughs*, p. 195.

woke up because someone was squeezing my hand. It was my other hand.' When his money was late in coming, his dear Kiki would undertake the task of selling or pawning Burroughs's clothes, camera, or typewriter.

On December 30, 1965, Jay Haselwood died of heart failure. Burroughs, who was in Tangier at the time, went to his funeral at St Andrew's cemetery. It was a very sad scene. For Burroughs, Haselwood's death symbolized the end of an era, an era whose slogan had been 'Live and let live'. Life in Tangier had been something outside the law, and Burroughs had taken full advantage. His visits now were sporadic, no more than a fleeting nostalgia, a greeting, a tour in a forgotten garden. The city no longer inspired him with that which was fundamentally necessary for his literary project.

Burroughs had never wanted to root himself in Tangier like the others: David Herbert (son of an English count), Margaret McBey (painter), Claude-Nathalie Thomas (Bowles's and Mohammed Mrabet's translator), or Claudio Bravo (Chilean painter) – those who maybe had loved Tangier more than Burroughs did.

My Meeting with Bowles

Edouard Roditi bought a house in the Kasbah, with a modest garden, in the middle of which were a large fig tree, a well, and a grapevine. Whenever the strain of his work as a simultaneous interpreter at international conferences – said to be an extremely stressful and exhausting job – gets to him, he goes there to rest and recuperate. He is fluent in English, French, Spanish, German, and Turkish, and conversant in Italian and Portuguese; he writes poetry, short stories, and criticism in both English and French, and has translated a number of Yunus Emre's poems from Turkish. Familiar with the most important Arab capitals, he has experienced a sexual adventure in each of them. 'They very nearly raped me but I miraculously escaped them,' he will say with a terse laugh. When he hyperbolizes while recounting one of his many adventures, I feel doubt about whether it really happened, but what can I say when his enjoyment of his story is so evident? Wherever he goes, there is always someone (and sometimes more than one) pursuing him, attempting to rape him, but he knows how to slip discreetly away. His fantastic sexual escapades are never-ending. In talking about them, Roditi entertains himself and diverts his audience, intrigued by the strangeness and novelty of it all. He takes obvious pride in his personal acquaintance with Ahmed Shawqi's two sons and his nephews, and he has a store of reminiscences, bitter and sweet, revolving around the Egyptian expatriate Nimet Eloui Bey in Paris, from the days when she and Rainer Maria Rilke, who was in love with her at the time, carried on a correspondence. Roditi also likes to tell the story of how, after a night of drunkenness and orgy, he woke one morning in a Paris hotel room asleep in the same bed as Lorca, with no memory of how he got there.

In Tangier, anyone adept at telling stories can invent anything and it will be believed and he, in turn, will believe the stories told to him by others. Such is the eternal pleasure of living in a land embedded in multi-colored myth. A certain truth has been imprinted in the minds of all those who have ever loved Tangier, regardless of the epoch: as in *The Thousand and One Nights*, boredom is expelled from its magical kingdom and the grandeur of its myth. Stretching back to the period of Antaeus and reaching up to the most recent conquest, it is a myth that continues to preserve and feed all the legends that are woven in Tangier, and all the stories that are told about it. Everyone who comes to Tangier desires to be its Shahrayar, with the city playing the part of Shahrazad. But the city promises subjugation, expulsion, and even death to whoever betrays it, or misinterprets its secret mystery. It doesn't forgive those who wrong it. Today as yesterday, no matter how other circumstances may change, Tangier remains just as coveted by adventurers and dreamers as it always was.

At one point in *The Sheltering Sky*, Richard Holland says to Dyer Nelson, in journalistic language: 'In New York you have the slick financiers, here the money-changers. In New York you have your racketeers. Here you have your smugglers. And you have every nationality and no civic pride. And each man's waiting to suck the blood of the next. It's not really such a far-fetched comparison, is it?'[1]

One evening, I accompany Edouard Roditi on a visit to Paul Bowles. Each of them loves what the other produces artistically, and they encourage one another to continue their work, whatever the value of what they create. They have a very old friendship and are nearly the same age, although Bowles's movements and reflexes seem livelier. One thing is noticeable about Bowles: his hearing has grown weak, and he has developed the habit of balling up his right hand around his ear to amplify

---

1 Bowles, *The Sheltering Sky*, p. 121.

the words of whoever is speaking to him, and saying in
Spanish: '¿Que?' (What?). I ask myself if it is an act.
Like most of those still in Tangier, Bowles prefers to
speak Spanish with everyone but his compatriots. (Some
twenty-five years later, April 26, 1994, my literary agent
informed me that, after having two successive operations
in Paris on his face, to remove a cancerous tumor, Bowles
can no longer hear out of his right ear.)

In his soft voice, Roditi introduces me to him: 'He's
a Moroccan writer from the Rif. He recited some of his
stories to me and their content is good. I hope that you'll
like them as well and that you might translate some of
them for him.'

Bowles looks at me calmly, searching, and enigmatic;
then he says, lowering his contemplative gaze as he always
does:

'Why not!'

At this moment, I don't know why, I thought of
Lautréamont, who had wanted to be exactly what he was:
the apogee of sadism and tenderness at the same time. I
thought also, maybe naively, that whenever the great die
it's as if a crime had been exposed. But an inner voice
whispered to me: 'Life always seems to envy true creators,
and as a result afflicts them with an absurd and early
death so that they don't rival it in its immortality. Carry
on then, Life; live eternally, but you'll do so alone. And
when those who outshine you in their glory pass away in

their turn, you'll be more alone than ever – you, Life, the ageless depository of crime!'

Bowles and Roditi are speaking in English. I understand the gist of what they are talking about. They are basking in their memories, while I beside them am lost in my own meditations. I, too, have a past to swim in, but I have no one with whom to share that delicious nostalgia. Day by day, time has distanced us, yesterday's boon companions, and divided us one from another. Some of us have aged badly, some have lost their marbles, some have emigrated, and some have died. I don't know whether we failed to make the most of the good times that came our way. In any case, there's no point in waxing elegiac about a fate that is still incomplete. 'The destiny of a human being only becomes clear to him when it starts to correspond with what his memory already contains,' as Eduardo Mallea says.

Awaking from my daydream, I hear them talking about Jane Bowles, who is sick and being cared for in La Clínica de Reposo de Los Angeles in Malaga. I hear the names of Ahmed Yacoubi, Mohammed Mrabet, Brion Gysin, and Norman Glass[1] repeated several times.

The next evening I took two of my stories to Bowles, 'Violence on the Beach' and 'Herbs of the Dead'. To help him render them into English, I translated the words he

---

1 An English writer who lived in North Africa, including Tangier, for a period in the sixties. He translated *A Journey to the East*, by Gérard de Nerval, from French into English.

didn't understand into Spanish. Bowles was very pleased with the two stories. He was still translating 'Bachir Alive and Dead'[1] when the British publisher Peter Owen arrived in Tangier. Bowles hadn't told me much about him. It was only after he had published my book *For Bread Alone* and given me an advance of a hundred pounds on the royalties, that I realized I was dealing with a vampire. He himself acknowledged that he was a gangster, but claimed, in self-defense, that he helped the unknown achieve a degree of prominence and fame.

Maybe the Iraqi poet Abd al-Qadir al-Janabi was right when he said: 'Create your reputation, then live up to it.' I wanted to live up to my role. First, all that mattered to me was to publish my first book, even if it meant being swindled and robbed. Peter Owen had already published *A Life Full of Holes* – or *A Humiliating Life*, as it was originally titled – the autobiography of Driss Ben Hamad Charhadi (whose real name is Larbi Layachi), and *Love with a Few Hairs* by Mohammed Mrabet. He had come back to Tangier in search of a new victim.

Edouard Roditi had already told Paul Bowles some fragments of the vagabond life I had led, and Bowles had passed these on to Owen. Owen suggested that I write my autobiography, to which I promptly replied:

'But it's written, I have it in my apartment.'

Bowles was taken aback and looked at me in surprise.

---

1 Bowles suggested this title in place of 'Herbs of the Dead'.

Owen's foxy eyes widened and he said: 'Then let's sign a contract right now. I'll give you an advance of a hundred pounds as soon as I receive Mr Bowles's translation.'

I agreed, and the three of us signed the contract that Bowles drew up on the typewriter without further comment. Later I came to realize that Bowles loves this kind of ambiguous enterprise; his entire life has been built on the vague and bizarre, leading ultimately to the nihilism toward which his stories' and novels' characters are driven. Bowles explains it thus: 'The characters in my stories, I might relegate them to a kind of pessimism, but without allowing them to fall into nihilism, as the average reader or the critics seem to think.'

In truth, I hadn't yet written a sentence of my autobiography *For Bread Alone*. I had dreamed of writing it some day, after I had achieved some literary renown. Its events had been simmering in my head, and I had already presented the tajine of my life experiences to my student friends in Larache, who lapped up the tales of my way-out adventures. Relying on my powerful memory as an erstwhile illiterate, I began to write the first pages that same night, sitting on the top floor of the Roxy Café, until I was overcome by drunkenness, weakened by hunger, and my pockets were empty, as usual.

I wrote every day, and then went to Bowles's place in the evening to dictate sentence after sentence to him in Spanish, which he put directly into English. It's been said that I dictated the book to him in Moroccan Arabic, but that's not true, as I've never mastered the art of telling stories in dialect. Even Ahmed Yacoubi, Abdeslam Boulaich, Mohammed Mrabet, and Driss Charhadi – the most skillful of such storytellers – used what they knew of the Spanish language when helping Bowles adapt their stories to English. They would tape-record their stories in Moroccan dialect interposed with some Spanish words. Bowles would then undertake to modify and adapt them (the result was far from a literal translation), while their creators helped him clarify and interpret what they had said. There's no doubt that Bowles revised each text more than once while he was in the process of editing it, before finally typing it out, but he has always denied this, either from loyalty or as an artistic stratagem.

Most of the time Mrabet would come while we were working. We would stop for a few moments to be nice and talk with him a little. Bowles never makes any effort to be in harmony with other people. On the contrary, he tries to undermine such concordance, in the manner of *No Exit*,[1] or like Tunner in *The Sheltering Sky*, when, with tedious persistence, he busies himself with wrecking the intimacy between Port and Kit, tagging along with them wherever they go. Port wants desperately to be alone with Kit, but Tunner is always there, trying to sleep with Kit himself. Finally, he manages it. Nevertheless, despite their brief coming together it remains that 'people could not

---

1 Sartre's play, which Bowles was the first to translate into English.

really get very close to one another; they merely imagined they were close,[1] as Day, Dr Slade's wife, comments in *Up Above the World*.

Bowles loved to observe the arguments that took place between Mrabet and whoever his guests were at the time, whether they were friends, acquaintances or first-time visitors. He seemed to derive a certain pleasure from these altercations, and if they led to embarrassing moments he would just smile sarcastically. More often than not, he would simply withdraw into himself like a 'hedgehog', as Mrabet called him. I never had to reprimand Mrabet, who, as soon as he came in, dominated everything, and this is something that delighted Bowles – a kind of game that everyone who visited him knew about. Whenever Mrabet interrupted our labors, we would break for another glass of black tea with lemon, prepared by Bowles, or by Mrabet himself, if he was in a good mood. Mrabet was in the habit of commenting with exaggerated zeal on any political event, local or international, that he had heard about on the radio, TV, or in one of the cafés. I preferred not to discuss with him in depth any subject that he brought up. Bowles most often resorted to his usual diplomatic neutrality: 'Ah! Is it true that happened? Too bad. I understand. Yes. No. It's possible the situation didn't need to be that way, as you say ...' If the subject was one that got Mrabet particularly agitated,

1 Paul Bowles, *Up Above the World* (New York: Harper Perennial, 2006), p. 178.

this is how Bowles would respond. As for me, I would content myself with a shake of the head. Mrabet might then either leave or stay.

Sometimes Mrabet would take me with him downtown in his car. Ordinarily in the evening, I would visit the same bars and my favorite prostitutes before going back to my wretched top-floor apartment, where I froze in the winter cold and frizzled in the summer heat. The ceiling corners were festooned with spider webs, and the humidity had decorated the walls with little maps of unknown countries whose outlines were forever changing.

By that time, Mrabet had given up drinking for several years, but he was still a devotee of *kif* and *majoun* and was adept at preparing it. Bowles had stopped smoking *kif* in the traditional *sebsi* (pipe), choosing instead to stuff it into cigarettes that had been emptied of their tobacco beforehand. Away from his home, he smoked only English cigarettes. If he had smoked *kif* and was going into the city, he would chew cloves to disguise the smell of it; he liked to adhere to the community's standards of social etiquette.

Mrabet kept in touch with the prostitutes he knew when he was young. Now their faces and hands had become wrinkled, the veins in their legs blue, their teeth decayed, and their bodies fat and flabby. He liked to visit them in their congenial quarters, preferably accompanied by one of his friends. He was very generous toward them. My company, I noticed, seemed to please him, maybe because we spring from the same soil, both of us being Rifians, and people from the Rif have rallied together, especially recently. Mrabet would drink only lemonade, while I drank beer or whisky. But, because of his prickly character, he often threatened my friendship with Bowles. He would interrupt us while we were working on the translation of *For Bread Alone*. Our work aggravated his jealousy severely, to a ludicrous degree, to the point where I considered pulling out definitively, but Bowles saved the situation in the nick of time. One night he disappeared into the kitchen and came back carrying a hammer, screaming in Mrabet's face: 'Get out of here or I'll kill you!'

I knew that Bowles could kill people in his books, but I didn't believe he could hurt a fly in reality. That night it became clear to me that he wouldn't allow his dignity to be insulted with the kind of puerile impudence Mrabet had been in the habit of displaying toward him.

Mrabet left the apartment with his head down. I had never before seen Bowles so angry as he was that night. We stopped working, and he lit a *kif*-filled cigarette. Once he started to smoke, he regained his composure. I lit a cigarette, too, and we each inhaled calmly and in silence. I had never imagined that Bowles would venture to threaten someone with a hammer, but I also knew that he was the same man who had conceived 'The Scorpion', *Let It Come Down*, 'A Distant Episode', 'The Delicate

Prey', 'The Garden', and 'Allal'.[1] After a few moments, Mrabet returned, apologized to Bowles, and left. This was the last time that he disturbed us while we were working. Bowles isn't in the habit of letting his anger last, or of commenting much on an incident like this. He's very tolerant, but I've never been able to tell whether such incidents bother him or not. One evening, I went to his place drunk, and I began to babble on about things that were of absolutely no interest to him. The next day I apologized. With his customary calm he said:

'Forget about what happened; it's just a pity that we didn't get any work done. But why did you want me to prepare a grilled boy for you to eat? Do you really want one?'

'Me?'

'Yes. You repeatedly said that you wanted to eat a grilled boy.'

'I don't remember anything of that.'

'That's for the best.'

---

1 Generally, terror, sadism, and violence dominate the works of Paul Bowles.

A Thing or Two about Jane Bowles

Jane (or Janie, as she's known to her friends) was not interested in making a career for herself. Today Bowles will say: 'Jane married me because she wanted to get away from her mother more than she wanted to escape from men.' It's clear that Jane hasn't shaken off her introverted childhood or her adolescent longings. It's as if she had satisfied the latter in order to turn them into old memories, so that she could become the refined, worldly-wise grandmother she had always wanted to be. Prophets and poets alone can leave their stamp on an era; Jane believed herself cut out for such a role, but her epoch rejected her. One can clearly see this from both her daily life and her writings. She wanted to be ahead of her time, not only in writing, but in love, in friendship, in conversation, even in the way she styled her hair like a boy.

To be free means that we are not under anyone's thumb, but Jane gave up much of her freedom to those who didn't deserve it. I remember here what the poet Muhammed ibn Ibrahim said: 'I was born a man, so I was not one.' This was the case with Jane: she didn't live as the woman she had wanted, or deserved, to be. In her literary audacity and personal comportment, she was a heroine of her time. But when someone of this caliber fails to prolong their moment of triumph, the public prefers to see them dead or paralyzed, and to meditate on their misfortune. In her youth, Jane had nurtured some radical revolutionary tendencies. She rejected all compromise, and shut herself out from the inner peace offered by Taoism. While waiting for her kindred spirits to catch up with and sustain her, she found herself unable either to keep frustration at bay to the bitter end or to conquer death by intense creative activity. If life is against the person, then the person has the right to be against life.

Fear, for Paul Bowles, is ever present. But Jane was both afraid and not afraid at the same time. She wasn't obsessed by fear, because for her fear was only circumstantial. Passionate beings can lose their minds when they go too far; and Jane went too far. Paul, however ('gloompot' as Jane would call him), possessed by fatalism, could remain steadfast.

What could an unattractive woman possibly want with a mirror? Jane was outstandingly beautiful in her youth, but psychological illness and physical debility took their relentless toll. Her attractiveness extinguished, there was nothing left for her to do but break all the mirrors and let someone else gather up the shards.

Up until now there is no written account of her early life, nothing that might disclose the secrets of her childhood, in contrast to the numerous writings devoted to Paul and focusing on the fundamental questions: Who had wanted to be rid of Paul when he was young? Was it his father? His maternal grandmother? Or both of them in collusion?

Jane and Paul had wanted to mythologize their lives, to defy their families and take revenge upon them. Perhaps they agreed secretly to make a pact of silence and throw away the key to the mystery. A mystery like Tangier itself, the key to whose labyrinth is yet to be found.

Jane found social events something of an ordeal. According to Mrs Gérofi, when she was invited to a party she would spend more than an hour hesitating between wearing this dress or that. From Paul's description, she was worse than this. In a letter to his parents, Rena and Claude Bowles, in which he talks about an honorific party thrown in the style of *The Thousand and One Nights* by Barbara Hutton and attended by two hundred guests, many of them from London and Paris, he writes: 'Since we had received an invitation, we went, and Jane was busy for a week beforehand trying to arrange her clothes. You can imagine the excitement! Anne was busy having a new evening dress made for the occasion. Every hour there were telephone conversations, and Jane changed her mind at least twenty times about going and not going. We did finally go, and everything came off all right.'[1]

Jane hesitated for almost six months before joining Paul in Tangier, finally arriving on January 31, 1948, accompanied by her new lover, Jody. She was afraid of what she might find in this city with its reputation both seductive and frightening: Tangier = Danger.

It shouldn't be overlooked that Jane had been coddled by her mother, who would choose her clothes and dress her until she was seventeen or eighteen years old. She spoiled her to a degree that ended up by being harmful. 'But if the salt has lost his savor, wherewith shall it be salted?' (Matthew 5:13)

All relationships were illusory for Jane. She had lost all discrimination between what was real and what was imaginary. Jane was idiosyncratic in her ideas. People, in her view, crossed paths without ever actually meeting each other; they never met face to face. Despite the many warm and intimate relationships she had enjoyed with women both American and foreign, she wouldn't allow Paul to sleep with her until they were married. Their sexual relationship lasted a mere two and a half years, after which they each took refuge in their homosexuality,

---

1 Bowles, *In Touch*, p. 314.

while continuing to live close to and apart from each other simultaneously.

Jane had met Paul in New York one night in November 1937. He was smoking marijuana with a group of young people in Harlem, and what she liked about him was his gentle smile. From that moment he became her beloved enemy. They married soon after, on February 21, 1938. But the marriage was undertaken against the will of her mother, who had wanted her daughter to marry a Jew like herself, regardless of the fact that Jane was incorrigibly anti-Semitic. Likewise, Paul married her to annoy his father, who was also anti-Semitic. Whereas Norman Glass had gone to the lengths of filing a lawsuit against his mother for being Jewish (we don't know whether he was serious or merely joking), Jane would be content simply to live as far away as possible from hers.

Jane was used to speaking and thinking in French (in which Paul was equally fluent), and it was the language in which she wrote her first novel, *Le Phaéton hypocrite*. The text is said to be lost, but Jane, who had a predilection for destroying whatever she wrote, may have torn it up and thrown it away. All her life Jane Auer lived in defiance of all social norms and traditions. In the end, worn down by chronic physical illness and her literary and romantic disappointments, she embraced the cross and declared her faith in absolution. According to what Paul told me, she had been made to embrace the cross and ask for forgiveness while she was so severely ill as to be barely conscious.

What destroyed Jane was her intense nihilism. To satisfy her masochistic urge, she took pleasure in the failure of her projects and in destroying whatever she produced, with which she was never satisfied in any case. For her, everything had to be created from scratch, for there was nothing in ordinary life that could offer comfort or diversion. Her writing was an original creation, self-generated; it depended on no external source, and so she often found it difficult to complete what she had begun. Paul, on the contrary, didn't spend much time revising or rereading what he wrote, as he himself admitted. The strange thing about Jane was that she had both a strong desire to destroy herself and a powerful will to live. Paul, though, was satisfied with his pessimism, or so he claimed. Pessimism, in his opinion, is a natural human feeling, while nihilism is not of this world. Yet Bowles is nihilistic to the core.

Though Jane may have wanted to live through writing, she never managed to control and deploy this skill as much as she would have wished. Unlike Paul, she lacked the self-discipline and egoism essential to excel in this field. Instead, she preferred to put her talent at the disposal of her friends, or even of those just passing through who didn't even know her. Whenever she happened by chance to pick up Ariadne's thread, it wasn't long before she dropped it again. She was certainly gifted, but she lacked the tenacity to sit for hours day and night, as Colette, Simone de Beauvoir, Marguerite Yourcenar, or Marguerite Duras did. She couldn't bear to be stuck to a chair – except, that is, when writing long letters to Paul or her friends, complaining about the erosion of her finances or the deterioration of her romantic relationship with Cherifa, and about the latter's female entourage, whom Cherifa encouraged to extort as much money as possible from 'that Christian infidel', as they would call Jane.

Everyone feels like crying at times. But what does one do with a person who weeps without stopping? We let them cry as long as they want, until they can't cry any more. We can't be held responsible for the feelings of others. You're all free to destroy yourselves as you wish. You can abandon yourself to drugs, greed, and debilitating masturbation. Don't worry about the disapproval of others. In this world you sing and then you vanish; paint, write, create what you wish, you will still disappear. It's best to leave this world to itself and not worry about how it's going to regenerate. It's true that we can, if we like, launch a revolution, but it never brings forth what we want. If only the wisdom of some prophet had given us infallibility!

Jane only loved things that fled from her. But was it writing that ran away from her, or she that ran away from writing? She seems to have loved people for themselves (inducing self-abnegation), rather than wanting to create literary works about them (leading to immortality). Like them, she was almost annihilated, dying without leaving any trace of herself behind, being insufficiently motivated to challenge the insignificance of either her life or theirs. Had she managed to conquer her weakness, she might have been capable of making such a challenge, but she was emotional to the point of fragility, and surrendered her life to the people among whom she lived.

Her successive frustrations – particularly romantic ones – embittered her towards life, and contributed to her paralysis and ruin, until she became a 'forgotten genius', incapable of writing.

Jane refused to submit to the discipline necessary for a writer; or maybe she just wasn't capable of it. Paul was able to write in even the worst of conditions, as he did when working on *Let It Come Down*. For Paul, the dullest, most exasperating, or most distressing situations could provide him with an incentive to write. In a letter to William Wright (July 23, 1954) he says: 'But perhaps boredom is what one needs if one is going to work well.' Adding further: 'I've usually found it the case. One must have the boredom in order to want badly enough to escape.'[1] He had needed to work in this self-absorbed way when he began studying painting, followed afterward by music, then finally switching to writing – 'like a chameleon', as he mentions in an interview with Ghila

1 Bowles, *In Touch*, p. 255.

Sroka (in *Tribune Juive*). He always remembered the advice of Aaron Copland: 'If you don't work when you're twenty, nobody's going to love you when you're thirty.'[1]

Shakir Nuri asked him in an interview here in Tangier: 'I noticed that you've put a group of your works aside; is that because they're especially dear to you or are you rereading them?'

'They're here because they're here. I'm here because I'm here and not because I chose to be here. When we're young we might think up a lot of projects that we'd like to accomplish. I, personally, never made any projects, since I was sure I'd never finish them. Since then I've decided to let life follow its own course. Today I can tell you I don't have any particular project in mind. And next year I'll turn eighty.'

'Do you like solitude?'

'I like silence. That's the reason I refuse to live in New York. Also, to work well, you need to be alone.'

Paul was lucky in that, being far removed from his family environment, he was free to meet people like Gertrude Stein, Aaron Copland, and Virgil Thomson, who encouraged and directed him in his creative work. Jane didn't have anyone of their ilk to guide her when she started writing. She created in solitude, arduously and painfully. She would frequently rip up what she had written, with no regrets. When her writer's block was

---

1 Bowles, *Without Stopping*, p. 166.

insurmountable, she would drown herself in alcohol, sometimes drinking an entire bottle of gin, alone in her apartment (much like Kit in *The Sheltering Sky*, who shares many of Jane's characteristics, and who drank an entire bottle of champagne in bed before breakfast). Or she would hang around the bars, firing off sarcastic remarks that could be wounding to those who didn't know her. She was always keen to break the rules, and had, unquestionably, been wiser than her years since childhood, like Paul. Her precociousness probably stemmed from her father's death when she was just thirteen, and from her position as an only child. Allen Ginsberg found her to be reserved and serious, reminding him of Burroughs's wife, Joan Vollmer.

Jane was terrified of the word 'inspired'. The phrase, 'In the beginning was the word', terrorized her. She believed that every word she wrote was lame, without knowing exactly why it was inadequate. She was born with a self-destructive impulse; it was her predetermined fate.

She was rather prudish, and a strict observer of the norms of propriety. Once, when suffering from a stomach ulcer, she refused to undress in front of the doctor who had to examine her. She didn't want children, fearing the pains of pregnancy and childbirth, or maybe even death itself. She possessed both an exaggerated courage and an excessive sense of fear. Here I'm reminded of Edgar Allan Poe, who in his stories brought the dead back from their tombs, but who in life was afraid to go to bed and sleep peacefully on his own. Jane had a similar profundity to Poe, even though no one in her writings ever rose from the grave. She had to anesthetize herself with alcohol and sleeping pills just to get to sleep, or when she wanted to take the elevator: going up in one of these would induce an attack of vertigo, and every descent would make her feel as though she was falling into a bottomless pit. As for tunnels, she was afraid they would never come to an end. Jane was equally scared of fire, dogs, crocodiles, and seaweed.

I didn't know Jane personally; at the time Edouard Roditi introduced me to Paul she was already in Malaga, in the depths of her unhappy, intractable illness, refusing to receive any visitors apart from her closest friends. But Paul has talked to me about her at length, as have those who knew her well, such as Temsamani (Paul's former driver), Ahmed Yacoubi, Larbi Yacoubi (actor and costume designer), El Hamri (Moroccan painter), and Mohammed Mrabet, who was her biggest defender among all the Moroccans who knew her. According to Paul, it was Mrabet who took charge of preparing her meals once she became ill. At first, she had asked Paul repeatedly to dismiss him; but with the passage of time they became very good friends. Other people have also told me a lot about her: Brion Gysin, Emma (owner of the BBC Bar with its pool on the beach), Roditi, and Lily (owner of the Parade Bar).

It may have been Jane's slow mental suicide that led

PAUL BOWLES IN TANGIER

her to drink so excessively, and to take sedatives and other medication. In a letter to Virgil Thomson referring to Jane, Paul writes: 'She is convinced no one can diagnose her illness and that suicide is the only solution.'[1] In her desire to rid herself of her soul, she had stabbed it and gnawed it down to the bone. From what Paul told me, he never made the slightest attempt to force her to abandon her capricious behavior, and this was the right thing to do. He showed compassion toward her, never trying forcibly to change her. Instead, he would tolerate her impulsiveness, even when she wrote checks, with no regard as to whether or not the funds were available, and gave them to whoever asked for help, even if she didn't know them. Or she would leave outstanding tabs in some of the bars, like the Parade, that Paul would then pay – the miser who swore he would never pay for anyone but himself. 'I've saved money systematically, by trying to spend as little as possible.' This is what he says about money, because 'money has no odor'.

Paul's stinginess could even be seen in the paper he used to write some of his letters to Jane. It was of extremely poor quality and she hated it, as she let him know in the margin of one of her letters to him from Paris towards the end of 1950. He experienced real poverty in his student days in America, and, later, when he ran away to Paris to escape his parents. But he never went so hungry

1 Bowles, *In Touch*, p. 272.

as to see dog excrement and imagine it to be mustard, as happened to Henry Miller in Paris. Nor did he have to sleep in the streets, his teeth chattering on bitter January and February nights, as did Genet, begging for his daily bread, tramping around the villages of Andalusia with no shelter from the cold or wind. Paul Bowles always managed to find a relative or friend who could help him and give him a place to stay. Maybe his miserliness was inherited from his parents, who would give him money only when he was on the brink of utter destitution. It's well known that Paul loves money, and that he's always trying to ingratiate himself with those who have it. People call him frugal, but in fact he's tight-fisted. He loves the good life, but doesn't want to pay for it. At the end of the forties, his financial situation greatly improved, but he hesitated a long time before buying his first car. Then, on the advice of the devilish Brion Gysin, he conquered his fear of destitution and bought a Jaguar convertible, hiring Mohammed Temsamani as his chauffeur, complete with a uniform suggested by the owner of the Hotel Villa Mimosa.

One side of Jane's body became paralyzed, she lost most of her vision, and finally became completely blind shortly before her death. Even before this, she had always found excuses for not writing: maybe because of the reading public's indifference to her novel *Two Serious Ladies*, or her family's disapproval of her for daring to write such an indecent work, or the reviews that failed to understand the book, considering it stupid and superficial. These were all things that caused her infinite pain, and took a toll on her sensitive disposition. In a letter to Phil Nurenberg, Paul describes a representative incident: 'Jane and I had just left a grocery store in Eighth Street, and I was carrying a very voluminous paper bag. The idea was to get home to Tenth Street as fast as possible. But Anais Nin appeared, and engaged Jane in the longest conversation on record while I stood trying to keep the melting snow from dissolving the bag. After forty minutes Nin went on her way; she had been telling Jane how much she disliked Jane's novel. So obviously I never forgot the meeting.'[1]

As Paul admits himself, Jane's presence in his life nourished his literary production. According to his own statements, he never wrote anything of any importance after her death. She, however, denied having any influence over his work, refusing to consider herself his equal, saying: 'There don't need to be two writers in the family.' Maybe this was simply an excuse for her lack of inspiration and inability to continue writing. She was modest to a fault. While Paul was gaining renown in the music world and working his way up in literature, she was fading, tormented by her inability to produce, if only to please Paul. She was acutely jealous of Ahmad Yacoubi, even though it had been she who, while in Fez with Paul,

---

1 Bowles, *In Touch*, p. 506.

had encouraged him to paint before he even knew how to mix colors. Now Ahmad Yacoubi was painting non-stop, while she was making no progress at all on her novel, *Out in the World*, begun in Paris in 1950 and destined never to be finished. The last story she wrote was 'A Stick of Green Candy', completed in March 1949 on a vacation with Paul in the Algerian desert.

Jane dedicated her brilliance to life itself, in contrast to Paul, who poured his talent into his musical scores and books, with little thought for sexual passion, excepting his love for Jane. Jane sacrificed literature for life, while Paul gave his life to literature, with his customary reserve. He conceals his secrets even from himself. He attempts to observe everyone without being seen; or, as Dyer in *Let It Come Down* says: 'It was the same old sensation of not being involved, of being left out, of being beside reality rather than in it.'[1] Rimbaud, in contrast, merged literature and life with no second thoughts. He put his heart on the table, as three or four geniuses in every century will do, as Céline said; the others are merely playing a game of writing and imitation.

His friend Virgil Thomson says: 'Paul had little sex drive ... Sex simply wasn't important to him.' Thomson, along with a number of Paul's and Jane's other friends, doubted whether the pair had ever slept together. But Millicent Dillon confirmed that they did, but then

---

1 Bowles, *Let It Come Down*, p. 230.

stopped after two and a half years,[1] as Paul himself told her. None the less, in Paul's life sex remains a sin. He also had a fear of being raped, particularly in a Moroccan bathhouse. Homosexuality fascinated Paul; but he elevated it to the level of an abstraction, sublimating it into an idea, in order to escape the physicality of it. In a letter to Bruce Morrissette, he confirms this: 'Homosexuality is a thrilling subject to me, just as sanguinary killings are and rapes, and tales of drug addicts. They are exciting because they are melodramatic. Struggle! And who would not give several years of his life could he but strangle with impunity?'[2]

This is Paul Bowles's understanding of sex. Insofar as he couldn't actually engage in this kind of deviant behavior, he remained protected by his puritanism, as if encased in a shell. Bowles had fostered in himself very early the inclinations that would form his conception of life, as he further confessed to Bruce Morrissette (February 20, 1930): 'I am too perverse. If I find I am doing a pleasing thing and that people like it, I switch; it must be bad what I was doing. I've got to displease them. Adolescence? Anger. Perhaps you will say it is part of "panemotionalism." Hooray! If it is, I can still be normal (by that I mean either hetero or homo) but if not, then I must wander down life seeking something to fall

---

1 An American writer, she wrote a biography of Jane Bowles and published a collection of her letters.
2 Bowles, *In Touch*, p. 42.

definitely in love with, and it is quite likely it will be with animals. That will be too bad, because there we have a vice more vicious than ordinary indulgence with humans. But I was long ago aware that whatever I put my hand to is made into some sort of vice. There can never be any love, affection, even any satisfaction "in my life". Whatever is to please me must be a vice. True, really. Being beaten, for instance. A vice. But how enjoyable. Burning woods. How exquisite. Biting myself for the pain. All the more enjoyable than misbehaving with some girl or man. Well, *Dieu soit loué*, at least I am abnormal in a "different" way. But it makes of Life a series of steps down into regions unspeakably foul and deep. There is no other conception of my existence I can form. Each day makes me meat-one-day-rottener. Nothing physical. The glow is in my cheeks, but ... *dans mon coeur, la flèche est fixée* [the arrow is embedded in my heart]. Talking to you about it interests me. It is like telling a friend about a gruesome accident one has seen and cannot forget. The recounting brings up the scene more brightly for the moment, it is true, but then it allows one to relax and forget all about it until some night when in dreams he shall see it re-enacted.'[1]

To Paul Bowles it is a place and its people that are important; he doesn't expect to be made happy by any one person. 'Once you accept the fact that life isn't *fun*, you'll be much happier',[2] as Dyer's mother says to her

---

1 Bowles, *In Touch*, pp. 39–40.
2 Bowles, *Let It Come Down*, p. 21.

PAUL BOWLES IN TANGIER

son in *Let It Come Down*. Bowles's goal is to reveal the
art while hiding the artist, as Oscar Wilde puts it in his
introduction to *The Picture of Dorian Gray*. Bowles goes
even further than Wilde: 'It's my personal belief that as
long as the artist is an enemy of society, it's in his best
interest to remain as hidden as possible; naturally, to be
indistinct from the masses. In the back of my mind I've
always had the prevailing assumption that art and crime
were linked together, incapable of being disentangled.
The greater the art the more severe the ramification will
be ...' Regardless, Bowles will crush any value that the
writer himself may boast of having, as can be seen in a
letter to James Herlihy (Tangier, April 30, 1966): 'Too
much importance is given the writer and not enough
to his work. What difference does it make who he is
and what he feels, since he's merely a machine for the
transmission of ideas? In reality he doesn't exist – he's a
cipher, a blank. A spy sent into life by the forces of death.
His main objective is to get the information across the
border, back into death. Then he can be given a mythical
personality: "He spent his time among us, betrayed us,
and took the material across the border." I don't think a
writer ever participates in anything; his pretences at it are
mimetic. All he can do is keep the machine functioning
and learn to manage it with decreasing (we hope)
clumsiness. A spy *is* devious and, as much as is possible,
anonymous. His personal convictions and emotions are
automatically "masked." This all sounds far too serious.

But you got me started.'[1] This idea was expressed by Rimbaud in his early youth in a few words: 'the writer, the poet, this man does not yet exist!' That said, a man must choose the least repellent form in which to cloak his existence: he can help to perpetuate whatever was created before him or, at least, help to restore it.

Bowles hasn't lacked the courage to create protagonists whom he would then torture mercilessly. He wallowed in the torment of his characters in order to avenge what he had suffered in his childhood. This rescued him from insanity: to find solace he put others in hell. Everyone must suffer. Why not? Perhaps this shows a desire to take revenge on humanity itself.

Many Westerners and Americans say that Tangier without Paul Bowles wouldn't be Tangier. But which Tangier are they speaking of? No doubt they refer to the Tangier that had been adored by Bowles and his kind, when it was chic and life there inexpensive, a place where money would seek you out without your having to look for it. They forget that it was Tangier that created and adopted them, and that precious few of them did anything to enhance its literary and artistic reputation. They forget that it is the environment, first of all, that nurtures the artists, and that those it nourishes will only come to nourish it in turn if they are exceptionally gifted: true artists, in other words. Peter Owen says on

---

1 Bowles, *In Touch*, p. 381.

the jacket of one of Bowles's books: 'Paul Bowles knows
Morocco better than the Moroccans themselves do.' He
also states, in *Paul Bowles as His Friends See Him*: 'In the
year 1962 I was relaxing with my wife in Chefchaouen. I
met an American there and we agreed that *The Sheltering
Sky* is Morocco summed up.' Owen doesn't inform
us of the intellectual caliber of this American whose
judgment so happily coincided with his own. He might
simply have been an average tourist. An ordinary tourist
would hardly be an authority on civilization and culture;
furthermore, most of the events in *The Sheltering Sky*
take place not in Morocco but in the Algerian desert. In
fact, Owen was at fault all along the line. About Bowles's
autobiography he says: 'Paul Bowles is too nice to write
an honest autobiography, because he hates to speak badly
of people.' He should have added: 'because he hates to
speak badly of himself, in particular.' Of course, it's widely
known that Owen makes ridiculous pronouncements,
which he uses to bolster his credibility as a publisher who
steals the rights of writers, as he did to me with *For Bread
Alone*. He's not the only one who does this. Miguel Riera
Montesinos, Daniel Halpern of Ecco Press, Jeffrey Miller
of Cadmus: all of these publishers are vampires. When my
literary agent asked Halpern for the publishing rights to
my book *Jean Genet in Tangier*, which Bowles translated,
his answer was: 'The rights are reserved for Paul Bowles,
Choukri is nothing but an illiterate.' Halpern had

MOHAMED CHOUKRI

forgotten, or was pretending to have forgotten, that there is a text and that it was originally written in Arabic.

Jane Bowles's talent continued to be put on hold, waiting for her to gain some discipline in her work habits, but frustration, both literary and in her personal life, continued to debilitate her, and kept her from producing what she wanted. She only liked the places she was familiar with when she was far away from them: she longed for Tangier when she was in Paris, she longed for Mexico or New York when she was in Ceylon (today's Sri Lanka).

Jane was known for her sarcasm, which she bestowed on everything, even in the bleakest moments of her life. It may have been a way of trying to free herself from the complex caused by her authoritarian mother, who, at any rate, wasn't as sadistic and ignorant as Rimbaud's. Nevertheless, her mother's despotism accompanied her throughout her life, even when she was on a separate continent. Paul, on the other hand, managed early on to shake off every family curse. He was more defiant than Jane in his rebellion against his parents' severity, especially that of his father, of which his mother was also a victim.

Jane Bowles met Cherifa in April 1948 through Bowles,[1] who knew her from Suq Zraa. She was selling grain in a cave-like store, enclosed to a suffocating

---

[1] She was born in Tangier in the village of al-Marain in the area of Cape Spartel around 1928. It's said that she died in 1989.

degree, in the scorching heat. She was a human mass that inspired pity, a functioning body without beauty or grace. According to those who knew her, she was coarse and malicious. Even Jane, in the letters she wrote to Paul and her friends, complained about Cherifa's cruelty towards her, describing the flagrant financial extortion with which she oppressed her – Jane, who was always generous and, more often than not, bankrupt. Or Jane would bemoan the sufferings Cherifa caused her by all her romantic equivocations. She was so manipulative of Jane that she tried to force her to fast with her during Ramadan, despite her chronic illness. Convinced that she would be miserable without her, Jane thought of her as her adopted daughter. She didn't suspect that she was nursing a serpent in her bosom, never giving it a thought, since she was naturally kind and trusting. Cherifa's magic, for Jane, lay in her utter lack of beauty. Since Jane, like Paul, was always attracted to whatever she found enigmatic and obscure, that which repelled others enchanted her. And so she remained under Cherifa's spell for an unconscionably long time. When she first set eyes on this exhausted and overworked woman, wrapped in her mountain clothes and *chaachiyya*[1] the size of a car-wheel, sweltering in the lair of her store, she took pity on her. Then she began to love her madly. There could be no

---

1 A big hat worn by mountain women to ward off the heat.

stronger proof of the love a woman can feel for another woman.

It was a love full of suffering, but longed for, potentially fatal, but from which there was no escape: a love that struck from out of the blue, beyond the strictures of reason or judgment.

According to the Moroccans who knew Cherifa, she was a 'sorceress', a schemer, capable of poisoning someone, according to Mrabet himself, who knew her better than anyone. Ahmed Yacoubi doesn't disagree; he confirms that Cherifa was practicing witchcraft on Jane, as evidenced by the hair, congealed blood and fingernails wrapped in a rag bundle that Jane found under her pillow. Paul believes that Cherifa poisoned his parrot, and that she may have been trying to poison Jane and himself.[1] Her firecracker of a laugh which exposed her gold tooth was the most frightening thing about her. The foreigners who met Cherifa when she was with Jane described her as inane, ugly, and malevolent. But the question is, when was Jane ever attracted by that which was conventionally beautiful?

Jane lived to destroy all that was important to her and to turn her back on the things that others found attractive.

---

1 Some think that Jane's illness was the result of poison that Cherifa gradually put in her food, which caused the paralysis that lasted until her death. At Jane's request, Bowles gave Cherifa a house as a gift in the 'Amrah' quarter, leading to Bab Al Bahr in the Kasbah.

She lacerated herself, whereas the sadomasochist Paul practiced his cruelty on the characters in his books.

Paul Bowles may not have killed or tortured anyone in reality, but in his literary works he surely killed and tortured a good number. Happily, his imagination never reached the level of the Marquis de Sade – not that he wasn't tempted to emulate the latter, but he probably lacked the capacity. But if he could have done so, one wonders what he might have written, especially since in his mind sex was always linked to crime and debauchery. And when he could no longer incriminate sex, he banished it from his life altogether. Paul Bowles is a potential sex criminal who never perpetrated his crimes.

Whenever the word 'happiness' was mentioned in Jane's presence, her eyes would widen while she laughed and said sarcastically: 'Happiness, what is happiness, where is it?' Naturally, no one dared answer her. Her sarcasm was disconcerting: even when reading her works, we find ourselves obliged to adapt to their irony. When Paul was informed that the troop Le Sorano at the National Theatre in Toulouse would be presenting her play *In the Summer House*, he sent a letter to those responsible for directing the actors, warning them: 'Whenever you begin to take yourselves seriously, you're losing Jane. Don't ever forget Jane's humor.'

I get out of Mrabet's car in front of the Monocle around one in the morning. Human apparitions are passing by. I no longer trust the vermin of the night. We

have just come from a dinner party thrown by Claude
Thomas in his old house, La Montagne. Paul is in raptures
about the singing and dancing of a Gnawa group. On the
subject of trance, he says: 'The point is to be possessed
either by God, as the Blacks in Central Africa are, or by a
saint, like here in Morocco or Algeria. They ask the saint
to come down: they generally implore him for a long time
while dancing. The music provokes the dancing and puts
them into a trance. They lose consciousness. This part is
necessary, without it the saint can't possess the person.
Nevertheless, this doesn't always succeed. Sometimes they
roll on the ground trying to open themselves up so they
can receive the saint. But nothing of the sort happens.
They wail, they cry. Only a Muslim can achieve it. Those
who aren't believers like you or me are incapable of it. It's
impossible. You have to have faith. It's what allows one
to enter into the trance: the evocation of the saint. If you
weren't Muslim you would be mocking the saint. But
they believe in it, and each person has their favorite saint.
He'll implore the saint to enter him. When the man or
woman finishes the *radh*, the violent dance, he generally
falls to the ground unconscious. When his consciousness
returns he always feels exceptionally well, as if he had
wings. From a psychological point of view, it's good. It's
excellent.'

Mrabet took part in the dance until he reached a state
of ecstasy and lost consciousness. He was marvelous. I
was a mere spectator. I'm incapable of taking part in this

sort of intoxication. It's a delirium I know nothing about; I was simply there, an unwilling witness to something that doesn't interest me at all.

One day, returning from Rabat to Tangier on the train, I saw a boy looking after three sheep, waving happily to the whole train as it sped by. No doubt many of the passengers saw him through the train's windows. Maybe some of them smiled at him without him being able to see them. Perhaps the train contained one little boy of the same age who returned his greeting with the same enthusiasm; or maybe no one did. What did the little shepherd want?

Four in the morning, the emptiness of my pockets expelled me from the Monocle. I smelled the seductive scent of women, but I went my way and they went theirs. I felt as if I wanted to exile myself to a place where even my shadow didn't know me. 'The best late night soirées always carry a certain sadness for me.' This is what Adonis said to me in the streets of Turin one Sunday morning in the middle of a conversation about religious wars. Between two churches, I insisted we enter a bar while we waited for Edward Kharrat and his wife to finish praying in one of the churches. We had planned to visit the museum where the shroud of Christ is kept (or so it's believed), but one of our companions was seduced by a young girl's legs, and had disappeared with her, giving us the slip.

While we were entering the bar, Adonis said, regretful

that he wouldn't be going to see the holy shroud: 'Listen Mohamed, religious wars have killed people in far greater numbers than political or economic wars have.'

At our second-to-last drink I asked him to write out for me the three verses for the unknown Bedouin girl that he had recited in Alba:

> Of what offence has the Bedouin girl been accused
> Adversities of intent from where you weren't suspecting
> If she remembers the fresh water and its sweetness
> And the coolness of its stones at the end of the night
> You would overflow with tenderness and longing
> She sighs in the evening
> And she sighs at dawn
> If not for those two sighs, you would have gone mad.

I inhaled and Adonis and I cursed the goat and she-goat who had prevented us from seeing the shroud of Christ. They could even be having sex right now ...

On the way back home, I stagger, raving incoherently. I find an empty can in my path, and I begin to kick it until I arrive at the premises of Radio Tangier. The hollow noise of the can rings and rings: it is my echo. The doorman of the Radio Bar says to his companion, who is sitting with him on the threshold:

'Poor guy! Books and booze have driven him crazy.'

To make myself feel better, and to ignore what I am hearing, I think about how no one life is more beautiful than any other, whether it's lived according to reason or to sweet madness, whether it's lived in lucidity or in soothing drunkenness. I curse this wretched night of accusations, these ragged remnants of a sweltering day. Silence at last in the kingdom of noise! Now who will rouse the dog Juba[1] from his slumbers? The cacophony of other dogs? No, no one. Maybe it is I who am now privileged, compared with those who are asleep. One in the morning. The music of Eric Satie tinkles away. Raindrops slide from leaf to leaf. Everyone is on their own. No one asks anything of anybody. On a night like this, I'm lucky not to be like Nelson Dyar or his victim.[2]

On the subject of drugs, Paul Bowles says: 'It's hard for me to settle in one place. I can't stay seated, I have to move around. If one wants to write that's impossible, but when we smoke we don't want to move or go out. We stay wherever we are, focused on what we're doing. This is normal. Generally, I wouldn't smoke before I began writing, it never happened this way. But to smoke out of the desire to keep one's concentration, that's possible. This is something people don't understand. They think that one smokes to hallucinate or come up with ideas

---

1 Mohamed Choukri's old dog.
2 The protagonist of Bowles's novel *Let It Come Down*. The protagonist here kills his friend Tahami under the influence of *majoun*.

when one's trying to write. This doesn't give one any ideas. In the most extreme of cases it might bring out ideas that are in the subconscious, but it doesn't create the ideas themselves. They existed there already. *Kif* isn't responsible because it can't generate anything. In and of itself it creates nothing. I've tried to explain this, and several times, to journalists and critics, but the majority of them don't understand.' In a letter to Alec France he states: '*Up Above the World* was written entirely under *kif*, if one may use the word "under". Perhaps "over" would be more accurate. And, if I recall, "The Hyena" and "The Garden". This doesn't mean that I wasn't smoking at all when I wrote some of the other stories.'[1]

Near my house, two young guys confront me. I let them steal my watch with no resistance or aggression. One of them laughs scornfully; they are scoundrels. It doesn't matter. They win. I am too weak to defend myself, and I wonder: 'What would be the point of looking to the Roxy Café's doorman for help? He's old. And now he's inside the café lethargically keeping his post, or he's asleep; a guard in appearance only: a human scarecrow, no more.' Some time ago, a guard in the neighboring quarter chased away two thieves who were trying to steal a car. The next night they returned, but now they were four. They bound his hands and legs, crammed paper into his mouth and inserted the *sepsi* he used to smoke

---

1 Bowles, *In Touch*, p. 463.

kif into his anus. The motto of the security guards in our quarter is: 'See and shut up'. The two louts continue to strip me of my possessions. The ear of one of them is close to my mouth. If I bit it, they'd smash my head in; and if I severed it completely, I'd be a goner for sure. Then there's the issue of the *sepsi*, and the papers crammed into the mouth. Best not to think about it. I let them do what they want. Adolescents high on ether.[1] Their glee and laughter confirm it. My watch. Maybe they need it more than I do. They laugh as they leave, the bastards. I'm surprised to find myself envying them. Stealing has its own pleasure. I felt it myself when I participated in robbing a kiosk in the Trankat quarter of Tétouan. In those days you didn't sign off a robbery by stuffing papers into the mouth, or inserting a *sepsi* into the anus. Stealing had its etiquette. One didn't resort to knives or daggers. If you were caught in the act, you showed them a clean pair of heels.

The watch they stole was given to me by a Moroccan poet. It's not surprising that poets' gifts should be stolen in the night's darkest hours, the only birthright of the poor.

Going up the stairs, I stumble. The electricity has been cut off to save money. Pitch-black darkness. On the stairway I trip over a body. She's here again! She's sleeping between my door and my neighbor's, waiting for him, whether he comes or not. She's wearing jeans and a short

---

1 A kind of glue or paste that some young people sniff to get high.

jacket. She must be drunk or high on hashish to sleep on the cold floor like that. For several nights now I've been forced to step over her in order to enter my apartment. I don't invite her in; I've had my fill of strangers.

After a short nap, I wake up and drink the remains of a glass of wine. I no longer have a watch, no hour or minute hand to consult. I thought of the barmaid in Bar Maroc. I remembered the time when sleeping with her was preferable to masturbation. Now I'd rather masturbate. Damned women! They're only kind when old age has begun to ravage them, or once they've been reduced to a state in which they sleep at your doorstep, waiting for you to return. 'You can have me whenever you like, my dear!' It might be quite comforting, though, to grow old together. That barmaid, I don't know why, but every time I see her I have a burning desire to strangle her. Maybe it's her filthy, vulgar way of speaking. It would make my day to see her eyes bulging from the strength of my hands and the weight of my body while I lay on top of her, squeezing and squeezing with all my strength, while she struggled in an effort to break free, or merely to breathe. And, finally, the release! She would be a dead fish lying on a deserted beach. The irritating faces of multitudes of strangers have inspired me with imaginary crimes of this sort. Who knows how many times I've committed murder in my imagination? Maybe my imagination has saved me from committing a real crime. Sometimes I don't know why we commit crimes at all.

I gaze at the ceiling: our communal ceiling in the house of the eternal future. I no longer have anyone in Tangier, except the ants, with whom I'm not on familiar terms. Invasions, first by 'Tartars', and then by 'Mongols', have scattered all the heroes of Tangier's nights far and wide. I think about Rachida, the hashish addict. She's mad now. She walks around barefoot or in plastic sandals, her *jelaba* stained with dirt and full of holes. The space between her index and middle fingers is stained yellow and black. When she goes into a café or bar, all she begs for is cigarettes. One day, at noon, she blocked my way, and cursed me between ruined teeth: 'If you had married me, you wouldn't see me like this today.' I gave her some cigarettes and a little money, and I thought to myself: 'We can't save everyone we love. This one lost her mind, another married someone who's now in prison, another divorced after her husband went bankrupt through gambling and drinking, another has grown old and crouches at the corner of the street mutely begging alms from passers-by, while another died without a soul by her side to ease her last breath by placing a few drops of water in her mouth, or a damp towel on her fevered brow. They are all at rock bottom, or continuing to bet on an impossible dream, or asleep for ever in the cosmic nothingness.'

I'm fed up with night-times in the mythical Tangier, sickened by its criminal scum, which I regurgitate each morning with my bile. But a Tangier night is like the song of the sirens that refuses to acknowledge the itinerary planned for Odysseus's journey. It's like a watch without hands, displaying the same spirit as my grandmother Raqqiyya or my aunt Fathma. Grandmothers and aunts resemble each other. And you, just as you have something of her in you, she has something of you in her. It's not equivalent, but there is surely some cross-pollination. I wouldn't want to return to the stage of the suckling nipple; it's enough for me to have been weaned before my time. There is no intellectual superiority between a man and a woman. Each has his or her own mentality. They melt into each other; it's the law of mortal passion. But each of us now lives alone with his thoughts. The more extreme the distance that separates us, the more exquisite is the coming together again. I've always preferred to be out and about at twilight-time, never in the bright light of the sun; that's for the near-sighted.

Now the silence is broken by the wind instruments accompanying a wedding procession that passes slowly and noisily. In this place the silence of the night is always broken by the wailing instruments of a wedding feast, or the blaring horn of a ship crossing the Strait of Gibraltar. The first expresses the resistance of those who would otherwise be overwhelmed by loneliness, while the second announces travels to unknown worlds, the obsessive longing for adventure. One would love to be able to hear nothing, not even the song of a nightingale, and then suddenly we find ourselves deafened by a raucous group of people and a troop of itinerant musicians! The silence of the hermitage is only known to us by report. We only know it historically. Your silence; the silence under your ceiling; the silence of silence. The ceiling that no one shares with you, sheltering your most private contemplations, your meditations. You can become yourself again once your work is finished. How I hate those who take their jobs with them wherever they go! Detach yourself, rebel against your boss, don't allow anyone to disturb the time set aside for your self-communion, for gazing at your ceiling. Withdraw into yourself, open the door to no one, not even to those who love you and whom you love. May the most solitary and least communicative win the day! Take care not to rejoin the herd.

When someone asked Paul why he married Jane, he replied: 'So that I could be finished with women and she could be finished with men.' But he denies ever having said such a thing, attributing it to malicious gossip.

Jane would flaunt her homosexuality while Paul concealed his, or evaded answering directly if asked about it. In the beginning they agreed that there would be no duplicity between them: she was to know about all his lovers and he would know about hers. Paul was always more of a puritan than Jane was. Throughout their long relationship, whenever they separated neither of them knew who had left whom. Maybe they undertook these periods of separation, which could be either brief or prolonged, to create a sense of longing between them. I, too, do this from time to time with those close to me, and even with Tangier itself. If I don't find Tangier within its own parameters, I search for it outside of them. I leave my apartment and set off on my travels, to other towns and countries, or even around Tangier itself. Sometimes I don't visit certain quarters for months or even years.

Jane was known to be the more stubborn of the two in terms of what she would demand before she consented to return to Paul. He would yield. I don't think that he ever loved anyone (if he truly loved anyone) as he loved her. Literarily and psychologically, he was more or less extinguished throughout the period of her illness. Once she died he began to grow old and sardonic, concealing his depression beneath a show of arrogance. Jane would hesitate a great deal before deciding anything, but once she made a decision she was stronger than Paul. When they were separated, which happened sporadically, she would write a story about a woman who had abandoned her husband and he would write a story about a man who had left his wife. Were they playing a game of literary existentialism? That was their secret, like their personal relationship. Occasionally, Jane would detest something he adored, and vice versa. She couldn't put up with annoyances, and reacted with an impulsive sarcasm to the monotony of the lives of those around her. Her irony could be biting, but she was well liked by her lovers and disciples.

Paul was known to be stronger than her when it came to handling the psychological torments he'd been concealing since he was a boy, as if he were made of stone. He would grumble, but not complain. He was grateful to those who helped him out of a tight spot, but he preferred to extricate himself by his own efforts. He would bury himself in his work, which always restored him to an even keel. Jane, on the contrary, was an erupting volcano. She would declare her grievances to whoever was physically closest to her, whether she knew them or not. She was consumed by the fatal desire to annihilate herself rather than suffer humiliation: 'I am always one step away from despair.' Sin, feelings of guilt, the pleasure of perpetual suffering, psychological disintegration, the ambition to achieve what she was incapable of accomplishing in writing and in love, the fear of solitude: these are what motivated her and gave her nightmares. She was more miserable than Charlotte Brontë.

In a letter to Libby Holman written from Tangier in December 1948, she wrote: 'I can get chicken heads and giblets for a penny a pile but have no eating companion so what's the use? I'm God-damned sick of having no one to eat with except on odd nights, and no reason to eat at one time more than another.'[1]

This was Jane, complaining of her loneliness. She tried to be herself, but it was no use. Was this from cowardice?

---

1 Jane Bowles, *Out in the World: Selected Letters of Jane Bowles, 1935–1970* (Santa Rosa: Black Sparrow Press, 1990), p. 129.

Jane could have throttled a python. From shyness, then?
Most certainly. She was excessively generous toward
those who sought her aid. Paul, on the other hand,
hasn't for a day in his life believed in the concept of
humanitarianism. All he cares about is that things should
carry on of their own accord, with he himself completely
missing from the scenario. He prefers to wear blinkers,
so that he can't be a witness to anything. For Jane, every
gesture had to be imbued with grace and good humor,
because life is a fragile thing. Paul remained her beloved
adversary, always more disciplined than she was when it
came to work. Each would derive their strength from the
other, but they also had their own way of doing things.
In the end, it was Paul who was the primary beneficiary,
while all that remained for Jane, bound to his side, was
to bask in the glow of his achievements. On occasion,
she would say: 'There is nothing detestable about men';
and at other times: 'There is something loathsome about
women'. Was she trying to please him? There's no doubt
that both of them loved each other in their own way,
whether expressed behind closed doors or publicly. But
Paul himself has admitted that he often didn't entirely
understand what she was 'fabricating', or trying to express.
Thus he couldn't remain completely outside the circle
of confusion that Jane created around herself. In her
writing, she was always trying to tap into whatever was
ambiguous in women, just as Paul focused on whatever
was obscure in men. Evidently, Jane and Paul were

friends, above all else, and what was of mutual interest to them were the ideas that they entertained, she about men and he about women. He undoubtedly married her for her intelligence and talent, not for her femininity; when her brilliance faded, his interest in her diminished. In her solitude, Jane deplored separation. But above all else she wanted to be far away from volcanoes, tunnels, stray dogs, rapists, and anyone who might desire her or want to sleep with her, regardless of their good intentions. It has to be kept in mind that she inherited some of her family's moral austerity. Throughout her life she struggled to purge herself categorically of this reserve, but couldn't do so. When Jane met Paul Bowles, she told him, verbatim: 'I don't want any sexual relationship with you before marriage. I want to be a virgin when I marry.'

This desire of Jane's remains incomprehensible. She seems to have forgotten here the numerous times she had allowed herself to be deflowered by lesbians when she was between twelve and thirteen years old, long before she met Paul. Jane would ardently love women, and Paul would love men, albeit with less enthusiasm. It was their fate. Even they didn't know why; nor did they ever try to explain it. They loved each other, but couldn't achieve a real union. They embraced intimately in a shared bed, touched, joked together, shared secrets and thoughts; they shared the same ideas, but not the same memories, nor did they have the same way of retrieving memories. One thing alone united them: the passionate love of illusion. How did they arrive at this secret concord? It needn't concern anyone but them. They remained committed to their mutual bond of sexual ambivalence right up until Jane's death. Since then, Paul has regretted nothing about their companionship, which had shocked society at the time. It's clear that Jane was more rebellious than Paul, but it was he who ultimately won, without having had to suffer as she had.

It's known that Paul Bowles was sexually frigid, as he would frankly admit himself. Once I asked him:

'Señor Paul, don't you still have sex at your age?'

'Not at all. I haven't had sex for more than ten years.'

That was towards the end of the seventies. We know that he didn't differentiate between boys and girls until he was seventeen years old.

Paul and Jane, in their writings, continued to be mutually inspired by one another, until her illness, which completely paralyzed her. Toward the end of her life she could no longer use dreams to feed her writing, nor use her writing to feed her dreams. Even dreaming just for dreaming's sake was beyond her reach. After her death, Paul devoted himself to translations, journalism, giving interviews, and editing his diary. He also composed some lacklustre poetry. If Gertrude Stein had been alive, she most surely would have persuaded him against this. One might be excused for saying that it's the poets alone who have the right to resist poetry, it being the divide between the sublime and the profane, the partition screen, the intermediary between God and man. As for the texts adapted into English from colloquial Moroccan, Paul mentioned in a letter to Allen Ginsberg and Peter Orlovsky (August 2, 1962): 'It gives me a pleasant satisfaction to work on them, even though I'm aware of it as a vicarious sort of creativity.'[1]

Maybe as a result of her own mercurial character, Jane could find pleasure only in a love that was fleeting. She would keep anyone wanting to love her truly or deeply at a distance; stability only doubled her anxiety and boredom. I'm not referring here to Cherifa or Titoum: to them, Jane was little more than a source of income, an unbeliever whom it was their duty to rob. With Cherifa, Jane had only one year of sexual pleasure, as she admitted to David Herbert. There were other women from America, but they were no more than ships that passed in the sexual night. As far as 'fat Zohra' was concerned, she was nothing but an amusing prostitute summoned from the brothel of Bencherqui.[2] She was strong and tall, ate and drank voraciously, and had an imposing presence without being intimidating, but she wasn't a significant factor in Jane's life. The name or shadow alone of her male protector in the brothel was enough to invoke fear in people; he was notoriously vicious when angry. Relationships like these, woven by Jane to assuage her anxiety, became a real source of irritation for Paul.

1 Bowles, *In Touch*, p. 340.
2 A brothel in Moroccan Tangier during the colonial period.

Jane loved others more than she was loved in return: she never obtained the love, nor fulfilled the literary aspirations, for which she strove. That was her tragedy. No one could come to her rescue because she didn't want anyone's help. She wanted to make a literary adventure of her life, but found herself encompassed by a hostile entourage. She never learned how to cut herself free from the familial complex that clung to her and pursued her, however far she travelled. In truth, no one despised her; she created a self-hatred of her own, without any outside encouragement. She felt that she was unloved, but this was a feeling she created herself. She could never rid herself of certain ideas that her mother had force-fed into her, while Paul had had the courage to throw his family's authority in the trashcan. He knew how to distil something of value from his suffering and alienation, his exile and adventures. He was able to make his way on his own, whereas Jane always needed the help of others to get her through her ordeals. Her letters to Paul and her friends abound in complaints about her inability to support her loneliness, and to finish what she wanted to write. Writing had potentially been her one salvation from the daily monotony of Tangier. Her most cherished friends were far from her. She certainly thought about them a lot, but she was never sure if they, in turn, thought about her. That's the suspicion inherent in distance. We were created to live with others, and we find ourselves always alone.

Jane was devoted to her family and friends. She didn't promulgate discord with anyone, except with herself. Her rebellion against her family was frivolous in comparison with Paul's, which was radical and initiated by an extreme decision. Jane had been damaged by her family, and didn't know how to transcend the damage as Paul had done.

It remains unknown whether Jane Bowles ultimately gave herself to God or to humanity. She wavered between the two throughout her life. From an early age she felt that her life was fragile, torn asunder, and didn't know how she could remedy this. She felt like the survivor of a shipwreck, and that's why she allowed herself to be swept along by prevailing currents. If she had devoted herself to honing her literary talent, she might have been saved from nihilistic defeat. She loved, to the point of intoxication, those who fled from her. On herself, she had no pity, deliberately rebuffing those who loved her and chasing after those who would never bring her satisfaction. It's true that her actions were tinged with a sense of guilt, like most of those of her generation who rebelled against their puritanical families. But generally, if one ignores her fear of the unknown, she comes across as someone who didn't give much thought to, or couldn't imagine, the consequences of her behavior. She might sit on men's laps, one after another, but it went no further than that. Her movement and gestures were those of an innocent child, even when she was astonishing her audience with her witty wordplay. It was noticeable that when she and

Paul separated, he needed her to be with him more than she did him. And she couldn't bear to be with him without the presence of a third party, not along the lines of Sartre's concept of hell in *No Exit*, merely a third person to generate a kind of intimate struggle, so that even when they were together a certain distance would remain. Jane's desire for a third party between them didn't extend to Ahmed Yacoubi, however, whose perpetual clinging to Paul was something Jane couldn't stand.

No doubt this century will remember Jane and Paul Bowles as a famous couple, along with Aragon and Elsa, Sartre and Simone de Beauvoir, Dalí and Gala, and Scott and Zelda Fitzgerald. It's said that 'behind every great man is a woman', and this isn't entirely unfounded. We don't need to know which of the pair is the villain. The couple who destroyed themselves with the most *élan* was undoubtedly Frieda and D. H. Lawrence.

Paul has always tended to be rather gloomy, and his sarcasm toward others is simply a way for him to lighten his funereal mood. His friend Aaron Copland described him as being as cold as a fish. But there was never a tense atmosphere that Jane couldn't dissipate with her charm; she was sardonic and childlike, even without uttering a word. She was a woman who imposed herself through her personality, which drew the respect and attention of the men of her epoch. To assert oneself in this way, whatever the period, is usually a masculine characteristic, but Jane was simply being herself. She made no distinction between the proper comportment of men and women. There can be no doubt that all the women in her family were severely critical of her book *Two Serious Ladies*, a text in which the assertiveness of her personality was crystal clear. But who are these women, apart from their family connection with her? Ordinary women, with ordinary digestive systems and nothing in common with Jane other than the triviality of kinship: puritanical women who helped precipitate her breakdown.

Jane never abandoned her affable childishness that some fools found irritating. To her friends and companions it was a feature to cherish. Aaron Copland said: 'I never knew what went on in her mind. In my opinion, she was more inscrutable than Paul. He's guarded, but open with those who know him well. There was a conspicuous childlike side to Jane's personality. She was exaggeratedly sensitive, her mood changed easily, but only for certain reasons. With that, it remained hard to assess her. All that we really knew about her were that her responses, whatever their character may have been, were always distinctive, outside the norm.'

It's known that Aaron Copland and Gore Vidal didn't respond well to Jane's behavior, but it never reached the height of the animosity that existed between Buñuel and Gala Dalí. Among Paul's friends, Truman Capote and Tennessee Williams were the ones who liked her most. If Jane's dream had been fulfilled, she would have been a literary prodigy. As it was, she died a martyr to literature, owing to her refusal to commercialize what she wrote. This was despite the extreme poverty she experienced intermittently in her life, taking her on occasion to the brink of destitution. Her sincerity and innocence impeded her progress in both life and literature. Paul, however, kicked aside anything that stood in his path. Interested only in self-realization, he had no compassion for anyone. Humanity in his writing scarcely exists; something that, even now, he doesn't regret in the least.

Jane loved to venture into places that scared her. Was this from waywardness, obstinacy, or defiance? One evening, she returned to Paul's from a mysterious excursion; her feet were bare, the weather cold and rainy. We don't know what happened to her during this nocturnal ramble, a daring one for someone like Jane who was always afraid of being raped. Perhaps nothing at all untoward occurred. At all events, it remained a closely guarded secret with her, just as she never explained how she could be terrified of a harmless insect, while at the same time she would risk her life, without batting an eyelid, by approaching a rattlesnake that was about to kill her feral cat. When Paul asked her where she had been that night, she replied: 'In the place I've always been afraid to go to.' Paul, as usual, let it go at that.

Jane Bowles was weird, or, perhaps more to the point, she was a genius. She would sometimes apologize for things she hadn't done. She was haunted by a guilt complex, and from that the peculiar magic of her being was drawn. Each being manifests its own particular essence; for Jane, that essence was somewhat twisted and misshapen.

In April 1940, Jane and Paul travelled to Chicago with someone called Boo. Paul never left Jane's side the whole time they were in the city. Jane introduced Boo to everyone as her brother, which annoyed Paul. At a dinner party attended by the American screenwriter Richard Brooks, a woman asked: 'How many siblings does Jane Bowles have?' Jane became hysterical, shouting: 'Can any of us really be said to have brothers and sisters?'

This was Jane, and she had to be accepted as she was. She had something in common with Zelda Fitzgerald: both of them created stories and diversions to amuse themselves, and destroyed the things that were precious to them, and to others. For them, nothing was stable, and nothing deserved to last. But the question of futility that they raised, maybe unwittingly, remains pertinent. Jane Bowles and Zelda Fitzgerald were born to shake up what other people found customary, to startle them out of their normal routines. In their eyes, since everything was futile, nothing was important. What mattered was to prick people out of their complacency. Zelda destroyed her husband because she was jealous of his work. She insisted that he throw roaring parties, and dragged him along to those given by others, until all the carousing and drunkenness exhausted him. He died, and she went mad. Jane, however, always supported Paul and wanted him to complete whatever he was working on. It was a kind of compensation for her own inability to produce. Moreover, she always came to Paul's aid whenever he was in difficulty, or had problems with other people. She would be there in good time, charming and irresistible as ever.

Paul Bowles has always concealed his emotions. One never knows what he's really thinking. He keeps his own counsel. This is his most attractive trait. He adores parrots, and from them he's borrowed the virtue of circumspection. He talks to them, and it may be that they're the only ones who know his secrets. He visited a restaurant in Paris, whose owner had a parrot perched on his shoulder. Marcel Proust had been one of his customers, and the man gave a copy of *In Search of Lost Time* to Paul as a gift. But Paul was more interested in the parrot, and would have preferred to receive that rather than the book.

Paul and Jane surrounded themselves with animals, wherever they went. At home they gathered an entire collection: a cat, a kitten, a duck, a parrot, two wild cats, and so forth. Once, one of Paul's two feral cats killed and devoured a pigeon, then choked on one of its bones. It's something he recalls with great sorrow.

Sex, for Paul, was always secondary. It wasn't necessary in his life. He utilized it in his writings, but never for the sake of titillation. When he was seventeen, Paul met an English girl named Peggy. Their friendship was strictly platonic, and Paul left her in order to avoid becoming entangled in a sexual relationship with her. In his reading choices, as well, he recoiled from writing that was too sexual. I asked him once about Henry Miller and he said: 'He's a laudable writer, but he's boring when he goes on at length in descriptions of sex. My favorite book of his is *The Colossus of Maroussi.*' About Anais Nin, he said: 'Oh, that woman obsessed with repressed sexual urges. I shall never forgive her for the perverse spitefulness she showed in her criticism of Jane's novel, *Two Serious Women.*'

Anyone who reads Paul Bowles's autobiography, *Without Stopping,* will realize that everything in his life has been minutely planned. In this, he closely resembles Truman Capote, though Capote was even more of an obsessive. Capote lacked decorum and the spirit of adventure, and was as incorrigible a braggart and as prone to hysteria as Tennessee Williams. Still, one isn't entirely convinced by *Without Stopping,* despite Paul's statement to Alec France (June 13, 1973, in Tangier): 'The autobiography is nowhere meant to be "cryptic".'[1] It is an autobiography that amounts to a catalogue of names, visits, and trips, apart from the chapters devoted to his childhood and family. The rest is a series of interludes, ponderous and boring. But he himself hadn't wanted to write it, having agreed to do so because he needed the

---

1 Bowles, *In Touch,* p. 453.

money to cover the costs of Jane's hospitalization in La Clínica de Reposo de los Angeles in Malaga.

When I left the Monocle, all I had left in my pockets were three dirhams. It was after three in the morning. With these coins I decided to have a café au lait at El Pilo. Jilali Gharbaoui was sitting on the café's terrace. I'd met him in the middle of the sixties. He visits Tangier from time to time, carrying under his arm the paintings he's done on cardboard. When his money runs out, he gives me one to sell for him. I always manage to find a buyer – from one hundred and fifty to two hundred dirhams for each painting. He called me over:

'Hey! Choukri!'

I sat down beside him, then he said to me in his falsetto voice: 'Do you know what happened to me tonight?'

'What happened?'

'You won't believe this. Just a little while ago I was in Moulay Driss Zerhoun.¹ Walking toward Fez, and staggering under the weight of my two suitcases, I felt the presence of two ghosts following behind me. I dropped my cases and ran like mad. I don't know how I come to be sitting here!'

He looked at me sharply, and added: 'Everything I own was in those two suitcases: my canvases, personal papers, clothes, money.'

'That's too bad!'

---

1 A small town located 20 kilometers north of Meknes.

'Do you have any money on you?'

'I'm in a bad way.'

'Give me what you have.'

I gave him the three dirhams with no hesitation, before becoming his third ghost. Then I went in the café to have my breakfast: café au lait and toast with butter. On credit.

The next day, in the evening, I found Gharbaoui again, having dinner at the Zagora restaurant. He was dressed to the nines. He invited me to have dinner with him. That was the last time I saw him before learning, about a year later, that he had sold all his paintings, and even his painting materials, to someone rich who liked his work, and that he had left Morocco for good, only to die in Paris one freezing night, on a bench in the Champ-de-Mars in April 1971. In Tangier, everything is surreal and everything is possible.

When we die suddenly, death has no geography. I've experienced coincidental encounters like this one more than once. Genet came looking for me in the Negresco bar-restaurant, but I wasn't there. He dined and, as a joke, left a glass of wine and the newspaper *France Soir* with the waiter for me. I never set eyes on him again, and a few months later he died. I had dinner with Tennessee Williams at the Parade; then we took what was left of our bottle of wine to drink by the pool of the Minzah. He suggested we sit on the terrace of the Café de Paris and have a drink. Before the waiter came, a young man sat next to Tennessee, blood running down his head onto his face. Tennessee took off, taking the half-full bottle of wine with him, without so much as a goodbye. It was the last time I saw him before he died. Paul told me that he choked to death in a hotel, in mysterious circumstances.

Towards the end of his life, Gharbaoui often complained about Morocco's art scene. The Moroccan audience hadn't yet been ready to accept his abstract style of painting. Ahmed Sharqawi suffered from the same incomprehension. Here in Morocco, Gharbaoui's take on painting seemed strange. Abroad, however, he had more freedom to produce his work. There were those who both understood it and received it well: critics, museums, galleries. In Morocco, painting, whether abstract or not, was still suffering from the prohibitions of Islamic tradition.

Gharbaoui was aware that abstract art attracted little interest in Morocco. In fact, abstract painting was practically non-existent in Moroccan art culture. Thus one saw very few paintings, other than third-rate works of no merit, from both the north and the south of the country, taken up by foreign cultural delegations, to pander to the taste of a naive public, hungry for images of the exotic and the fantastic.

Gharbaoui was like a bird with no legs: a tiny body and huge wings. He was like the 'Blue Bird', Mohammad Khaïr-Eddine, who died on November 18, 1995. The two of them had almost the same temperament, the same passions, and the same desire to overturn all the conventions of artistic creation.

In his autobiography, Bowles writes: 'Today one has to be devoid of feeling in order to continue being an artist.' But this doesn't apply, for example, to Gharbaoui and Khaïr-Eddine, who were both from Azrou-Ouadhou, literally 'the rock of the breeze', in the south of Morocco, where the people of the village sit in the shade to talk when the heat is at its most oppressive. In their lives, both were steadfast amid life's storms.

Gharbaoui was born in 1930 in Jorf el-Melh, in the west of Morocco. Today his work can be found in the homes of rich Moroccans, or in a few European and American museums, and God knows where else.

At the age of sixteen, the naked human body began to disgust Bowles, at the time when he began to study painting. By the time he turned seventeen, the difference in male and female anatomy seemed weird to him. Why was there this distinction?, he asked himself. But stranger still is the question of why he chose to paint the human body using only the color blue. Did he think that Adam was blue because he had fallen from the sky? Everything came to him late in life. Even his worldwide literary fame came to him only after the age of sixty. As the proverb says: 'You will be given bread when you've no longer got teeth.'

Between the rosy freshness of youth and the vagaries of age, Paul engaged in what could perhaps at a stretch be called sex – as he admits in his autobiography – with a Hungarian girl named Hermina, in the middle of a field of nettles. In a Paris hotel, he had a sexual experience with another girl, cold and unresponsive, disappointing him even more than her predecessor. Who would want to continue the pursuit of love after such let-downs? As for his sexual experiences with men, we know very little. To be fair to him, we oughtn't to show much interest in them, since he himself never gave them much importance, saying only that he'd nothing to regret on that score. One thing is sure: women were never his cup of tea. As far as his homosexual experiences are concerned, we know that he lived with Billy Hubert, a relative of his. Billy came to see him in Paris, and was extremely generous toward him – Paul was more or less broke at the time. He even convinced him to return to New York with him, so as to be reconciled with his parents, assuring him that they wouldn't reproach him for deserting them. Paul regretted his return, nevertheless. He's admitted that he wasn't mature enough then to decide his life for himself without allowing others to interfere in it.

'Paul, in his youth, had an outstanding elegance that attracted men and intelligent women,' Edouard Roditi told me.

Paul Bowles wrote in his autobiography: 'The life of a writer is of no significance. The depth of my thought is in my writing and music.' But shouldn't one be wary of the soul that hides itself behind the mask of art? Art's goal is to become master of reality, to remove the veil from the hidden reality. Bowles invested a lot of his life in art, but he rarely managed to achieve the sublimation of the one into the other that he so fervently desired.

Paul was always excessively cautious toward other people and things, even though he tempered his mistrust with his sense of humor. To render his self-isolation more complete, he had his telephone cut off. He even found a justification for his refusal to travel, saying: 'I don't travel anymore, because there are no more steamships.' Perhaps for him this was a valid excuse, since he always took about thirty suitcases and two large trunks on his travels. People called him 'dandy, old steamship lover'.

It was toward the end of the fifties that he began to live this sedentary and indolent existence in Tangier, like one ensconced in a shell. As Pascal says, 'All of man's misery stems from a single source: his inability to stay put in one room.' Or: 'In the end, living in hotel rooms is dehumanizing,'[1] as Mrs Rainmantle says to Mrs Slade in *Up Above the World*. Due to his illness over the last few years, he's essentially been living in a corner of his room. It has never been his way to go knocking on anyone's door. Just like the philosopher Santayana, if no one asks about him, he won't ask about anyone.

After Morocco's independence, Paul cut down his visits to coffeehouses, bars and restaurants, deeming them to

---

1 Bowles, *Up Above the World*, p. 35.

be the haunts of secret police and intelligence agents. He therefore contented himself with a daily trip to the post office and the new market on Fez Street, accompanied by his driver, Abdel Wahid. He would take in the smell of the flowers mixed with those of the meat, vegetables, and fruit, and he would play with the stray kittens. Paul loves cats and hates dogs. One day he said to me: 'Their place is the desert, not the city. They're aggressive. But cats, despite their haughtiness, are tame.' Regardless, after Jane entered the 'rest clinic for the Angels' in Malaga, no cat took refuge in his home any longer. There had been a black female kitten that would always come at a specific time; he would feed her milk in front of his apartment door. One day she disappeared. When I didn't see the dish in front of the door or her resting in the building's entrance, I asked him about her. He answered me in a sorrowful voice: 'The poor thing died. She was a nice cat, even if she was a stray.'

Unlike Jack Kerouac, Paul didn't consider the death of a cat to be always and necessarily a bad omen. One afternoon I found him in the market on Fez Street playing with a small cat. I asked him his opinion on the Gulf War that was in full flow at the time. With his usual calm, he answered: 'Playing with this kitten now is more important to me than any conversation about that filthy war.'

Even so, Paul had an opinion about the war: 'The bombing of Iraq has been executed with extreme violence. It wasn't necessary to reach this point, but Mr

Bush wanted to demonstrate that he was powerful. I'm convinced that the Americans were pleased. When it happened, they said: the horrors of Vietnam have been erased. Here we've recovered our power and greatness. This is ridiculous. However, in Tangier, there are no tourists anymore. The Americans have received a request from their government asking them to leave Morocco. And it's true that everyone who had been working here has now completed their evacuation to Washington. The streets have become deserted. Even the Moroccans no longer go out on the streets.'[1]

This situation lasted around a month, after which things returned to normal. Nothing else happened. The Americans, and probably the Europeans as well, had thought that the people here would be irate and would take to the streets in protest. In fact, that occurred only once, on the first day after it was announced that a coalition authorized by the United Nations had bombed Iraq. This aroused their anger, because they're Muslims. Naturally, they don't like to see a situation in which Christians are killing Muslims; they tend to forget that

---

1 It should be said here that Paul Bowles, after independence, was, to all intents and purposes, living in a room that was indeed located in Tangier, but he was hardly ever in the city itself. Of what would the Moroccans have been afraid? Of the war? It was their war, though they knew that it was already a lost war with the West – apart from a few fools who believed in a real victory. Bowles here is thoughtless, and completely divorced from reality.

their own king had sent troops to kill Muslims. In the end, everyone forgot all this, and that's for the best. I hate the war, and I think there are very few people who like it. It gives those who bombarded Iraq feelings of power and greatness, and deep down that's what they were after. We don't fear what we know; we only feel threatened by those people and things we can't fathom. Knowledge alone can conquer fear. When Jane stopped writing literature, which after a certain point meant her short stories, she would find compensation and a creative outlet in drafting long letters to Paul and her friends. She would recount the simplest daily minutiae. To expel her boredom and assuage her incurable loneliness, she would explore Moroccan life and try to learn the country's language and traditions. Before Jane had fallen in love with anyone here, or had melted into this part of Africa, she wrote to Paul from Treetops, Connecticut (September 1947): 'I wish to hell I could find some woman still so that I wouldn't always be alone at night. I'm sure Arab night life would interest me not in the slightest. As you know I don't consider those races voluptuous or exciting in any way, as I have said – being a part of them almost.'[1] And in another letter (October 1947): 'I don't know about the Arab town of Tangier (I *refuse* to use that Arabic word).'[2] On another occasion she said: 'Of course I think I shall

1 Jane Bowles, *Out in the World*, p. 55.
2 Ibid., p. 62.

simply never be interested in anyone who is Latin or Arab or Semitic.'[1] She preferred the Scots and Irish.

From the beginning of the sixties, she began to suffer attacks in which she would lose large chunks of her memory. This was initially caused by the stroke she had in 1957, as she mentions in a letter to Libby Holman written from Tangier in 1965: 'Last night I had dinner with Mary. I suddenly forget her name – (this happens since I had the stroke), but it will come back. Here it comes – BANK CROFT.'[2] Similarly, during this period her letters were filled with mistakes: a letter or more would be dropped in some words, for example. Between two different hospitals in England and Spain, she would receive twenty-three electric shocks to treat her depression and calm her nerves. In 1966, when she had difficulty using a pen, Jane began to dictate most of her letters to her friend Carla Grissmann, without even signing the majority of them. In the middle of April 1967, Paul took her to Malaga, where she was admitted to the clinic for mentally ill women. There she underwent electric-shock treatment again. Her letters from Malaga were handwritten, noticeably unsteady, and almost illegible. From this stage onwards, the transcription deviated from the norm not only in its grammar and punctuation but also in the words that were frequently crossed out or left unexplained.

While Jane had always feared tunnels, mountains,

1 Ibid., p. 42.
2 Ibid., p. 263.

heights, and elevators, Paul always wanted to live in a dark cave. What he wanted – in the style of the Romantics – was to escape civilized society and live a more primitive life. He, unlike Jane, lived a fully independent life. Further, natural scenery held no attraction for her, since she was usually afraid of it, particularly the jungle. In a postcard to Gertrude Stein during their honeymoon in Central America, Paul wrote: 'I married a girl who hates nature, and here we're surrounded by volcanoes, earthquakes, and monkeys'. And he wrote to Peggy Glanville-Hicks from Lisbon on March 25, 1958: 'I know the south of Portugal – the province of Algarve – and it's pretty. But I'm not looking for prettiness.'[1]

In one of her letters, Jane wrote to Paul: 'You would do just what you've always done and so would Helvetia [her close friend] but I don't exist independently.'[2]

Jane's major anxiety stemmed from her inability to continue writing. It was intellectual death that she feared most. This is a very different scenario from that of Lawrence of Arabia, who deliberately stopped writing, committing intellectual suicide, to become an average person, as he remained until his death from a motorcycle accident. He was more attracted to adventure than the writing of poetry, and, in order to continue along these lines, he extinguished the daring genius so evident in *The Seven Pillars of Wisdom*. Rimbaud, on the other hand,

1 Bowles, *In Touch*, p. 281.
2 Jane Bowles, *Out in the World*, p. 86.

traded poetry for financial adventure. Once, after he was already well immersed in the slave and weapon trades, he was asked about what would have happened if he had continued to write poetry. He merely answered: 'Ah, poetry!' He had outgrown his poetic maturity without knowing it. Perhaps, had he continued writing, he would have done no more than recycle the same old stuff.

Writing became a heavy burden for Jane: 'I have to write, but I can't.' Burroughs, too, feared that he would be unable to complete *Naked Lunch*. At the beginning of January 1955, he was utterly beaten down by his excessive drug use, and afraid of a permanent writer's block.

Rimbaud didn't want to bring literature down to the level of life, nor did he want to transcend life to arrive at the heady heights of literature. Instead, he tried to blend the two together, before devoting himself completely to adventure, seeking anonymity among the masses. He managed to find adventure, but not anonymity. There was a small but elite minority who considered him a prophet, praised him to the skies, and begat the generations who pay homage to his memory to this day. 'Death transforms life into destiny,' as Christopher Marlowe said.

In writing, Jane's ambition was greater than what she, despite her promise as a young prodigy, was able to produce. Maybe she lacked a certain guile, a certain malice; she was too kind for that. Paul, however, entrenched in his shell, could be hard and cunning when he had to be. It's good to have faith, and even better to know exactly what you've got faith in, and to understand it. Jane had faith, but the things she believed in often bewildered her.

Every time she found herself devoid of inspiration, she was afraid of being ignominiously expelled from the realm of literature. She never knew where her pen would lead her, and that is what tortured her. She promised to complete a book without even having written its first sentence. And no sooner had she begun, than she would tear up whatever she had written, claiming that: 'Everything is futile, like trying to catch the wind.' Even what she published didn't mean much to her. She only had one urge: to throw it in the trashcan. In her troubled life, anything could happen. Paul felt the same. Both of them believed that living was only possible if one mythologized one's life. Scott and Zelda Fitzgerald preceded them in this tragi-comic vision of life, but there was less spectacle and buffoonery with Paul and Jane.

About Jane, Beatrix Pendar said: 'In the forties, everyone around her was charmed by her indecision and nonchalance, but, unfortunately, she had gotten older and the charm of it was no longer there.' Gore Vidal, on the other hand, found Jane to be completely insufferable, as he did Truman Capote, with whom he frequently quarreled, and who was like a dear brother to Jane. Likewise, Jane hated Gore Vidal, as opposed to Paul, who was much taken by him. It reminds one of Buñuel's aversion to Gala, despite his perfect accord with Dalí.

I met Beatrix Pendar at Paul's; she was very refined, gentle, and kind. She wrote romantic poems for her own pleasure and would read them to her friends. In her day she had been beautiful and her features still bore witness to this. She drowned herself in alcohol until she began to be robbed, both outside and inside her home. She frequently invited me to her apartment, where she would read me her poems, a glass of whisky never leaving her hand. Rarely have I met a woman with so much tenderness and compassion. I would meet her in Madame Porte's tea room, and we would drink together until intoxication got the better of her and I would accompany her home. There she would offer me one for the road, and I never refused. She lived in the utmost seclusion, as solitary as I was. Once, while she was reading one of her poems, it occurred to me that poetry is one big family, regardless of time or place. No visa is required for entry to its kingdom. It will sustain and fraternize with anyone, no matter where they are.

Jane was very jealous of Paul's relationship with Ahmed Yacoubi, but she concealed her jealousy. Moreover, she preferred to have a rival between herself and her beloved Paul, as in the ménage of Kit, Port, and Tunner in *The Sheltering Sky*; yet she didn't want any tension to flare up, as it does in *No Exit*. Port and Kit loved each other a great deal, like Paul and Jane, but couldn't live happily together. Emptiness and privation were just around the corner. One could never know when Jane would take exception to you, and when she would be favorably disposed. She gave no sign beforehand. When Paul asked her one day for her opinion of Ahmed Yacoubi, she answered him calmly: 'He has two holes in place of eyes.' Maybe it was a moment of anger directed against herself or someone else, and not against Ahmed Yacoubi specifically. She was known to be capricious, but, according to those who knew her here in Morocco and in the Americas, she wasn't in the least malicious. She created a life for herself and submerged herself in it completely, not bit by bit. It was all or nothing.

Nothing in her life was stable. Everything she accomplished had to be destroyed, so that it could be replaced by something bigger and better. What would that be? She didn't know herself. When she refused to answer, it was because she didn't want to titillate those of a more ordinary, or more imbecilic, disposition. She reserved her replies for the chosen few. In vain, Paul would threaten her by saying: 'I don't want to see you if you're not working.' But she wasn't working on anything. She was sunk in inconsolable despair; it was useless to try to snap her out of it. She let herself be destroyed by her own thoughts, wallowing in her delectable forced idleness. No one could blame her for it; it was her choice. Her one desire was to produce that which she was no longer capable of producing. She lost herself in writing, and writing was lost in her. She continued to struggle to bring her creative endeavors in harmony with life, but life is not as she, or we, would like it to be. What sickened her, perhaps, was that she could never accomplish in prose what Rimbaud had accomplished in poetry, before he quit it in his prime, to gain the peak of a silence that was heroic, beautiful ... and suicidal.

'The children who haven't yet been born are happier,' Jane would say to Paul. She considered herself to be like a loving mother to her friend Cherifa, and she, in turn, was like a daughter to Jane, who would never have children. 'Why do we insist on bringing children into this world?' she liked to say, with an ironic smile.

Whenever relationships with her friends became strained, she had a way of consoling herself. 'We only live with those who are temporarily passing through,' she once said sardonically to Lawrence Stewart. She also declared: 'I haven't yet lived a single happy day in my life, but I've never given up searching for happiness.' The characters in her books resemble her in this. As for Paul, in most of his texts, he drives his characters towards complete annihilation, or reserves for them a painful end. Brutal crime is omnipresent in his novels and stories; his doctrine has been built on the hatred of one person toward another. All human relationships are grounded in manipulation, betrayal, fraud, and murder. Jane is more merciful toward her characters; she allows them to keep the hope that one day they might be happy. For Paul, no iota of hope can be entertained! But he, too, struggled to find happiness through writing. This struggle is also reflected in Paul's statement: 'One experiences the same guilty feelings as a thief, but with an extra piece of stolen property to boot.' It is as if Yorick's skull has never been exorcized from Bowles's imagination. Nihilism has taken root in him like the very marrow of his bones. Most of the characters in his novels and stories don't escape the deluge. Port, for example, in *The Sheltering Sky*, wants to travel deep into the desert and not leave a trace behind him, since sandstorms can be relied on to cover one's tracks. He is plunged into the profoundest nihilism. Paul knows well that 'Man is hated in the Sahara ... one feels it in the sky, in the stones, in the air,'[1] as he wrote to Peggy Glanville-Hicks. In his story 'A Distant Episode', the tongue of his protagonist is cut out and he is forced to act the buffoon, never mind that he is a professor of linguistics. It's a spectacle of the utmost cruelty. Nor do the heroes of his two stories 'The Delicate Prey' and 'Allal' evade a sadistic fate, either. The first has his penis cut off and thrust into his stomach, which has been sliced open; while the second's head is severed with an ax. For Bowles, an equation underlies his writing: the real is transformed into the imaginary and the imaginary into the real, with the imaginary the more powerful of the two. Sartre, in *Nausea*, has his hero say, *'Je me survis'* (I outlive myself); and Paul Bowles says, in 'Unwelcome Words', *'ma vie est posthume'* (my life is posthumous).[2] However, in *Days:*

---

1 Bowles, *In Touch*, p. 189.

2 Paul Bowles, 'Unwelcome Words', in *The Stories of Paul Bowles*, p. 587.

Tangier Journal: 1987–1989, he retracts this notion of eternity: 'Now that the prognosis [for immortality] is doubtful, the desire to leave a trace behind seems absurd. Even if the human species manages to survive for another hundred years, it's unlikely that a book written in 1990 will mean much to anyone happening to open it in 2090, if indeed he is capable of reading at all.'[1]

---

1 Paul Bowles, *Days: Tangier Journal: 1987–1989* (New York: Ecco Press, 1991), p. 5.

One Sunday in 1972

Bowles and I went to Rmilat. It was the only time we worked outside his home while we were translating *For Bread Alone*. He was in need of the sun's vitamins, as he said. It was a fine sunny day in spring. We sat in a grassy, tree-filled spot covered with wild flowers, violet in hue. In the distance, Moroccan and foreign families were enjoying their picnics; we could hear the joyful cries of the children. I could see, in Bowles's expression, a certain allergy to children that reminded me of Simone de Beauvoir. Like her, he liked them, but from afar.

In the assembly hall for the presentation of the Grinzane Cavour prize in Turin, in 1993, a reporter asked me: 'What's your opinion of marriage, bringing up children, and love?'

'I'm not against the institution of marriage, though I wouldn't want to start a family. As for children, they're around everywhere, there's no need to insist that they be from your loins or mine specifically.'

These days, Paul Bowles is allergic to the sun, though he used to adore the suns of the desert and tropical climes. He hasn't gone swimming in the sea for years, despite living close to some beautiful pristine beaches. He contents himself nowadays with inhaling the odor of iodine, when his driver takes him past the lighthouse at Cape Spartel. His illness has deprived him of all the things he loves. His skin has become ultra-sensitive, and sunstroke soon lays him low. So he now shuns the sun, his one-time god, which he hasn't soaked up since the days when he made the characters in his books, and even his traveling companions, expose themselves to it, whether they wanted to or not. Paul has seen many things, and these days he doesn't want, or is unable, to see anything more. He has reached the point of satiation. For him to desire anything now, it would need to be unspeakably seductive, or marvelous. But the magical days are gone, destroyed by the population explosion, by wars, economic crises, and the collapse of social values and liberal governments. And then, there are no longer any steamships.

Among the people who were picnicking not far from us, I recognized the Gérofi family, Isabelle and Yvonne.

'I'm going to say hello to them', I said to Paul.

He discouraged me, gently.

'No, don't do that. People get away from town to unwind a little, but also to get away from other people.'

He's right, I thought. You've got to be Bedouin in the desert and civilized in the town. Ever since I've lived in the city, I've still hung on to my Bedouin ways. I remain faithful to our traditions. No sooner do we set eyes on each other, in town or elsewhere, than we rush to embrace, sometimes several times in a single day.

It's a lovely day, neither too warm nor too cool. Paul's driver, Abdel Wahid, has wandered away from us. He drifts in and out of our vision as we continue to translate the pages of *For Bread Alone*. Abdel Wahid once asked me: 'Are a lot of foreigners really interested in the stories that you and Mrabet recite to Paul for him to translate?'

'I don't just recite. I write what I have to write; it's for others to decide whether to read it or not.'

'I don't understand.'

'I don't know how to explain it to you any better.'

'But Mrabet doesn't write, he only recites.'

'Yes, but Paul writes it down, and adapts it in such a way that people can read it.'

On the way back, Abdel Wahid buys some eggs from a young mountain boy standing on the edge of the road. We drink tea in a small café whose owner has known Paul for a long time. Its clients are all *kif* smokers and excellent at telling stories. Tangier these days only inspires them with feelings of regret and alienation.

January 17, 1993

Sex, according to Paul, is a lot of effort for small gain.
Tolstoy thought the same. One should only copulate in
order to reproduce. But Paul goes so far as to deny the
reproductive instinct itself. All a man can hope for is to
save himself from the futility of existence, even if it be
through deviance. Once we have entered life, the only
thing we can do is struggle to disengage ourselves from
this polluted existence. Here the extent of his nihilism
is clear; because, if there were this error, this imbalance
at the very start of our existence, then we wouldn't be to
blame for our inability to understand ourselves.

I visited Paul today with Hans and Rubio. Paul was in
bed, very tired. There was a little table in the middle of
the room, covered in medicines. Abd el Wahab (a young
man I saw at his place for the first time) helped him to sit
up in bed. When I introduced Rubio to Paul by saying

that he was from Tafraout, he cried out: 'Ah! I was there in the forties. I really liked its Wednesday market.'

'And the rock whose peak looks like Napoleon's hat?' asked Rubio.

Paul went on: 'I remember the racket the foxes made at night, when they attacked the stray dogs. The foxes always won and the dogs would run away whining and howling. [He imitates them.] Awww ... Awwww ... Are the foxes still there?'

'*Abghoughen*? [Rubio uses the Berber word for foxes.] Yes. But not as many as before. There are still some in the mountains far away from the villages, but they're too scared to come any nearer. Today in Tafraout you're more likely to see *boutaggant* (wild boar), *anzidh* (squirrels), and *tharoucht* (polecats).'

Paul, his interest aroused, remarked: 'The world has changed a lot everywhere.'

I started to sweat. The logs in the fireplace crackled. Even at the peak of summer, Paul tries to keep himself warm with a fire. He says that he is always cold. I never heard him complain of the heat, either indoors or out. In front of the fireplace there is a row of plastic bottles filled with water, probably to absorb the humidity. Hans wanted to take some photos of Paul, but he had to excuse himself, saying the state of his health wouldn't allow it. His memory is still intact, his eyes lively and bright, but, as I noticed since the start of the 1970s, he has a problem with his hearing. I banish from my mind the idea that he might be using this disability to his advantage.

When we left, Rubio said to me: 'Amazing, that man!'

'Why?'

'He still remembers in detail things that happened fifty years ago, but he forgot the rock in Tafraout whose peak looks like a lion's head.'

'Maybe he never saw it.'

'Impossible. All the tourists who visit Tafraout know the rock that looks like a lion's head.'

'In my opinion, it's the lion that looks like the rock. In any case, Paul Bowles doesn't do tourism like others do.'

'What does he do, then?'

'He may not know what other tourists know, but it could be that he knows things that they don't.'

'You writers don't talk the same way as everyone else!' says Rubio in exasperation.

Hans asks me what we are talking about.

'About a rock that all the tourists who visit Tafraout know, but Bowles doesn't, or he forgot it.'

'Whether he knew it or not, it's only a rock.'

Rubio is getting worked up: 'Not at all, Monsieur Hans. It's a very important rock. Everyone who sees it is amazed by its shape.'

Hans laughs and says no more.

June 6, 1993

I push open the door of the Cosmopolita.[1] Because of its small size, like the Hole in the Wall bar,[2] six or seven people would fill it completely. Virginie has never been here before; but I've invited her and she's agreed to come with me. At eighteen years, she is ready for anything. Temsamani is there in a corner, looking like a kindly marabou stork. In front of him sits a small bottle of wine. It looks as if that isn't the first, for his face is as red as a cherry. He is daydreaming, but pulls himself together when he sees us approaching, and welcomes us. After several drinks, we lead him back to his memories of Paul Bowles, Jane, and the rest of the group: Brion Gysin, Tennessee Williams, William Burroughs, Truman

---

1 The most famous bar of its time, established by the singer Antonio Sevilla in 1927, it was originally a small club for artists.

2 Another bar even smaller than the first, established by Madame La Marquise.

Capote, and the others. I tell him about my book on the Bowleses and their coterie. He is quiet for quite a while, and I let him be. At last, he begins to speak – in English, for Virginie's benefit.

'Paul, Jane, Ahmed Yacoubi, and Mrabet. Ah! Those were the days!'

Slowly, he empties his glass. He has a charming way of fighting off tiredness by recounting his memories. Temsamani's manners are impeccable. He hasn't been corrupted by this other civilization into which he fell unexpectedly. He lives in the village of Briyich. He invites me and Virginie to his place. We accept the invitation for another day. He's nice to her, like a father. When she asks him if Paul had really killed Jane's cat by pushing it from the edge of a window in his fourth-floor apartment, he answers her sharply: 'Never! Paul might be capable of cruelty, but only in his books, as I've heard him say. In truth, he was a good man. Literary imagination is another thing entirely. Everyone is free to imagine whatever they like.'

'It was Larbi Yacoubi who told me that story,' I tell him.

'Listen! Larbi Yacoubi is our friend, yes, but what he says about Paul isn't true. He doesn't know Paul the way I know him. It's true that I haven't read his books, but I've heard a lot about them. I speak English, but I can't read it, apart from letters.'

Virginie asks: 'You knew all of Paul's old friends.

What's your opinion of Jack Kerouac?' (She admires Kerouac to the point of worship.)

He emptied his glass in one shot, then answered: 'Ah! That one, I knew him well. He could sense things before they happened. Very intelligent. Paul would be disconcerted by his spontaneous way of speaking. When I asked Paul about it he told me he didn't consider him to be much of a writer. Kerouac, like the rest of his generation, was a young man rebelling against his family and society, but he wasn't mature. This is what Paul told me. But his personality impressed me because he was simple and didn't overcomplicate things. With Burroughs, for example, it was a different story. He was always in his shell. [He is silent for a moment, taking another mouthful of wine.] How exquisite it is, the drink before the last! [He looks at Virginie, then at me.] Listen. I'll tell you both something before I go. Paul taught me many things. He has his tastes and I have mine, but I still respect him. He sees things from afar, and all his predictions about his friends' futures have turned out to be true.'

I asked: 'And Mrabet, what do you have to say about him now that he's no longer on intimate terms with Paul?'

'Paul is like Jane, neither of them ever knew how to choose Moroccan friends. I asked him a few weeks ago, the last time I visited him: "Hasn't he come even once since he left?" Paul said: "No, and there's no reason for him to come, because he no longer works for me."'

Bowles's birthday in 1994 is being celebrated at Mrabet's place, despite the estrangement between them, in the traditional Moroccan way: a group of Jilala musicians, and the slaughtering of a sheep. To Pedro,[1] Paul is singing the praises of his driver Abdel Wahid: his dependability, his excellent care of him, his good cooking. At this, Mrabet,[2] sitting nearby, says: 'Señor Paul [they always speak in Spanish], I, too, did the same for you, and better.'

Paul replies, with his well-known icy coldness: 'I don't think so. You did nothing for me. You only worked at my house when it suited you.'

Mrabet became absorbed in the music, so Pedro said to Bowles: 'But you were such close friends.'

'With whom? Mrabet? That's not true. He was never my friend.'

'What was he then?'

'He was an employee like all of those who worked for me.'

---

1 A young Spanish painter.
2 Mrabet is a very good cook.

July 22, 1993

I drop in on Paul Bowles accompanied by Pedro. Abdel
Wahid receives us. We find Paul lying in bed, fatigued.
After we've exchanged greetings, he says to us: 'You see me
here a prisoner. I'm just waiting for death now.' I thought
to myself: yes, he surely will die one day or another,
but he won't have to suffer the painful deaths that he
bestowed on so many of the heroes of his novels and
stories. Resolved to stir up a little life in him, I venture:
'Señor Paul, don't you think that by giving yourself so
wholeheartedly to music and writing you might have
contributed a little to the paralysis that took hold of Jane,
disabling her from finishing any of the books she started
to write?'

'That was her problem, not mine. I didn't interfere in
her life, except in things that concerned her health, or
when I saw that she was running into a danger she wasn't

aware of. In the end, I left her to do what she wanted with her life. I never arrived at the point where I thought I might force her to do something against her will.'

'But it's well known that you refused to accept that she should die and be buried as a Christian.'

'This is true. Jane was originally Jewish, of Bulgarian descent. What happened is that the nuns managed to convince her to convert to Catholicism. They plied her with pressure day after day, and, thanks to her weakened physical and emotional state, they gained the upper hand. But I don't think she really embraced Catholicism. She was forced to. I had to go to her aid. Moreover, once when I visited her and found a cross around her neck, I didn't say a thing to the good sisters. All that mattered to me was that they should take good care of her. I was always happy with Jane, whatever people say.'

I felt that Paul was very much affected by these recollections, but I didn't forbear from further probing:

'Jane said that when you were busy pursuing your musical and literary compositions, she felt insignificant, as if her light was dying out. What were your feelings toward her as a creative writer? And I'm not saying as a rival ...'

'I appreciated her talent. I don't feel at all to blame for what she wasn't able to accomplish in her writings, or in her life. She alone was responsible for herself and her literary ambitions. She achieved some of them, while some of them remained where they were – in the land of dreams. In my opinion, each of us must be responsible for our successes and our failures. It's true that I helped her correct her mistakes of grammar and punctuation, but this wasn't a big deal. Any language teacher could have done that. She knew this, too, and told me as much, but she wanted me to be the one who took charge of it. Jane gave me a good deal of happiness, and we were rarely at loggerheads, no matter what the rumors spread about us say. Jane had her own unique writing gift, and it's absurd to compare her writings with mine. We each had our ideas, and wrote accordingly. There was never any rivalry or jealousy between us, either in life or in literature. We shared the same affection for certain of our friends, whatever their sexual leanings, their moral principles, or their artistic ideas. One time I advised her not to show anyone the manuscript of *Two Serious Women*, riddled as it was with faults. But she just shrugged her shoulders, saying: "If I happen upon a publisher, he'll take care of those things (meaning correcting the technical aspects of the writing). They don't publish a book because the grammar's correct, Mr Pessimist."'

'Señor Paul, people say that since Jane's death you haven't written anything comparable to the kind of things you liked to write before. And they say that that's when you turned to recording and adapting the stories of your young Moroccan friends.'

'I don't deny that Jane's presence with me was a big motivating stimulus, an incentive for me to continue writing, but when she became sick another trajectory in writing opened up for me. I don't regret it. It was another experience. Jane always thought that only one of us had to be a writer. I didn't agree with her on that. The issue here doesn't have anything to do with whose talent was superior or inferior. It was more like a gift from her, as if she were saying: "You work because you're more capable and disciplined than me. I was born to live on my own terms, but they wanted me to live on theirs, so in the end all of us failed, both me and them" (she means her family). It's true that she found it hard to knuckle down and discipline herself, but many of the writings that she tore up I thought were very good. But that was Jane. Who could stop her from doing or not doing anything? I've never blamed her. She was tremendous company. In the life they share together, a couple has to learn to love each other, even in the very depths of disharmony.'

Jane was fifty-six when she died; for the last sixteen years of her life she had been ill. She was buried in the San Miguel cemetery in Malaga, in an unmarked grave.¹ Because it's a Catholic cemetery, a cross has to be placed on the grave. But Paul didn't put a cross on Jane's grave, because she herself wavered in her conversion. He says:

---

1 On November 13, 1996, Jane's body was re-interred in the cemetery of Marbella. One of her female admirers took charge of the removal – at her own expense, and with Paul's agreement – once she discovered that Jane's remains were scheduled to be placed in a common grave, in order to allow the construction of a highway through the old cemetery.

'There'll be no grave for me. I don't believe in cemeteries or graves. What good are they? So one can cry over death? Or overcome it? Transcend it? One can never defeat death. It'll always be with us. In any case, I can't get rid of death, as that would deprive me of my connection to the world. I think I've lived vicariously, in every aspect of my life, without being aware of it. And when I can no longer live through someone, or even without them, I will no longer be in life.'[1]

Fortunately, Paul fears death like everyone else, without turning it into a personal tragedy. At the same time, he has no regrets, even if he's hurt some people through his behavior, or through his books, replete as they are with all manner of evil, atrocity, and violent death. Moreover, he never took a vow of piety, and so has no need to seek forgiveness for anything.

During all the years that Bowles has lived in Morocco, he has been possessed by a single idea: he is a foreigner, and no one can get along with him. In an interview with Jesus Ruiz Mantilla for the newspaper *El País* (May 30, 1995), he says of Moroccans: 'They don't accept me, they'll never accept me. For them, I'll always be a foreigner.' In the same interview, he issues a warning about Islam, and affirms that the coming century will witness a confrontation between Muslims and the West.

---

1 Michelle Green, *The Dream at the End of the World: Paul Bowles and the Literary Renegades in Tangier* (New York: Harper Perennial, 1992), p. 344.

This alleged hostility of Moroccans toward him was nothing but a figment of his imagination. Wherever he was, as is well known, he always lived in a state of siege and paranoia. He saw spies everywhere, along with thieves and wicked ones who wanted to deprive him of everything he had, and of whom he spoke with awe. Paul was miserly in the extreme, which he had every right to be. He didn't, however, have the right to commandeer the profits from the publishing rights of my books that he had translated, without giving me any share in them. I never received a cent from these books, apart from the meager advance I was allowed when the contract was signed. What's more, in each of these contracts, he collared 50 per cent of the translation rights!

When I was in the habit of visiting him several times a week, I found that he had few visitors. Today he's inundated with them. They bear down on him, to take down his words, while he rarely leaves his bed. This is much like what they did to Tolstoy, when he left his family in order to seek a quiet conclusion to his life, far from the wife whose one desire was to take over his authorial copyrights and the lands he had bequeathed to the poverty-stricken serfs. Paul, though, never aspired to become a saint in a country whose people he considered to be barbarian, backward, and simple-minded. He had a horror of poverty, which he had a right to do, but he didn't have the right to despise the poor. His fortune amounts, according to Pedro, to more than 700,000 dollars, which he has entrusted to a bank, to invest the money and donate the profits to help artistic and other foundations. These days, people come to see him from all over the world.

It's not unusual to find half a dozen journalists in his home, interviewing him in English, French, and Spanish. His sense of propriety won't allow him to turn anyone away, unless it's someone who's visited him before and aggravated him with questions he didn't like. Mrabet, if he was there, took on the job of showing the door to any undesirable visitor, or to anybody he personally disliked, even if Paul had agreed to see them. What would really irritate Paul was to be asked for a loan, no matter how paltry the amount. He would swallow with difficulty several times, look at the supplicant in embarrassment, grow pale, then lower his eyes in thought before either agreeing reluctantly or refusing with exaggerated politeness. When I was working as a teacher, I sometimes needed to borrow some money from him. At the end of the month, he couldn't wait to remind me: 'Don't forget that you owe me ...' and of course the amount was never more than fifty or a hundred dirhams. When Norman Glass, a fellow writer in need of help, asked him for 300 dollars, Paul refused, sending him a letter filled with apologies, prevarications, and aphorisms (December 16, 1968): 'In any case, I can only write you my decision and hope that you don't take it amiss. I have friendship to give, but not money. Others have more money than friendship, some have both, some have neither. But anyway.'[1]

In his visitors' presence, Paul displays his deep intelligence, which flashes forth from him without any showing off. He is witty, ironic, and frank, but can be reserved if he needs to be. He offers his opinion freely, and doesn't quibble over minor details. If the discussion becomes too acrimonious, he attempts to lower the tension with some conciliatory words. He joins in with everything, but won't take a position on anything. He always believes he's being cheated, so when he sees someone other than himself being swindled, he takes comfort in the fact that he's not the only one.

I went with Tennessee Williams to Louise de Meuron's house. There was quite a crowd of guests there. I hadn't been invited, but I went along because I was in good company. Besides, I was broke again, and couldn't face the prospect of returning to my own place without having eaten something and knocked back a few drinks.

A couple of days before he was due to leave Tangier, Tennessee invited me to dine with him at the Djinina restaurant, with Paul, Mrabet, and Abdel Wahid. Naturally, Tennessee would foot the bill. I think that Paul's avarice is pathological: he puts money aside so as to not be poor, but, since he never spends it, he lives in a state of permanent indigence.

1 Bowles, *In Touch*, p. 419.

Once I asked him: 'Why do you publish your books with thieving editors like Peter Owen?'

'Because I don't have a choice. I'm not living over there, and I can't control things from far away. Most publishers are scoundrels, anyway. When you're not on the spot, they can do what they want. There's nothing you can do about it.'

I said to myself: Señor Bowles, you're a bloody liar. For the publishing rights of his books and mine, William Morris, his literary agent, was sending him hard cash, or copies of the checks that he'd deposited directly into his bank account in New York. At that time, I didn't have a cent, and I didn't even know that literary agents existed. This is another of life's miseries reserved exclusively for the third world. People profit from your ignorance by pretending that they're going to blazon your name, and the names of other gifted but unknown artists, across the world. They behave as if they have to perform an act of kindness and altruism, instead of simply giving talent its due, and treating it fairly. Paul wrote to Carol Ardman (November 19, 1972): 'Choukri comes every day. He and Mrabet have a new custom, which is to eat together in the Petit Socco every night. What this presages, I can't imagine at present. But I imagine that if anyone is to influence anyone (literarily), it will be M. influencing C.'[1]

First of all, I don't know where Bowles got this story

1 Bowles, *In Touch*, p. 446.

about our dining together. I've never eaten with Mrabet at the Petit Socco. Occasionally we would go to the bars on the boulevard to have some fun with the barmaids and hostesses, recalling with some of them the good times we'd enjoyed in the past. Further, when Bowles talks about influence, his conjecture is off the mark. Mrabet has his world, and I have mine. But, confined to his room, Bowles gets carried away by his imagination, and frequently invents no matter what. I state categorically, and not for the first time, that Paul Bowles has been deeply influenced by the tales and stories of Mrabet, and by his manner of telling them – sometimes to the point of imitating Mrabet, and even of identifying with him.

Paul Bowles enjoys the privilege of being American wherever he goes: but I, according to him and his buddies, can be Moroccan only in Morocco. On the covers of my books, the ones I dictated to him, his name is linked with mine, and written in characters the same size as mine, as if he was the co-author. It's possible that an editor like Peter Owen would engage in this underhand practice for his own commercial ends, but Bowles, the famous writer, wasn't ashamed to endorse such skullduggery, and didn't have the decency to oppose it, telling me instead that it would help me become famous! Far from feeling ashamed, he went so far as to place his name beside mine on the copyright page: 'Copyright Mohamed Choukri and Paul Bowles'! He did the same with Mrabet, but Mrabet had been a close friend of his for a long time, and managed to recover his right in his own way. I, however, always remained outside the circle, and kept my distance from its *habitués*.

In the last few years, R. has become the literary agent of Mrabet and Rodrigo Rey Rosa,[1] and, at Mrabet's suggestion, he has also become mine.

R. found out about Bowles's acts of embezzlement from Mrabet, who showed him the contracts that Bowles had typed out himself, in English, and which I'd trustingly signed. He also showed him the photocopies of the checks Bowles had received in his name. When R. asked Bowles to explain these misappropriations, Bowles replied with his usual icy sarcasm: 'Well, Choukri is a drunk, what is he going to do with the money other than ruin his health, ruin his writing and produce less!? When he doesn't have any money he writes better and devotes himself to his work. I know him well enough and I've been told a lot about him.'

This is the kind of rotten thing that Paul Bowles, the 'wise man', says about me. But that's him all over. All his life, he's never had anything but scorn for others – for the characters in his books just as much as for those who have kept him company and looked up to him all these years.

---

1 A young writer from Guatemala who lived in Tangier for years. He translated some of Bowles's stories into Spanish, so Paul Bowles followed suit and translated his stories into English. It's probable that this close friend of Bowles will inherit the publishing rights of all his writings, as R., the source of the rumor, told me.

That said, there are certain of his writings that I regard very highly; a feeling that is, I think, reciprocated. But that's another story.

August 6, 1993

Around four in the afternoon, Paul Bowles passes in front of the Negresco bar. I get up to greet him. His voice sounds choked. He's in pain. He's on his way to the dentist, and walks slowly, leaning to the left. Abdel Wahid holds him by the right arm. I return to my table, overlooking the street. And, sipping my whisky, I meditate on the hardships of growing old.

October 28, 1993

Accompanied by Ibrahim El Khatib, I pay Paul a visit at around five in the afternoon. When we arrive, he has already dined. He is in the bathroom, bent double. No doubt the pain from his sciatica is troubling him again. When he returns to his bedroom, Abdel Wahid and I help to lay him on the bed. Ibrahim, who is interested in Paul's work and reads all he can about him, talks with Paul in Spanish about some literary studies on the translations of his books. Then Paul turns to me: 'What's new?'

What he wants to know is where I've got to in my work. I've already told him that I'm writing a book about him and about Tangier in general.

'I've got to page 107.'

'I look forward to reading what you've written about me.'

In fact, he doesn't seem enthralled at the idea of my

writing a book about him. One day, he said to Pedro: 'I wonder what Choukri can find to write about me. He doesn't know my family, and knows practically nothing about my life.'

When I tell him that I'm in the process of reading *Paul Bowles: An Invisible Spectator*, Christopher Sawyer-Lauçanno's biography of him, his face creases in disgust: 'It's a petty book. It was maliciously written. Its author asked me to cooperate with him when he visited me while he was writing it and I refused. I was preoccupied with other important things, and my health wasn't good enough for me to answer all his wide-ranging questions about my life and work. I abhor that book. I couldn't finish reading it because he falsifies all the particulars of my life and I find it deeply offensive. He interprets the facts however he wants. He's a contemptible person.'

In a letter to Regina Weinreich, Paul said he regretted not having poisoned Sawyer-Lauçanno the first time he laid eyes on him. Ibrahim asked to be given something to remember him by. Paul responded somewhat reservedly: 'What would you like me to give you exactly?'

'One of your books with an inscription.'

'But that would require me to get up and look for one. Choukri can take care of that.'

Ibrahim handed him five copies of a group of stories (*The Garden*) that he had translated from English into Arabic, and said: 'When I read these stories, I thought that translating them would be easy, but once I'd begun I realized it would not be so straightforward.'

'That's true. Everyone who translates my stories says the same thing.'

Paul asked me to go and ferret out a book from the next room. Abdel Wahid helped me rummage through a heap of books piled up on a table. I came upon *The Sheltering Sky* in a Spanish translation. I took it to Paul, and he signed it with the inscription: 'I thank you for translating my stories.'

Paul is delighted to see his stories translated into Arabic. I have a copy of *Let It Come Down* with me, and I ask him if he would mind signing it. He says: 'What, it's enough for me to just sign it?'

'As you like.'

He writes: 'To Mohamed Choukri, with my admiration.'

Paul is having difficulty breathing. He looks a lot worse than the last time I saw him. For the first time I notice a television set in his room; yet, since I've known him, he's always despised television. Later I was told that Claudio Bravo had given it to him as a gift. What did he watch on it? It's one of his secrets.

Once Paul said to me: 'Before, when I had a telephone, the calls would annoy me, because people would call to see if they could visit or not, but today it's even worse, and more awkward. When I open the door to whoever's knocking, I find that I'm compelled to let them in. Would they believe me if I told them I was busy or tired?'

I indicate to Ibrahim that it's time for us to go. This evening, Paul seems really exhausted.

Once outside, I say to Ibrahim: 'So he's finally given you a copy of *The Sheltering Sky*. It's "a delicate prey"!'[1]

Ibrahim made no comment, contenting himself with a short, enigmatic laugh.

---

[1] A reference to one of Bowles's stories.

March 6, 1994

I leave my place around eleven o'clock in the morning, at rather a loose end, not knowing what to do with myself. I've just spent a long time staring up at my ceiling, and I'd seemed to see the message there that what is called true love can only be achieved through dreaming of, and experiencing, the pleasure of betrayal, when an unknown voice called me on the telephone:

'Hallo! Mohamed Choukri?'

'Yes.'

'I'm the girl from the future!'

'Congratulations!'

'Get me connected, you pimp!'

'Go and find someone else to plug your festering holes, you plague-ridden hag!'

In front of the Café de Paris, I meet Ramon and his girl. They're on their way to visit Antonio Fuentes, the painter, who asked them yesterday to buy two loaves of black bread for him. I agree to go along with them. It's years since I've seen him. He buys his meals from a small restaurant near his house. When he ventures a little further, he seldom goes beyond the Petit Socco. He's always on his own. I only spoke to him once, during one of his exhibitions in the sixties.

'I'm sure he won't have us come into his house today', says Ramon. 'We went only yesterday. Even his closest friends he only receives at long intervals. Anyone who wants to buy a painting from him has to go there with someone he knows, but he won't receive more than three persons at the same time – and never before eleven in the morning, or if there's any fog around. And if the prospective buyer doesn't buy a painting, he'll never be allowed in again. He's nearly ninety, and he's still got the memory of an elephant.'

The paint on the old door has faded to a nondescript shade. Ramon knocks several times and shouts: 'It's Ramon and Sonia!'

He's wearing a woolen bonnet. His face has been colonized by white hairs; it's evidently several days since it last saw a razor. Ramon introduces me to him:

'A Moroccan writer.'

'You're from Tangier. That's good!'

He turns to Ramon and Sonia: 'He's an artist. I see it in his face. There's something very distinctive about it!'

Maybe it's my hooknose that's aroused his interest,

I think to myself. He glances at two workmen who are whitewashing the walls of the New Mosque, calling down God's help and blessing upon them. He greets everyone who passes in Moroccan Arabic: '*Allah ya'aouanak* (God be with you).' Then he explains to us: 'For Moroccans, work is sacred. To work and to pray, it's the same thing.'

Ramon offers him the two loaves of bread wrapped in a plastic bag. Fuentes says: 'It doesn't matter; it's bread, after all. But it's not the real black bread that I know. You can still get it in the Grand Socco. Only it's a little more expensive than the regular adulterated black bread, and you have to know where to buy it.'

We say goodbye to him and leave.

Ramon remarks: 'He hardly goes out anymore. It's the children of the quarter and the neighbors who bring him what he needs. Cleanliness horrifies him. His dusty furniture, all piled up, is infested with rats and mice. Some of his canvases have been ruined by the humidity. One day the Spanish consul and his wife offered to have his place refurbished – the walls repainted, and so forth. He was indignant, as if someone were trying to take something from him by force: "Everything you see here is going to remain the way it is. That's my way of life, and I've grown used to it."'

I say to Ramon: 'I heard that he's very rich and miserly.'

'He once told me: "The two most marvelous things man has invented are art and money."'

'Who's he leaving his wealth to?'

'It's said that a bank in Tangier will have the responsibility of investing it. To what end? Nobody knows what he wrote in his will.'[1]

I remark: 'He's a bit like Paul Bowles, who's lived a pauper and will die rich.'

Some of Bowles's stories that were inspired by the Moroccan environment are based on *Es'heur* – not *Tseuheur*, as Bowles pronounces and writes it – meaning a light kind of magic based on deception, and invoked by an incantation written on a piece of paper, an egg, or an everyday object. It's also based on *Ettoukal* – not *Tsoukil*, as Bowles says it – which is 'something eaten or drunk', and given to someone without their knowing it. This particular magic is witchcraft pure and simple, and its goal is to subjugate a person physically and spiritually. It aims at complete submission, and even paralysis, which may be partial or total – depending on the amount of ingredients absorbed. It can lead to death, as can be seen in the story 'The Wind at Beni Midar'. The lightest of its effects is amnesia, as in the story 'The Garden'.[2] *Es'heur* by incantation is practiced by men who have studied in Qur'anic school, and whom the uneducated wrongly call *fuqaha*. *Ettoukal*, on the other hand, is practiced mainly by women who can't read or write. The type of 'witchcraft'

---

1 He died in the summer of 1995. They found 4,000 dirhams in his house and several drawings and oil paintings of little value.

2 Two of Bowles's stories.

story that Bowles was inspired by traditional Moroccan culture to write are generally well-known tales, but when told amongst a group of *kif* smokers or eaters of *majoun* they have a distinctly bewitching effect.

Majoun doesn't feature in Bowles's short stories, except for the terrifying 'Allal'. Maybe this is because the effect of the drug, as evidenced in the events of *Let It Come Down,* is infinitely more hellish, and because its preparation requires special skill and attention. Also its cost – unlike *kif*, which is widely affordable – is out of range for many people. The Moroccan characters in Bowles's stories are usually poor, and *majoun* is an extravagant luxury. As exemplified in 'A Friend of the World' and 'The Fqih', trickery, deception, roguery, revenge, and terror are the things generally brought forth by sorcery, *kif*, and *majoun*. Perhaps what the protagonist of the story 'Madame and Ahmed' says epitomizes the prevailing theme in these stories as a group: 'Everybody plays tricks nowadays, Madame. Everybody.'[1] Deceit, fear, distrust, despair, and murder: these are the subjects that regularly nourish Bowles's writings.

In some of his Moroccan stories and memoirs, Bowles shows a fascination, in a way that is almost mystical, with the voice of the muezzin. But he believes the loudspeakers that predominate today have caused the call to prayer to lose much of its beauty, reverence, and charm. This is a

---

1 Paul Bowles, 'Madame and Ahmed', in *The Stories of Paul Bowles*, p. 508.

legitimate observation, and one with which I tend to agree. But I would very much like to know from which source he took the following edict about women in Islam, related in his story 'Tea on the Mountain':

> With the passing of the day the countryside had attained complete silence. From the distance she could hear a faint but clear voice singing. She looked at Mjid.
>
> 'The muezzin? You can hear it from here?'
> 'Of course. It's not so far to the Marshan. What good is a country house where you can't hear the muezzin? You might as well live in the Sahara.'
> 'Shh. I want to listen.'
> 'It's a good voice, isn't it? They have the strongest voices in the world.'
> 'It always makes me sad.'
> 'Because you're not of the faith.'
> She reflected a minute and said: 'I think that's true.' She was about to add: 'But your faith says women have no souls.'[1]

Paul Bowles disclosed to me one day the pain he felt at still being considered by Moroccans to be not a resident but a tourist, albeit one who has extended his stay longer than most.

When his driver Abdel Wahid brings him his mail, while still in the car, where he has been waiting for

---

1 Paul Bowles, 'Tea on the Mountain', in *The Stories of Paul Bowles*, pp.138–9.

him, the first thing Bowles does is search the letters for checks.

'I don't have a family anymore. Everyone who I once knew has died. Fortunately, this keeps me from having to go to America. I surrender to fate.'[1] Paul Bowles has always been hesitant about returning to America, afraid that his passport might be confiscated, because of his communist past. On February 17, 1996, he wrote to James Leo Herlihy: 'And about the hatred of America: naturally I mask it.'[2] Today, with his illness, his Sphinx-like reserve, and his international renown, he no longer has anything to fear.

With the passing of time, Paul's distinct style began to be influenced by his translations from Moroccan Arabic. This is particularly noticeable in the tales that one could label 'Moroccan'. Some of Mrabet's Moroccan friends, who had listened to his tape recordings and compared them to the printed translations that Bowles had made of them, told him that Bowles hadn't been very faithful in his adaptations. This made Mrabet livid with anger. The strange thing is that Paul erased all the copies of his recordings with Mrabet.

What happened was that Bowles had thought it would be easy to 'transform' the stories related by Mrabet. He forgot that story-telling is first and foremost a matter of style, and not simply a question of delivering a story

---

1 From the film *An American in Tangier*.
2 Bowles, *In Touch*, p. 381.

orally that could just as well be given in writing. Jane was opposed to Bowles devoting himself to this activity. She wanted him to write his own books, not record the recitations of others. For her, this was not the proper work of a writer.

In the evening, I meet Guillermo Carlos, a 'mystic', who's been around the world. We're drinking at the Negresco, and he says: 'Throughout the world, there are still people in a state of innocence. The authentic Moroccan face expresses this innocence, but the Moroccan lacks a self-reflecting mirror, where he could see his true self, instead of the distorted version that he keeps seeing in the mirrors of others. He's a little lacking in self-awareness. Fascinated and dazzled by modern technology, he's lost his points of reference. Today culture has become global, but Morocco has still a role to play: it can bring forth human innocence to the attention of the world.'

I never saw Guillermo again after that. Perhaps he returned to one of his caves!

Bowles, intentionally or not, resembles the protagonist of his story, 'If I Should Open My Mouth':

> Traffic moves past at some distance from where I am reclining on the ground under the trees. The time – timeless. I know there are streets full of people behind the trees, but I will never be able to touch them. If I should open my mouth to cry out, no sound would come forth. Or if I should

stretch my arms toward one of the figures that occasionally wanders along the path nearby, that would have no effect, because I am invisible. It is the terrible contradiction that is unbearable: being there and yet knowing that I am not there, for in order to *be,* one must not only be to one's self: it is absolutely imperative that one be for others. One must have a way of basing one's being on the certainty that others know one is there. I am telling myself that somewhere in this city Mrs Crawford is thinking of me.[1]

Elsewhere, Paul Bowles has elucidated how he came to embark on a literary career, after achieving fame as a composer and a music critic for the *Herald Tribune*:

I had been reading some ethnographic books with texts from the Arapesh or from the Tarahumara given in word-for-word translation. Little by little the desire came to me to invent my own myths, adopting the point of view of the primitive mind. The only way I could devise for stimulating that state was the old Surrealist method of abandoning conscious control and writing whatever words came from the pen. First, animal legends resulted from the experiments and then tales of animals disguised as 'basic human' beings. One rainy Sunday I awoke late, put a thermos of coffee by my bedside, and began to write another of these myths. No one disturbed me, and I wrote on until I had finished

1 Paul Bowles, 'If I Should Open My Mouth', in *The Stories of Paul Bowles*, pp. 230–1.

it. I read it over, called it 'The Scorpion,' and
decided that it could be shown to others. When
View published it, I received compliments and
went on inventing myths. The subject matter
of myths soon turned from 'primitive' to
contemporary, but the objectives and behavior
of the protagonists remained the same as in the
beast legends. It was through this unexpected
little gate that I crept back into the land of
fiction writing. Long ago I had decided that
the world was too complex for me ever to write
fiction; since I failed to understand life, I would
not be able to find points of reference which the
hypothetical reader might have in common with
me. When *Partisan Review* accepted 'A Distant
Episode,' even though I had already sold two
or three other tales to *Harper's Bazaar,* I was
triumphant: it meant that I would be able to go
on writing fiction.[1]

1 Paul Bowles, *Without Stopping*, pp. 261–2.

May 3, 1994

Around nine in the evening, I call on Paul, accompanied by Pedro. Paul has just finished eating. I ask him: 'Señor Paul, how are you?'

'As you see me, all alone.'

'But to live alone, a man must be either a genius or an idiot.'

He laughs thinly, and replies: 'And why not both together?'

May 8, 1994

This morning, Paul will fly to Paris, then to Atlanta, to have an operation to remove a cancerous growth. In the end, we're all scared of death. My dog Juba, though, never thinks about it.

September 16, 1994

This evening Natalya, a friend of mine who had just returned from Dakar, said that she had read somewhere that: 'When you first arrive in Africa, you can't wait to write a book about it. After several months you decide that an article will suffice, and at the end of a year you've not got the slightest wish to write anything at all.'

Eisenhower once said to the American people, 'Everything is for the best in this brave new world.'

Jane was always threatening to give up writing altogether, at times when she was unable to compose even the first sentence of a new work. A thousand projects jostled with each other in her head, but not one of them could find a way out. She was talented and intelligent, but, for want of will and determination, all her projects turned into illusions. Paul neither mapped out nor announced any of his projects, in contrast to Truman Capote, who planned what he was going to write, down to the last detail. Paul wrote in one go, rarely correcting what he'd put down on paper, or so he's always claimed. Jack Kerouac said the same thing,[1] although his publisher, Malcolm Cowley, has formally denied this, asserting that Kerouac altered, corrected, and fine-tuned his texts constantly, in an endless quest for perfection. It was as if the idea of revising texts and polishing them up would make them lose the aura of unsullied spontaneity that both Bowles and Kerouac wished to lay claim to.

In his novels and stories, Paul rarely uses first-person narration. He says: 'I don't want to be associated with my stories. I've always remained distant from them, except for three or four that are in the form of monologues or letters. In such cases, I had no choice but to use the first-person pronoun.' Thus Bowles confirms his belief that the writer must not introduce his personal life into his work. 'If one gives a lot of importance to a writer's life, that means his writing can't be up to much. One's personal life is a private affair; it doesn't concern anyone else. My past doesn't mean anything to me. It was full of meaning at the moment I was living it, but now it has no significance, for me or for anyone else.'

Today, like yesterday, Tangier continues to embody the goal of dreamers. Paul Bowles is a prime example of

---

1 It's said that he wrote his favorite novel, *The Dharma Bums*, in three or four weeks.

such people. To the Japanese, for example, suicide is not a defeat but a kind of victory. But Paul doesn't wish to be 'victorious'; he is withdrawing from the battle, physically and morally, when he writes: 'There's nothing left to wait for except death. I'm awaiting my death in Tangier. Nothing is more certain.' *'Mann muss nur sterben'*[1] ('man has one certainty, death'), as Daisy muses in her interior monologue in *Let It Come Down*.

Before his death, Antaeus wrestled with Hercules. Paul, however, has surrendered to fate, and now waits only for a death worthy of the literary artist he once was.

Jane Bowles loved people as they were, but people didn't love her as she was. She never disowned anyone, nor did she ever beg favors or compliments. To her, everyone was trustworthy, apart from the palpably insane. But by how many honest, warm, humane, kind, and intimate friends was she really embraced? She never really got along with anyone. Everything she loved most deeply would slip away from her; or she would purposely drive it away from her, in order to love it better. Her inability to establish stable relationships with her female Moroccan lovers only confirmed her in her false opinions. She forgot that, all over the world, love itself may be subject to negotiation, and that Moroccans are neither more nor less disloyal than any other group of two-legged, two-handed humans. In fact, Jane only loved

---

1 Bowles, *Let It Come Down*, p. 219.

what she couldn't have, or what was shrouded in the mist of the unknown. She possessed, or was possessed by, a kind of Buddhism mixed with nihilism: suffering, self-abandonment, and non-being. This was equally the case for Paul, with some significant exceptions.

In 1968, Jane reached the nadir of impotence in her writing. Affected by the deterioration in her health, Paul had stopped creating in his turn. I think it was Lamartine who wrote: 'Let one being be lost to you, and the whole world is lost.' Paul was compelled to wait for Jane's depression to reach its bitter anticlimax, perhaps as he had been waiting since the beginning, since their first meeting. Their destinies were welded together. Like Kit and Port in *The Sheltering Sky*, neither of them could live without the other. Of course, Paul had no regrets for staying with Jane right to the end, despite all the premonitions he had had since the beginning, but he hadn't anticipated the extent of the tragedy that would overwhelm her.

Based on my acquaintance with Paul, one that lasted nearly a quarter of a century, I think I can say that he never gave particular importance to what he, or any other writer, produced. The essential thing was that excellence should ultimately prevail and flourish. It was the high quality of a literary work that mattered, not who was producing it. This was a principle by which he always abided. I have rarely met a creative artist, major or minor, who renounced his artistic ego, his 'I,' with so much modesty and self-deprecation. It's one of his ineluctable qualities. He even let people create his legend in the way they wanted, a legend that eventually began to feed off itself, growing bigger by the day. Bowles could only go along with this, helping to cultivate the myth, and develop it in line with his chameleon-like contradictions, so that he wouldn't disappoint his admirers, or hurt their feelings.

Paul wrote in an effort to fight the banality of the daily life around him, and in the world in general. This is normal. But what would one think of the woman who uncovers her backside as if to show us, by this means, an image of the world; or, more probably, simply to show us her backside without any metaphorical intent? I think she would only do such a thing as a way of resisting an expected snowstorm, which, on its next attack, would continue to surprise with its whims and caprices: a storm sharp and merciless, carrying all before it. However noble the trace we leave behind us, it won't give more than an inkling of the mammoth struggle we underwent to create it. Who among us deserves immortality? Perhaps only the one who thought up the idea of immortality in the first place.

Today, Bowles constantly complains of the changes that have occurred in Tangier (and in the world as a whole, of course, near and far). In his opinion, only *el charqi*, the eastern wind, is always the same. He's not entirely wrong about that. Most of the people of Tangier, the Tangerines, live hemmed in by their tiny apartments, having sold their finest lands for a fraction of their worth.

El charqi continues to blow for two long months each year. Isaac Laredo says in his book *Memorias de un Viejo Tangerino*: 'In reality, the only things left of the genuine Tangier are the air and the wind. With the eruption of so much frenzied activity, shortly before 1939, and carrying on right up to the time of the troubles in 1952, everything changed. Even in the Kasbah, there is only one alleyway that has, miraculously, remained unchanged. The Muslims of Tangier, like people across the world, are mad about altering the shape and appearance of everything.'

Paul Bowles loved Morocco, particularly the Morocco of the 1930s, but he has never loved Moroccans. In which case, why did he think that Moroccans should make an effort to like him? At all events, he was adamant about remaining in this country, as he confirmed in a letter to James Leo Herlihy (October 4, 1972): 'Somehow I can't imagine getting myself across the Atlantic. At least, not unless I'm forced out of Morocco. (I don't really like the U.S., but don't tell anyone.)'[1] Here Bowles shares the sentiment of Henry Miller, who once said: 'Returning to New York, from another angle, was frightening. Because that city, in which I know every street, of which I have a book-like knowledge, and where so many of my friends are, has become the last place on the face of the earth to which I'd like to return. I'd prefer death to spending the rest of my days constrained in my birthplace.'

1 Bowles, *In Touch*, p. 445.

Bowles used to say in a high voice: 'Those strictly conservative Arabs are firmly convinced that Westerners only visit Morocco to mock the traditions and customs of a different country.' Today, however, it's little more than a rattle in the throat. Paul Balta[1] remarks: 'In the past, in the West's perception, the Arabs were courageous and noble; today they're considered lazy, deceitful, conservative, and malicious.'

The problem with Paul Bowles is that, despite being a seasoned traveler, when it comes to particular countries and their respective peoples, he hardly distinguishes between past and present. The future is nonexistent for him. In fact, what he wants is to live in a world that is static and primitive – but civilized! How could a people be civilized and primitive at the same time? Bowles never enlightened us with an answer.

This obsession with the dichotomy between the civilized and the savage is also noticeably present in most of the works of D. H. Lawrence, who was disappointed with Mexico, where he wrote *The Plumed Serpent*. Likewise, the utopianism of Aldous Huxley, who was preoccupied with the same struggle, as depicted in his novel *Brave New World*, came to the same sticky end. Most of Paul Bowles's writings are replete with an excessive nostalgia for the colonial era, in Morocco and elsewhere.

---

1 Director of the Center for Middle East Research.

July 11, 1995

I ran into Mrabet in front of the Spanish-Moroccan bank. I don't know whether he was waiting for someone, or just waiting for himself. His health deteriorates more and more. He's growing old gracelessly. We exchanged a few words about the miserable tourist season in Tangier this year, and about the crisis over water, the precious liquid that people have started to call 'white gold'. He gave me a wan smile.

August 21, 1995

Encarna dropped in on me this evening. She came straight from her visit with Mrabet, who has been suffering from stomach cancer for the past year. He is thinking of selling his small farm to cover the cost of an operation in Spain or Germany. When she told him that she was going to see me, he said: 'Tell him that I'm dying little by little. It's *maktoub*, predestined.'

August 23, 1995

Encarna visited Bowles this evening. He still smokes black cigarettes stuffed with *kif*. She told him that Mrabet's cancer was worse. His response was: 'He doesn't visit me anymore. I don't have any news of him, and I don't know any person who could give me any. He must be suffering a great deal, because he's always placed so much importance on his physical appearance.'

November 11, 1995

Pedro and Mrabet call on Paul, to ask him to help pay the expenses of Mrabet's operation in Germany. In principle, Bowles agrees to pay the hospital bills. Once Mrabet left, Paul says to Pedro: 'Jane was always afraid that the Moroccans would one day realize that I knew they were lying to me.'

Starting from 1950, Jane began to feel incapable of writing. At the end of January, she wrote to Paul from Paris: 'I do feel very strongly that I should give up writing if I can't get further into it than I have. I cannot keep losing it the way I do much longer.'[1] Paul, however, never once considered giving up writing. In a special issue of the French daily newspaper *Libération*, published in March 1985, there was a survey in which several writers, Paul Bowles among them, were asked the question, 'Why do

---

1 Jane Bowles, *Out in the World*, p. 150.

you write?' Bowles answered: 'I write because I'm still in the land of the living.' But there is another question that has not yet been asked of him: Would he have become a writer, in the broad sense, if he hadn't made Tangier his home, as Lawrence Durrell had made Alexandria his?

He confirmed his lack of national affiliation when he declared to Ammar al Joundi, in *el Wassat* magazine, March 1992: 'I'm not American nor am I Moroccan. I'm a visitor on earth. You have to be Muslim to really be accepted in Morocco, to be a part of it.' What would Peter Owen, who claims that Bowles knows Morocco better than any Moroccan, think of that?

In a letter to Charles Henri Ford (November 19, 1947), Paul explains why he's so keen to remain in Tangier: 'I haven't met any new friends in the few months I've been here. The reason is that I have a hovering feeling of not being really in Tangier at all. It is terribly changed, and I can't bear to try to imagine what it used to be like. Part of what it used to be like was of course what I used to be like, and since that too is gone, it seems that it would be needless torture to search for a past which has left no vestige. I've found I'm always happiest in a place I've never been before and about which I know nothing. There is absolutely no way to be again in a place. Whether or not it has changed, it's never the same. Isn't that true? And by never being the same one means of course, not being alive any more. Every place one revisits seems to have lost the life that made it exist the first time one knew it. Certainly

I never meant to stay in Tangier again, but for no reason at all I have remained on and on, perhaps because one can get everything one wants here and the life is cheap as dirt, and travel is so damned difficult ... visas for Spanish Morocco and currency restrictions for French Morocco, and suspicious men in the trains ... and mainly the great fact that I haven't the energy to pack up and go anywhere else.'[1]

Among John Hopkins's memories of Paul Bowles in his book *The Tangier Diaries* appears this:

> February 7, 1964
> Last night he [Paul Bowles] admitted to me he is not interested in flesh and blood characters, but in people as fictional expressions of ideas, etc. Situations and ideas interest him more than people, as they did Camus.[2]

And again:

> August 23, 1964
> Irving Rosenthal entered Paul's apartment, screamed, and covered his eyes with his hands.
> 'What's wrong?' Paul asked.
> 'That thing in the cage! What is it?'
> 'A parrot.'
> 'I've never seen one before! Take it away!'
> Ira Cohen: 'I know he is guilty, but I am not sure of what.'

---

1 Bowles, *In Touch*, pp. 179–80.
2 John Hopkins, *The Tangier Diaries: 1962-1979* (Tiburon-Belvedere: Cadmus Editions, 1998), p. 54.

> Norman Glass: 'Filing a lawsuit against his
> mother "for being a Jew"'.
> Tangier is a magnet for wandering artists and
> writers. They all migrate to Paul's apartment.[1]

Paul has always been intrigued and alarmed by sex. He's
always tended to disregard it, since for him it's linked to
debauchery. New England's puritanical traditions, which
he inherited, have a good deal to do with this reaction.
He wrote to Charles Henri Ford (November 19, 1947):
'You ask about Tangier's sex life. I have a feeling it is now
completely changed. I never knew it very well, even when
I was young.'[2]

He also recounts: 'At the age of nineteen I was
astonished one night to discover that I had just thrown
a meat knife at my father. I rushed out of the house,
shattering panes of glass in the front door, and began to
run down the hill in the rain. Before I had gone three
blocks Daddy caught up with me in the car, then parked
and came along behind me on foot. I stopped and turned
around to face him. "I want to talk to you," he said. "You
can't do this again to your mother. It wasn't my idea to
come after you."'[3]

As a result of this incident, Paul Bowles may have
realized that man can, if necessary – and even if he's
destined to lose in the confrontation – take up arms

1 Ibid., pp. 59–60.
2 Bowles, *In Touch*, p. 179.
3 Bowles, *Without Stopping*, p. 104.

against his god. Paul, however, wasn't able to stand up to all those who denied his early talent. He arrived in Paris on April 10, 1931, and visited Gertrude Stein, guardian of all the expatriate American artists, as he himself would later become in Morocco, after he had transformed himself into the Sphinx. One evening, Paul showed her the poems he had written in imitation of the Surrealists. After he had guardedly read them to her, she pronounced the following judgment: 'Well, the basic problem is that all of this is not poetry.'

Gertrude Stein refused to acknowledge his poetic talent, and predicted an early end to his career in this field. But he stubbornly persisted in writing poetry, which constituted a résumé of the same subjects that would recur in his novels and stories. His prose, however, remained rather ordinary. He didn't try to improve or refine it by revision, or to poeticize it in an effort to compensate for what he had failed to accomplish in poetry.

For Paul, it was more important to prove to himself that he was a poet than to be considered one by others. But this aspiration slipped away from him without ever having been realized, though he still dreams of it even now, and he's just turned eighty-six. Until the seventies, he remained intermittently haunted by the obsession to write a poem.[1] He wanted to take root in the realm of

---

1 He published two books of poetry, *The Thicket of Spring* in 1971 and *Next to Nothing* in 1981, collections of his published poems from the twenties to the end of the seventies.

poetry, even though he knew he would never amount to much as a poet. As Stravinsky said: 'The others are still romantic, but I am a Romantic.'

Gertrude Stein told Paul: 'You are a born savage.' He struggled throughout his life, by means of his writing, to purge himself of the notion that he was the product of his parents, or, for that matter, of anything outside of himself.

The financial instability of which Paul Bowles always complained was something he knew how to surmount in his special way. His friend Virgil Thomson has observed: 'He had an effeminate way of acting, and this helped him acquire money and women friends, but in reality he had never been interested in the physical end of things.' Further, Edouard Roditi has noted: 'Paul Bowles was, physically, a great success in the most brilliant clubs in Paris. He always seemed averse to it. The thing with him was that everything was intellectual.'

In connection with this, it should be understood that at twenty Paul rejected sex outright, and would have preferred to believe that it did not exist at all. That said, he didn't altogether reject heterosexual relationships, which at the time he found more acceptable than homosexuality. But were his heterosexual relationships ever a success? His puritan upbringing always dominated his private life, and it even left its mark on the characters in some of his 'American' stories. Sex was to remain his biggest adversary, and the reason behind most of the misunderstandings and tragedies in his characters' lives.

In many of the world's capital cities, Paul has had the opportunity to relieve his sexual frustration, but he couldn't uproot what had been so deeply implanted within him. He adored the sexual world, but only for its perversity, and without really taking part in it. He was content to be an onlooker, gazing from afar, a voyeur. In his fear of being violated, this was enough to arouse his sexual pleasure. This form of pleasure was like trying to catch a fish in water with bare hands. It developed into a kind of sadism that Bowles projected onto the characters in his books, as Flaubert had done in *Salammbô*.

Paul has always shied away from lived reality by hiding behind a thick veil; but life, for all its fragility, ended up by rendering this veil thinner and thinner, until it became transparent. The fatalism, in which Bowles had hitherto taken refuge, is of little use to him today. He has given up, conquered by the life in which he never believed. When he wrote his first novel, *The Sheltering Sky*, between 1947 and 1948 in Bab El Hadid in Fez,[1] he surely never anticipated the old age that has slowly overwhelmed him, along with its train of illnesses (sciatica, skin cancer, and so on); nor did he foresee how the Tangier he cherished in his memory would grow more and more estranged

---

1 It's said that he first wrote it in French, like Jane, who also wrote her first novel in that language.

from him. We always end up by dying as far away as ever from discovering the secret of Tangier.

At the time, booklovers were not much attracted to the work of Bowles. But these days the circle of those who appreciate his work is growing wider and wider. The considerable interest shown nowadays in his books and in his life is the just reward of a literature subtly attuned to the spirit of its era. Bowles managed to transcend his legend, something of which only a genius is capable. Has the phoenix kept its word, after all?

At noon, I'm on my way home. Near the Lycée Regnault, I encounter Mekki. Like me, he hadn't foreseen the onset of his madness. He used to be a very bright boy. He had passed his baccalaureate and wanted to continue his studies in England. Today he is taciturn, and takes refuge in vagrancy, cadging cigarettes – even butt-ends. He doesn't extend his hand. I give him a few coins, as I do every time I see him. He says to me, in the act of squashing his lice with skinny, grime-blackened fingers: 'I'd like you to help me exterminate all these lice clinging to my skin.'

'They were my companions, too, for a long time and I've killed my share of them. So please excuse me.'

'Lice today are more ferocious than they were in the past.'

'I know. They're also hungrier.'

He stares at me, and smiles.

A little further on, I run into Mucho. He used to be a longshoreman in the port of Tangier. One fine morning, after unloading three or four sacks, he suddenly lost his mind, and was dismissed from his job. He was the sturdiest lunatic in Tangier; anyone who annoyed him would bite the dust with one blow from his fist. Nowadays, though, he's old and shriveled up. As usual, he puts out his hand:

'Alms, my son!'

'What have you eaten today?'

'I ate shit and drank blood.'

Then he passes along, dragging his worn-out shoes. Before, it had been I who followed the madmen wherever they went; today it is they who follow me. I attract them. Maybe they want me to watch over them while they sink into a madness even more profound and impenetrable. There is one – he was my student more than thirty years ago – who is always dogging my heels. He knows by heart the route of all my regular perambulations. When he doesn't manage to track me down in one of the bars, he lies in wait for me outside my home, to extort the usual five dirhams from me. He's beginning to get on my nerves. One day, he said to me: 'You've wronged me, m'sieur.'

'How come?'

'When I was your student, you took a book of mine with a picture of a squirrel in it, and you still haven't given it back.'

'Then I'll buy you a book with a picture of squirrel, and other animals as well.'

'Impossible.'

'Why?'

'Because that was an extraordinary squirrel. It was the only one of its kind.'

'But squirrels are all the same.'

'Not at all. Are people all the same?'

'No.'

'It's the same thing with my squirrel. No other squirrel looked like him.'

'So now what do we do?

'God forgive you, but you've wronged me and you've wronged my squirrel.'

He regards me mournfully, turns his back, and shuffles off. In front of the Roxy Café he stops, directs his inscrutable gaze at me once more, before disappearing at the corner of the street. I hasten to disappear, too, before another idiot can emerge.

In his story 'Unwelcome Words', Bowles writes as if he's addressing himself: 'You may remember (although probably not, since you never crack open a book written in our century) a phrase used by the Castor in *La Nausée*: "*Je me survis*" (ineptly translated in the American edition as "I outlive myself"). I understand the Castor's feeling of being her own survivor; it's not unlike my feeling, save that I'd express mine as: "*Ma vie est posthume.*"[1] And, in the same text: 'No dream without at least subliminal anxiety'.[2] This is what Paul said in the days of his restlessness, yearning for distant travels. Today there's nothing to which he looks forward with any enthusiasm; nothing that can engender dreaming. His one concern is the form his end will take. For years, since his operation for sciatica, he goes to sleep and wakes up wincing with pain, piercing to the marrow. Another worry torments him: the fear of being forced, should his health deteriorate rapidly, to leave his room in Tangier and find himself in a ward in a European or American hospital.

Some time ago in an interview for a French television channel, Paul said: 'A person has to stay where he is. The world has changed a lot, not just the Morocco to which I first came, but everywhere.'

On February 25, 1951, Paul wrote to Peggy Glanville-Hicks: 'Inside I am waiting to escape to somewhere else. I don't quite know where. Naturally one always wants to escape if one has no reason for being anywhere. And I have no reason for being anywhere, that is certain. If I work, I don't think of that, and feel the escape urge less, so that work is largely therapeutic. But when one feels that the only reason for working is in order to be able to forget one's life, and the only reason for living is in order to work, one is sometimes tempted to consider the work

---

1 Bowles, 'Unwelcome Words', p. 587.
2 Ibid., p. 586.

slightly absurd, like the pills one takes to make one's digestion easier. There should be something in between, but what it is, is anybody's guess.'[1]

Jane, however, chose to escape inside herself, contenting herself with 'burning up questions' in her isolation. To travel outside of herself, to go far away (by herself), was something she found very difficult. She had to be prodded into everything. Someone always had to push her and take her tenderly by the hand. Then she would be guided, even if the path led to hell.

Jane suffered a stroke on the evening of April 30, 1973. She didn't regain consciousness before her death on Friday, May 4. Paul remained seated by her side until seven in the evening, when he returned to his hotel. At nine o'clock, the head nurse informed him by telephone that Jane had passed away. The next day, there was a private burial at the Church of the Sacred Heart.

After Jane's death, Paul wrote to Audrey Wood from Tangier (May 11, 1973): 'There is nothing to keep me here now, save habit, but I shall probably stay on until circumstances force me to leave, since each time I've gone back to the States I've found it less a place where I want to live.'[2]

---

1 Bowles, *In Touch*, p. 231–2.
2 Ibid., p. 450.